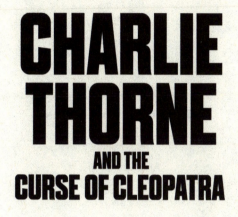

CHARLIE THORNE
AND THE
CURSE OF CLEOPATRA

Also by Stuart Gibbs

The FunJungle series
Belly Up
Poached
Big Game
Panda-monium
Lion Down
Tyrannosaurus Wrecks
Bear Bottom

The Spy School series
Spy School
Spy Camp
Evil Spy School
Spy Ski School
Spy School Secret Service
Spy School Goes South
Spy School British Invasion
Spy School Revolution
Spy School at Sea

The Moon Base Alpha series
Space Case
Spaced Out
Waste of Space

The Charlie Thorne series
Charlie Thorne and the Last Equation
Charlie Thorne and the Lost City

Once Upon a Tim

The Last Musketeer

A CHARLIE THORNE NOVEL

CHARLIE THORNE

AND THE
CURSE OF CLEOPATRA

STUART GIBBS

Simon & Schuster Books for Young Readers

New York London Toronto Sydney New Delhi

SIMON & SCHUSTER BOOKS FOR YOUNG READERS

An imprint of Simon & Schuster Children's Publishing Division

1230 Avenue of the Americas, New York, New York 10020

This book is a work of fiction. Any references to historical events, real people, or real places are used fictitiously. Other names, characters, places, and events are products of the author's imagination, and any resemblance to actual events or places or persons, living or dead, is entirely coincidental.

Text © 2022 by Stuart Gibbs

Jacket design and illustration by

Lucy Ruth Cummins © 2022 by Simon & Schuster, Inc.

Supplemental jacket illustrations by iStock

SIMON & SCHUSTER BOOKS FOR YOUNG READERS

and related marks are trademarks of Simon & Schuster, Inc.

For information about special discounts for bulk purchases, please contact Simon & Schuster Special Sales at 1-866-506-1949 or business@simonandschuster.com.

The Simon & Schuster Speakers Bureau can bring authors to your live event.

For more information or to book an event, contact the Simon & Schuster Speakers Bureau at 1-866-248-3049 or visit our website at www.simonspeakers.com.

Interior design by Hilary Zarycky

The text for this book was set in New Caledonia.

Manufactured in the United States of America

0422 FFG

First Edition

2 4 6 8 10 9 7 5 3 1

CIP data for this book is available from the Library of Congress.

ISBN 9781534499348

ISBN 9781534499362 (ebook)

For my father, Ronald Gibbs,
who taught me to love history and science

It has forever been preferable to attribute a woman's success to her beauty rather than to her brains.

—STACY SCHIFF,
"Rehabilitating Cleopatra"

PROLOGUE

August 10

30 BC

Alexandria, Egypt

Cleopatra was running out of time.

As her royal procession passed through the streets of Alexandria, she could think of only one course of action. It was drastic, but she had no other choice.

Over the past few months, she had suffered many cruel twists of fate. Now the gods had delivered a final one: She had been betrayed.

Cleopatra was returning home after visiting the tomb of her second husband, the Roman general Mark Antony, who she had buried only a week before. She'd had to beg for the privilege of even doing that, as she was being held prisoner in her own palace. For years, she and Antony had been allies in a war against Octavian for control of the Roman Empire, but they had lost. Ten days earlier, the final blow had been struck; their army and navy had gone to confront Octavian's superior forces—and promptly switched sides. Octavian and his soldiers were now camped outside the city while his ships blockaded the harbor. Cleopatra was trapped. All she could do now was negotiate the terms of her surrender.

Luckily, she had something that Octavian wanted.

Every ruler of Rome had coveted it, as had the leaders of all rival kingdoms to Egypt. Mark Antony had come to Alexandria seeking it, as had Julius Caesar and many others before him. Cleopatra had never given it up; it was the key to her power. But now Octavian had leverage over her: her children.

Cleopatra had four. Her oldest, Caesarion, was seventeen, the son of the great Julius Caesar himself and the true heir to the Roman Empire. Then, there were her children with Mark Antony: Alexander Helios, Cleopatra Selene, and Ptolemy Philadelphus. Cleopatra had sent each of them into hiding before Octavian had reached Alexandria; they had scattered across Egypt, accompanied by guards and tutors she trusted. But despite their head start, she knew they could never be completely safe; Octavian's forces would scour the world for them.

And so, two days before, Cleopatra and Octavian had reached an agreement. She would give him the treasure he desired; in return, he would let Cleopatra continue to rule Egypt—and allow her children to live. Caesarion would never rule Rome, but the Ptolemy Dynasty would survive.

However, Octavian had lied.

Cleopatra held the proof in her hands. A message from a spy inside Octavian's camp. It had been slipped to her at Mark Antony's tomb. Octavian intended to go back on his word, take Cleopatra and her family prisoner, drag them to Rome, and parade them through the streets as a display of Rome's power.

Throughout the world, even in Rome itself, many people considered Cleopatra more than human. They thought her to be a goddess, the living incarnation of Isis. If Octavian could make her his captive, he could conquer the entire world.

Then, at the end of the parade, he would execute her. And her family as well.

Cleopatra wasn't surprised. She had suspected Octavian would betray her. That was why she had placed spies in his camp—and why she had taken other precautions to protect the great treasure of the Ptolemy Dynasty. Now it was time to put those careful plans in action.

A goddess did not walk through the streets of Alexandria. Instead, as the procession returned to the royal palace from Mark Antony's tomb, Cleopatra was being carried. She rode in a luxurious chair, gilded in gold and jewels, shaded from the sun, and borne on the shoulders of her soldiers. *"Grigorotera!"* she ordered them, not in Egyptian but in Greek.

Even though Cleopatra's family had ruled Egypt for nearly three centuries, they were not Egyptian. They were from Macedonia, direct descendants of Alexander the Great. In fact, Cleopatra was the first Ptolemy who had even bothered to learn Egyptian at all.

Her soldiers picked up their pace and hurried through the streets.

Cleopatra's subjects gathered along the way, cheering as she passed, crying out in joy when they caught so much as a glimpse of her. She did not smile or wave to them but instead projected calm, doing her best to hide her inner turmoil.

She tried to savor the sights of Alexandria as her procession went by them: the glistening marble temples of Isis, the immense lighthouse that towered over the harbor, the elaborate Caesarium she had built to honor Julius. Alexandria was the greatest city in the world, the center of education and commerce, a crossroads where people of all nationalities gathered, taught, celebrated, and made fortunes. It was beautiful and clean, unlike Rome, which was dusty, ugly, and built in a swamp. Even now, it was shocking to Cleopatra that Rome had managed to conquer her empire.

That was because the Romans cared for nothing but war. They had little interest in art, music, architecture, or culture. Children in Alexandria, boys and girls alike, got the finest education in the world, while Roman boys began training for battle almost as soon as they could walk.

Cleopatra's procession wound through the royal quarter, passing her lavish palace and heading instead to a building she had ordered to be constructed only recently. It was a two-story, windowless box, nowhere near as grand as many of the other structures in Alexandria. But then, it had not been built for beauty.

The soldiers lowered Cleopatra's chair to the ground before it. The queen of Egypt stepped out, called for her two most trusted servants, Iras and Charmion, then entered the building with them and ordered them to bolt the doors behind her.

This was highly unusual. The two women instantly understood what was happening; Cleopatra had warned them of her drastic plans for an instance such as this. But neither woman showed any fear; it was their duty to serve Cleopatra no matter what.

Outside the building, things were different. Cleopatra's other servants and soldiers sensed that something was wrong; concerns were voiced, speculations were made, and rumors quickly spread.

And one young Egyptian, fearing the worst, raced back through the streets of Alexandria to Octavian's camp.

Inside the building, Iras and Charmion went to work. They dressed Cleopatra in her most regal robe and placed her crown upon her head. Then they opened a golden box and removed the glass vial that had been hidden inside it.

All around them the riches of Egypt glinted, each more rare and beautiful than the last. Gemstones, works of art, Cleopatra's royal robes—and gold. Tons and tons of gold.

Over the past few weeks, it had all been delivered here in secrecy.

And below it all, under the floor beneath them, was something else Cleopatra had covertly arranged for: kindling.

Cleopatra was troubled by her failure in the war against Octavian, but she had no regrets over how she had ruled. She was only thirty-nine but had been the queen of Egypt for over half of her life. Twenty-two years. A decade longer than even Alexander the Great had ruled. During her reign, there had never been an uprising. She had led wisely and been respected by her subjects, and by leaders around the world.

Now all that she had left to do was protect her most valuable treasure from Octavian.

Cleopatra's servants had been experimenting with various poisons for some time, fearing this day would come. They had even toyed with the idea of having an asp bite her, but feared the snake wouldn't do what Cleopatra wanted in her moment of need.

The vial she held in her hand would be far more effective.

Cleopatra ordered her servants to set the kindling on fire. It caught quickly. Almost instantly, the floor was warm and smoke was billowing through it.

Despite this, Iras and Charmion remained calm. It would be their honor to die serving their queen.

Cleopatra was not quite so relaxed. She was dismayed by the thought that she would never see her children again. She feared the plans she had made to keep them— and her treasure—safe from Octavian would not succeed. But there was nothing more she could do to protect them—except to take her secrets with her to the great beyond.

While her mausoleum burned around her, the queen of Egypt drank her poison and imagined how horrified Octavian would be when he learned what she had done.

He was.

The man who would rule Rome was not an impressive sight. He was only thirty-three, pale and puny. He hated being out in the sun and always wore a floppy, wide-brimmed hat to protect his fair skin. In the heat of Egypt, he was wilting.

When he learned that Cleopatra had locked herself inside her mausoleum with only her two most-trusted servants, Octavian immediately realized that she had either learned of his plans to betray her—or deduced them on her own. He sprang from his throne and exited his tent, only to see the telltale column of smoke billowing into the air.

Enraged, he ordered his men to hurry across the city. Then he leapt astride his own horse and galloped ahead of his army.

By the time he reached the mausoleum, it was consumed by fire, blazing out of control.

Still, he ordered his men to douse the flames. Bucket brigades were formed, hauling water from the harbor, but it was no use. Within an hour, the building collapsed. By the time the fire was out, almost nothing remained but smoldering rubble.

Octavian ordered his men to search it anyhow. They recovered some of the gems and melted heaps of gold. The gold wasn't in good shape, but it was still worth many times more than what lay in Octavian's own vaults back in Rome.

However, the great treasure that Octavian truly

desired wasn't there. Perhaps Cleopatra had hidden it elsewhere. Or maybe it had been destroyed in the fire. Whatever the case, it was gone.

And it wouldn't be found again for over two thousand years.

PART ONE
THE TABLET

Egypt, thou knew'st too well,
My heart was to thy rudder tied by the strings.
—WILLIAM SHAKESPEARE,
Antony and Cleopatra

ONE

Giza, Egypt
Present Day

On the evening of her thirteenth birthday, Charlie Thorne committed a crime.

As crimes went, it was a minor one, merely illegal entry. Charlie had no intention to steal anything or hurt anyone—although she knew from experience that even the most carefully thought-out plans often went wrong.

Which was exactly what happened that night.

The location was the penthouse condominium of Ahmet Shah, the oldest son of an extremely wealthy Egyptian shipping magnate. Charlie had been plotting the crime for two weeks, surveying the building, doing research, learning everything she could about Ahmet and his home.

Charlie was exceptionally smart. She had an extremely high IQ and a gift for languages; since arriving in the country, she had taught herself Egyptian Arabic. She could have hacked Ahmet's computer to get the information she wanted—although that hadn't been necessary. Ahmet loved the spotlight and was extremely active on social media, and so he had unwittingly posted everything Charlie needed to know online.

Ahmet was a vice president at his father's company, but he didn't appear to work very much—if at all. Instead, his main profession seemed to be spending money. He had vacation homes in Aspen and Malibu and an eight-bedroom yacht that was currently anchored off Ibiza. He belonged to seventeen different country clubs around the world, three of which he had never even visited. He had just returned to Giza after spending two weeks in a $10,000-a-night hotel room in Bali.

And now he was throwing a massive party to celebrate being home again.

Charlie had briefly considered breaking into Ahmet's condo while he was in Bali, but the security system was elaborate and state-of-the-art, and the building was patrolled by armed guards. Charlie had many talents, but breaking and entering wasn't one of them. Besides, there were far easier ways to get into someone's home, no matter how well protected it was.

Under the right circumstances, you could just walk through the door.

Ahmet Shah loved entertaining. It hadn't taken Charlie long to learn that about him; her first Google image search for the young man turned up hundreds of party photos taken at his penthouse. Large, crowded, glamorous parties, the kind that certain types of people were desperate to score invitations to.

The condo had also been featured in several architectural and design magazines, which allowed Charlie to easily memorize the layout of the rooms and catalog most of the artifacts on display.

Including one artifact in particular. The one Charlie had been trying to locate for the past two months. In a magazine photo, it was in the background behind Ahmet as he showed off another piece of art that wasn't anywhere nearly as important.

An artifact so powerful and significant should never have been in a private collection. Ahmet Shah would have been wise to keep its location a secret. But then, Ahmet did not appear to be a very wise person. From Charlie's research, he was a wealthy brat who wanted to be famous—and he didn't even know what he possessed.

Charlie took it as a good sign that the party happened to be on her birthday. She felt like celebrating, but unfortunately, she was no longer in touch with any of her friends. Four months earlier, circumstances beyond her control had forced her to cut ties with all of them and vanish from their lives. None of them had heard from her since then. None had the slightest idea what had happened to her.

And as for celebrating with family, well . . . Charlie had some very unusual family issues. Her half brother Dante was a CIA agent who had blackmailed her into working for the US government. He was the reason she was now on the run, pursued by intelligence agencies and criminals around the globe.

Although, Charlie had to admit, thanks to Dante, her life had become quite exciting. If it wasn't for him, she wouldn't have even known about the artifact in Ahmet Shah's penthouse.

To access the party, all Charlie had to do was pretend to be a member of the catering staff, which was easy. The party was going to be a big one, with more than sixty servers. And caterers all over the world wore virtually the same uniform: white shirt and black pants. The clothes were cheap and readily available—not that Charlie had to worry about money.

Charlie was tall for her age and behaved with a maturity that made her come across as someone who was several years older. In addition, she was extremely multiracial—partially Latina, Black, Asian, Middle Eastern, and Caucasian—and multilingual; with her caterer's uniform and her newfound mastery of Egyptian Arabic, she easily blended in with the other hired help.

The building where the party was taking place was imposing and opulent in the front but basic and industrial in the back. There was a rear entrance for nights like this, so that the catering supplies and staff wouldn't have to come through the main lobby and tie up the elevators. As Charlie had expected, the scene at the rear entrance in the hour before the party was chaotic; the catering staff was scrambling to unload truckloads of food, glassware, serving dishes, utensils, and linens and get them up to the penthouse. Charlie simply grabbed a tray of canapés and fell in line. The single security guard stationed there was distracted, trying to get the phone number of an attractive young caterer; Charlie walked right past him and into the service elevator without any trouble at all.

The penthouse was even more spectacular than she had expected. The magazine photos hadn't done it justice. It was extremely modern in design, which served as a stark juxtaposition to the ancient treasures in Ahmet Shah's art collection: papyrus scrolls and sandstone sculptures that were thousands of years old. But for most visitors, the most amazing feature was the view of the pyramids.

The western walls of the penthouse were floor-to-ceiling glass, fronting an outdoor deck with an infinity pool. All of it faced the famous Giza pyramid complex. Although the ancient tombs were still surrounded by the sands of the northern Sahara, the modern city came surprisingly close to them, creating a jarring clash of the old and the new. The edge of the pyramid complex was lined with other luxury condominium towers, high-end housing developments, ghettos, shopping centers, school campuses, and even a golf course, whose irrigated green fairways looked bizarrely out of place beside the desert sands. At night, the great pyramids were lit with flood-lights, so they practically gleamed against the dark sky.

However, as impressive as the view of the pyramids was, Charlie was far more interested in something inside the penthouse.

And yet she couldn't go see it right away. There were security cameras in every room and plenty of guards patrolling the condo. So Charlie bided her time, wait-ing for the right moment. For a few hours, she worked dutifully as a caterer, first by helping set up for the party, arranging banquet tables and prepping food, and then, once the guests began to arrive, by carrying around trays of hors d'oeuvres and collecting empty glasses. When the party finally reached its peak, and the rooms were jammed with guests, Charlie decided it was time to make her move.

She ducked into a bathroom and took off her cater-ing clothes, revealing the party dress she'd been wear-ing underneath them all along. Ahmet Shah's guests were rich, and so, to blend in, Charlie had splurged on a designer outfit. It was sleek and stylish—although not so stylish that it would grab attention. Attention was the last thing Charlie wanted. She quickly put up her hair, did her makeup, and crammed the caterer's uniform into a cabinet under the sink. Then she stepped out and joined the party.

Charlie had little concern about the other caterers recognizing her; the lights were dim and the condo was packed. She even managed to pluck a few sliders and a soda off the trays of passing servers without being noticed. She worked her way through the crowds, ignoring two separate attempts by young male guests—unaware of her age—to flirt with her, and finally reached what she had gone through so much trouble to find.

It was in Ahmet's office at the more private end of the penthouse, where the bedrooms were. The door had a simple lock that Charlie picked with a hairpin in twenty seconds. Then she stepped inside and locked it again behind her.

The walls of the room were thick and soundproofed, immediately reducing the raucous noise of the party to a distant murmur. A security camera was mounted at the far-upper corner of the room, facing the door; Charlie couldn't do much about it except keep her head down so that there wouldn't be a clear view of her face—and hope that if anyone was monitoring the system, they were too distracted by the rest of the party to notice her.

The office was designed in traditional Western fashion, with a large oaken desk and built-in bookshelves. There was nothing on the desk, save for an unused notepad and a desk calendar that still showed April, even though it was June, indicating that Ahmet didn't do much work in there. And there were very few books on the shelves, two of which were upside down, indicating that Ahmet didn't read much either. Instead, the shelves were mostly lined with pieces of art: sculptures and bits of pottery, some of which were tacky junk, and some of which were incredibly valuable.

The wall opposite the desk was dominated by a large, garish piece of modern art. The tablet Charlie was looking for was mounted to the side of the artwork, toward the corner, as though it wasn't important.

Still, it took Charlie's breath away.

Because Charlie, unlike Ahmet, knew what it was.

In Ahmet's defense, the tablet didn't look very impressive. It was a pale slab of sandstone into which words had been crudely etched in Latin, and so old that the surface had been worn down, leaving much of the inscription only faintly visible. Furthermore, it was broken; a thin crack split it from top to bottom, and its edges had crumbled away, leaving the sentences—and many of the words—incomplete. As a result, even though Charlie knew Latin, she still couldn't fully translate the text.

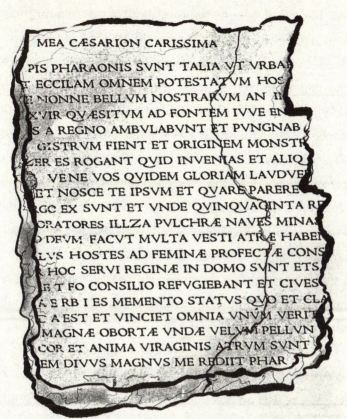

MEA CÆSARION CARISSIMA

PIS PHARAONIS SVNT TALIA VT VRBA
T ECCILAM OMNEM POTESTATVM HOS
H NONNE BELLVM NOSTRARVM AN II
X VIR QVÆSITVM AD FONTEM IVVE EN
S A REGNO AMBVLABVNT ET PVNGNAB
GISTRVM FIENT ET ORIGINEM MONSTR
ER ES ROGANT QVID INVENIAS ET ALIQ
VENE VOS QVIDEM GLORIAM LAVDVE
ET NOSCE TE IPSVM ET QVARE PARERE
GC EX SVNT ET VNDE QVINQVAGINTA R
CRATORES ILLZA PVLCHRÆ NAVES MINA
D DEVM FACVT MVLTA VESTI ATRÆ HABE
LVS HOSTES AD FEMINÆ PROFECTÆ CONS
HOC SERVI REGINÆ IN DOMO SVNT ETS
E T FO CONSILIO REFVGIEBANT ET CIVES
A E RB I ES MEMENTO STATVS QVO ET CL
C A EST ET VINCIET OMNIA VNVM VERIT
MAGNÆ OBORTÆ VNDÆ VELVM PELLVN
COR ET ANIMA VIRAGINIS ATRVM SVNT
EM DIVVS MAGNVS ME REDIIT PHAR

The tablet was mounted to the wall with steel brackets. As Charlie had noted in the magazine photos, Ahmet hadn't even bothered to put it in a protective case.

Which was good, because Charlie needed to touch it.

She snapped a few photographs with her phone first, but assumed those wouldn't tell her everything she needed to know. The photos could barely capture the faint words, let alone the texture of the stone.

To do that, Charlie removed a roll of thin, almost translucent paper from her dress, as well as a stick of red graphite. Then she set to work creating a rubbing. She unfurled the paper, pressed it firmly against the tablet, and then dragged the graphite back and forth across it. Wherever the paper touched the stone, the graphite left a coating of red, while the places that were sunken, like the etched words, remained white. In this way, Charlie was able to duplicate the tablet on the paper. The technique was simple but effective; even the faintest words on the tablet were easily readable on the rubbing. Although Charlie feared getting caught, she didn't rush, making sure her rubbing was as accurate as possible; any mistakes she made in haste could alter the message left in the stone.

She was almost finished when she heard the office door rattle. Someone was putting a key in the lock.

There was no place for Charlie to hide. All she could do was back away from the tablet and drop the rubbing and the graphite in a wastebasket beside the desk.

The office door opened, and Ahmet Shah entered. He froze in surprise upon seeing Charlie in his private office. And then his surprise turned to suspicion.

"What are you doing in here?" he demanded in Arabic.

Despite her fear, Charlie smiled at him brightly. "It's a funny story . . . ," she began.

TWO

CIA headquarters
Langley, Virginia

Six thousand miles and seven time zones away, Jamilla Carter was having her final lunch as director of the CIA. To her great annoyance, she was being forced to spend it with the man who was replacing her.

They were eating in Carter's office, which wouldn't belong to her much longer, having sandwiches that Carter's assistant had brought up from the commissary. Carter would have preferred to have her final meal as director in the Agency's executive dining room, which was far more comfortable and served a poached salmon that she loved. But she wanted privacy today, because she was still somewhat embarrassed about being fired—and because their topic of discussion was extremely classified, even within the CIA itself.

Carter was briefing her replacement on Charlie Thorne

and Pandora. And how the operation to recover both of them had failed. Which was why she had been dismissed from her job two weeks earlier by the Director of National Intelligence.

The office was large, as befitted the director of the most important intelligence agency in the United States, if not the world. It was on the top floor of the headquarters building, with a sweeping view of the Agency's forested grounds, which were lush and green with summer foliage. There was a great, imposing desk, a sitting area, and a small conference table, where Carter was now dining with Arthur Zell.

The classified files concerning Charlie and Pandora were spread out on the table before Zell. He was so engrossed by them, he had only taken two bites of his sandwich in the past fifteen minutes.

Zell said, "Let me see if I have this straight: Pandora is an equation that was devised by Albert Einstein. It explains how to access the energy within an atom cheaply and easily, which could solve the world's energy problems . . ."

"Or allow almost anyone to build a nuclear bomb," Carter finished. "Which is why we didn't want it getting into the wrong hands."

Zell chuckled nervously. "Makes sense."

Unlike Carter, Zell had not worked his way up through the ranks of the CIA to get this job. He was a political appointee, a middling congressman who had risen by making friends in all the right places. Carter didn't trust him one bit. Although Zell had been nothing but friendly to her, she suspected that the moment she was out the door, he would immediately try to take credit for all her successes (of which there had been many) and blame all his failures on her.

Carter said, "Einstein recognized how dangerous Pandora was and didn't think humanity could be trusted with it. So he hid it, hoping that people would be able to handle it better in the future. He originally constructed a complex series of clues to its location but then had second thoughts and tried to ensure that Pandora was never found. He almost succeeded. The equation remained hidden for decades—until a few months ago, when we became aware of a terrorist organization known as the Furies that was closing in on Pandora's location. Faced with this news, I made an . . ." Carter paused for a moment to consider her words. ". . . *unorthodox* decision."

"Operation Hope," Zell said.

"Correct." Carter went on to explain how a young, innovative agent named Dante Garcia had come to her with a proposition: The best way to find something that Albert Einstein had hidden was to recruit someone who was as smart as Einstein. Dante even had someone in mind: Charlie Thorne.

"A twelve-year-old girl," Zell said, disdain evident in his voice.

"She's not a *normal* twelve-year-old girl," Carter told him. "Her IQ is off the charts, she speaks at least fourteen languages, she has a photographic memory, and she was acing college courses in theoretical physics without even bothering to show up for class." She glanced at her calendar. "And, as of today, she's no longer twelve. She's thirteen."

"Still," Zell began dismissively, "I've got kids that age, and I wouldn't trust them to load the dishwasher properly, let alone protect the safety of the planet."

"This was not a decision that was made lightly. Desperate times called for desperate measures."

"But it ended in failure."

"It did not," Carter said curtly. "With the help of Thorne and Agent Milana Moon, Garcia prevented the Furies from obtaining Pandora and neutralized the group."

"And yet, from what I understand, Thorne escaped with Pandora."

"There were complications, as is the case with any mission. The fact is, if it hadn't been for Thorne, Pandora would have been lost forever. Einstein's copy was destroyed, but Thorne still has one."

"Where is it?"

"She memorized it."

Zell's eyes widened in surprise. "Do our enemies know?"

"We believe that the Russians do. And maybe others."

"So then, this girl might be the most powerful asset in the world."

Carter hesitated a moment before answering. "Yes."

"Do you have any idea where she is?"

"We have a few. Garcia and Moon are still on the case, although it's off the books." Carter went to her desk, unlocked a drawer, and removed another classified file from it, which she brought to Zell. It was marked PRO-METHEUS. "Although we failed to contain Thorne, Operation Hope led to a success that we hadn't anticipated."

Zell opened the classified file. Inside were dozens of photographs of what looked like math problems.

Carter explained, "Einstein had devised an ingenious code to hide his clues to Pandora. What looked like mathematical equations were actually encrypted messages. Once Thorne cracked the code, I suspected that perhaps there were other encoded notations throughout Einstein's work, which had been overlooked. So I deployed a team of agents across the globe to comb through all of his papers."

"And you found something?"

Carter flashed a proud smile. "Einstein wasn't the only great scientist who concealed a landmark discovery.

It has happened repeatedly throughout history. Einstein had been researching them . . ."

"But how did *he* know about them?"

Carter shrugged. "It's unclear. Our best guess is that the information was passed down by the great thinkers themselves—as though there has been an exclusive society throughout the centuries, tasked with making sure these secrets stayed safe. Or maybe, as usual, Einstein simply noticed things that other people didn't. Whatever the case, he detailed the starting points to tracking down many of these discoveries."

Zell flipped past the photos to some other documents, each stamped CLASSIFIED multiple times: the translations of Einstein's notes. Zell's jaw dropped as he skimmed through them, noting the names of the great historical figures who had hidden their findings. And yet, as badly as he wanted to believe what Carter was saying, disbelief nagged at him. "This can't possibly be true."

"We have no reason to doubt it. As well as some evidence to back it up."

"What?"

"Two months ago, Garcia and Moon caught up to Charlie Thorne in Ecuador. Together, the three of them uncovered evidence backing Einstein's claim that Charles Darwin had made a landmark discovery in the Amazon."

"What was it?"

"Sadly, that remains unknown. The team found a few clues but ultimately lost the trail. And they had some unexpected interference from Russian intelligence."

Zell sat forward, concerned. "Were the Russians after Darwin's discovery—or Pandora?"

"Pandora. Thankfully, they failed to capture Charlie, but their actions allowed her to escape . . ."

"Again?" Zell snorted. "Are you sure Garcia and Moon are up to this task? They've lost this girl twice now."

Carter bristled. "They're two of the best agents the CIA has. Read their files if you don't believe me."

"I've read them."

"Then read them again. Like I said, Charlie Thorne is no ordinary girl. Not only is she brilliant, but she has extensive financial resources."

Zell looked to her curiously.

Carter explained how Charlie had managed to steal at least forty million dollars from the Lightning Corporation via cybercrime—although, in Charlie's defense, Lightning had stolen something from her first: a computer program she had written as a child that had ultimately earned Lightning considerably more money than the millions Charlie had stolen. Charlie had covered her tracks well—but not well enough. Dante Garcia had suspected she was the thief and used that information to blackmail her into working for the CIA.

"How did he figure out it was her?" Zell asked.

"Garcia had inside information about Charlie. He's her older brother. Well, half brother, really."

Zell dropped the Prometheus file on the conference table. "They're siblings? You can't possibly keep Garcia on this operation! He has a conflict of interest!"

"Maybe, but he's still the best person for the job. I can't task some random agent to work with a thirteen-year-old girl. Plus Garcia knows Charlie better than anyone else. In fact, he thinks he knows where she is right now."

"Where?"

"Egypt. Looking for whatever Cleopatra hid."

"And why does he think that's the case?"

"He believes Charlie feels a connection with Cleopatra."

"A gut instinct isn't much to go on."

"That's still more than we'd have with anyone else."

Zell nodded thoughtfully. "Obviously, I'll need to know how you stay in contact with your operatives on this mission. I want to get a message to Garcia and Moon right away."

"What do you want to tell them?"

Zell gave Carter a pitying look. "I'm sorry, Jamilla. But since you only have a few hours left as director, I'm afraid that information is classified."

THREE

Giza, Egypt

Even though Charlie Thorne was smarter than almost anyone who had ever lived, she often found it was to her advantage to let people think she wasn't smart at all. People tended to be more relaxed and talk a lot more when they thought they were more intelligent than you.

Sadly, it was quite easy to fool people in this way, especially men; Charlie had discovered that most men tended to assume they were smarter than women anyhow.

"I was looking for the bathroom," she told Ahmet, using a slightly more high-pitched voice than normal. She spoke in English, which she knew he understood, and kept her hands loosely balled into fists, so he couldn't see the red graphite on her palms. "But I ended up in here instead."

Ahmet's suspicions quickly began to fade, although

they didn't entirely go away. "Wasn't this room locked?"

"If it was, then how could I have gotten in here?" Before Ahmet could usher her back out, Charlie turned her attention to the tablet on the wall. "I was going to leave, but then I noticed *this*. Why do you have this old piece of rock on your wall? Is it important?"

"My great-grandfather used to think so. Many years ago, he paid a lot of money for it." Ahmet came farther into the room, staring at the tablet as though he hadn't noticed it in a long time. He had a glass of scotch in his hand and was slightly unsteady on his feet; this obviously wasn't his first drink of the evening.

The office door swung closed behind him, although not all the way, so that the sound of the party still filled the room, forcing Charlie to raise her voice to be heard.

"How much money?"

"I'm not sure. But it was plenty."

"What did he think this was?"

"A message from Cleopatra."

None of this was a surprise to Charlie, although she had only been guessing at the truth up until this point. So it was nice to receive confirmation that what she had deduced was correct.

Two months earlier, Charlie had hacked into the CIA's computers and accessed the translations of Einstein's notes. According to those, a stone tablet rumored to bear a partial inscription from Cleopatra had been discovered on an archaeological excavation of an Isis temple near the Red Sea in 1947. The inscription didn't make sense, which led Einstein to believe it was a clue to something important that Cleopatra had hidden. The tablet was supposed to be delivered to the Egyptian Museum in Cairo—but the caravan delivering it had been robbed by bandits en route and the tablet, along with several other artifacts, was never seen again.

The story had been big news at the time; the tablet was even rumored to have been cursed by Cleopatra. However, over the decades, the tale of the tablet had mostly been forgotten. Charlie had spent much of the last few weeks in Cairo libraries, piecing together what had happened. It was assumed that the tablet had ended up in the hands of a wealthy collector, a fate that was unfortunately common with ancient artifacts, even in the modern day. Thousands of precious items that should have been in museums for everyone to see were instead hidden away in private homes. Back in 1947, the police even had suspicions as to who had been behind the theft: Ahmet Shah's great-grandfather. But the elder Shah had been wealthy and politically connected, and a full investigation never seemed to have taken place. Instead, the story from the police began to change, which Charlie suspected meant that they had all been bribed to let the case drop.

Charlie had found photos of the tablet in the original newspaper stories. They were too grainy for her to read the inscription, but she could at least learn what the tablet looked like. Then, figuring that it was still in the Shah family's possession, she had scoured every photo she could find of their homes until discovering the one where the tablet appeared behind Ahmet, right on the wall she was facing now.

Despite all this, she pretended to be impressed. "A message from Cleopatra? *The* Cleopatra? The queen of Egypt?"

"Don't get so excited. The whole thing was a hoax."

"Why do you say that?"

"It doesn't make any sense. Plus, it's in *Latin*. Why would the queen of Egypt write in a Roman language?"

"I don't know," Charlie replied, although she did. Cleopatra had spoken at least seven languages. The two loves of her life had been Roman leaders, Julius Caesar and Mark Antony, and with them, she had given birth to four children, all of whom were potential heirs to the Roman Empire. They would certainly have known Latin, so it made sense that if Cleopatra wanted to leave them a message, it would have been in that language.

And this message was clearly directed to her eldest son, her only offspring with Julius Caesar. It was evident in the very first line: *Mea Caesarion carissima*. My dear son Caesarion.

"Great-Granddad thought that maybe there was a code hidden in this," Ahmet said, pointing to the tablet. "He apparently had every specialist in the country look at it. But no one could find anything. Either it's a fake—or there's too much missing to figure it out."

Charlie frowned, despite herself. The latter possibility was her biggest concern. The chance of a clue from Cleopatra surviving intact for over two thousand years was extremely small. Stones eroded and broke apart over time—while anything written on papyrus would have deteriorated centuries ago. Almost nothing remained from Cleopatra's day. Even much of Alexandria, where she had lived, the greatest city in the Western world at the time, had vanished. The locations of Cleopatra's palace—and her mausoleum—had never been found.

And yet, even now, staring at the tablet on the wall, Charlie had a sense that there *was* a message hidden in its words, although she couldn't quite grasp how. She needed more time—and a complete rubbing—but that was in jeopardy now that Ahmet was here. Sure enough, he took her arm and tried to guide her out of the room. "Why don't we get back to the party?" he said. "Besides, you still need a bathroom, right?"

Charlie held her ground, continuing to stare at the tablet. "Are you sure you can't just let me stay here a little longer? I mean, if that's really something Cleopatra wrote . . . it's amazing."

"If only it were real. If you don't mind, this is kind of my private place. I'd like to lock it up before anyone else wanders in." Ahmet gripped her arm more tightly and tugged on it.

Charlie had been hoping to avoid a situation like this, but she had also planned for the possibility. She pulled away from Ahmet suddenly, staring at the tablet as though she had just noticed something on it. "Oh wow," she said in fake astonishment. "What is *that*?"

Intrigued, Ahmet turned back to the tablet himself. "What do you mean?"

"There's a little mark down at the bottom. It's very faint. Looks like a scarab."

"Where?" Ahmet crouched in front of the tablet and squinted hard. "I don't see anyth—"

That was as far as he got. Charlie had tricked him into turning his back on her. Now she clamped the chloroform-soaked rag she had concealed in her dress over his nose and mouth.

Ahmet gasped in surprise, which was exactly the wrong reaction, as that only brought more chloroform into his lungs. Then he tried to fight back. He was bigger and more muscular than Charlie, but his struggles were in vain. Charlie simply leapt onto his back as though he were giving her a piggyback ride, wrapping her arms around his head and keeping the rag pinioned directly over his face. Ahmet flailed about for a few seconds, then sank to his knees.

Charlie jumped off him as he thudded to the floor.

"Sorry," she told his prone body, then quickly locked the office door once more. "I was really hoping something like this wouldn't happen." She removed her rubbing and graphite stick from the garbage can, then resumed her place in front of the tablet.

She finished the rubbing, working faster now, concerned about the unconscious party host sprawled on the floor behind her. It wouldn't be long before someone noticed he was missing and came looking for him. She couldn't take the time to get the level of detail she wanted on the remaining portion of the rubbing, but she did the best she could. Then she carefully rolled up the rubbing and slipped it into the lining of her dress. She held on to the stick of graphite for the moment, not wanting to leave a clue behind, but grabbed some tissues to wrap around it and to wipe her hands.

Ahmet moaned drowsily. "Beware the curse of Cleopatra," he murmured in Arabic, then began snoring.

Charlie momentarily considered going out the window.

She could avoid passing back through the party, but the walls of the building were sheer glass. Charlie was an adept rock climber, but even for her, trying to climb down the building would be suicidal. It would be much safer to leave through the office door, casually move through the crowd, and go down the elevator. Hopefully, she would simply look like an invited guest who had chosen to head home early.

She pressed her ear against the office door, trying to determine if anyone was approaching from the other side, but the party music was blasting. It was all she could hear.

She had to leave. Every moment she stayed in the office with Ahmet's unconscious body was a moment too long. She yanked open the office door.

Only to find two bodyguards standing outside.

FOUR

efore the bodyguards could even react to the scene, Charlie shifted back into her ditzy fake persona again, pretending to be on the edge of panic. "Thank goodness you're here!" she exclaimed in Arabic. "I think Ahmet had a heart attack!"

The bodyguards instantly grew concerned. They looked beyond Charlie to the prone body of the man they were supposed to be protecting. Both shoved past her, racing to Ahmet's side. "What happened?" one demanded.

"He was showing me his art and he just collapsed!" Charlie explained breathlessly. Then, while the bodyguards were focused on Ahmet, she slipped out the door, intending to melt into the crowd.

She figured that she had bought herself only a few seconds. If the bodyguards were any good, it wouldn't take them long to realize Ahmet was only sleeping.

They were even better than she'd expected.

While one looked over Ahmet, the other returned his attention to Charlie and spotted her slipping away. "Hey!" he shouted, instantly growing suspicious. "Stop!"

Charlie didn't stop. Instead, she ran.

The bodyguard came after her. He was built like an ox, muscular enough to really do some harm.

During the brief time Charlie had been in the office, the party had grown even bigger. Guests were packed into the condominium's common rooms, eating, drinking, dancing, shouting to be heard over the music. Charlie gracefully snaked through them, heading for the exit.

The bodyguard showed no such care. Instead, he bull-dozed through the crowd, roughly shoving guests and catering staff aside in his pursuit of Charlie. Platters of food and crystal glasses crashed to the floor. The bodyguard shouted for someone to stop Charlie, but his words were drowned out by the thumping music. If anything, it looked as though *he* was the problem, drawing all the attention.

Charlie ducked back into the kitchen, slamming into one of the caterers in her haste. She accidentally dropped the stick of red graphite but had no time to pick it up again; she had to keep moving. Along with the service elevator, there was an emergency stairwell access door in the kitchen. The service elevator was busy, so Charlie took the stairs.

The stairwell was a stark contrast to the rest of the glamorous building. Not one bit of effort had been expended to beautify it. It was lit by flickering bulbs and the walls were industrial concrete. Given the large number of cobwebs and dead insects, it appeared as though the stairwell was rarely used, which was exactly what Charlie had been hoping for.

Once inside, she dropped any pretense of being a party guest and raced down the stairs as fast as her legs could carry her. She was already eight floors down before she heard the bang of the penthouse fire door being thrown open. The bodyguard peered down through the shaft between flights and shouted, "There she is!"

Suddenly the stairwell was filled with noise. Heavy footsteps and more shouting in Arabic.

But Charlie had a big lead on the bodyguards, and she was faster and more agile than they were. She flew down the stairs, passing one landing after another, her only real concern being who might be waiting for her down below.

Sure enough, she was almost at the bottom when a guard—the same one who'd allowed her to walk right past him to get into the building—burst through the exit door.

Charlie didn't falter for a second. Instead, she saw the numbers.

Part of Charlie's genius was an unusual gift with mathematics. When needed, the numbers would come to her, detailing exactly what force she had to apply, what angle to attack from, how much pressure to exert. Sometimes she needed to make delicate and precise calculations, which she could do instantly.

But at the moment, precision wasn't that necessary.

Charlie launched herself off the staircase, leaping down the last few stairs and slamming into the guard. Charlie was slight of build, but she caught the hapless guard by surprise, knocking him backward off his feet. His head banged into the concrete wall, and he dropped like a sack of potatoes.

Charlie bolted out onto the loading dock, where the catering staff was bringing more food and alcohol into the service elevator. Everyone stared at her curiously as she ran past but made no move to stop her. Charlie had already reached the corner before Ahmet's bodyguards emerged from the stairs, screaming at everyone to stop her, claiming she was a thief.

Most of the people on the street pretended like they hadn't heard anything, not wanting to get involved, although two different men tried to grab Charlie. She was more nimble than they were and easily slipped away, but she knew it wouldn't be long before her luck ran out. She couldn't keep running forever.

It was a good thing she had planned for trouble.

Her motorcycle was parked a half block up the street,

wedged in the narrow space between two cars. Charlie had considered several types of vehicles for making an escape but had picked the cycle for a few reasons:

First, the traffic in Giza was horrendous, and a motorcycle allowed her to maneuver through the cars more easily.

Second, Charlie didn't have a driver's license. Buying a car would be tricky—and practicing getaway driving would be even trickier. But there were plenty of teens who rode motorcycles in Giza, and Charlie had little trouble finding a dealer who was willing to sell her a slightly used one for cash.

Over the past few days, Charlie had taken the motorcycle on plenty of test runs through the streets around Ahmet's building, mastering how to ride the bike and working out potential escape routes.

To her relief, her helmet was still hanging from the handlebars; no one had swiped it. She quickly strapped it on—and then headbutted another man who was trying to catch her. He staggered backward, tripped over his own feet, and sank to the sidewalk.

Charlie had parked the motorcycle facing the road so she could make a quick exit. She straddled the bike, turned it on, and sped away. The street was choked with cars, but she was able to race through the gaps between them, leaving Ahmet Shah's bodyguards in the dust.

Only a few seconds later, two other motorcycles swerved into traffic behind her and immediately took up the chase.

The drivers wore leather cycling gear and black helmets, while the bodyguards had all been wearing two-piece suits. Which meant the motorcyclists probably didn't work for Ahmet Shah.

"Dang it," Charlie muttered.

Someone else was after her.

FIVE

The metropolis of Cairo, which included Giza, was infamous for its traffic. Cars jammed the streets at all hours and the rules of the road were rarely heeded. The sound of honking was almost constant. This night was no exception. Charlie found herself in a sea of vehicles that were barely moving. Many drivers had their windows down and were in deep conversations between cars, as though they didn't expect to be going anywhere anytime soon.

But Charlie had to move. She did everything she could to navigate the congested streets, squeezing through the thin gaps between cars, veering onto sidewalks, speeding through plazas full of diners and shopping stalls. Her mind raced, furiously calculating the timing needed to negotiate all the obstacles in her path. Sometimes she cut things awfully close, racing through a gap only a second before it closed, or leaving herself so little room that she sideswiped a car. She accidentally clipped off three side mirrors and upended two tables at outdoor restaurants, provoking tirades of insults in Arabic.

And yet she couldn't shake her pursuers. They were better motorcyclists than she was, doggedly following her through the streets. Each time she managed to gain ground, they would make it right back up again.

However, Charlie had one last trick up her sleeve. There was another reason she had selected a motorcycle for her getaway: It could be driven over sand. Charlie had splurged on thick, studded sand tires and inflated them to the optimum pressure for going off-road. That didn't mean driving over sand would be *easy*, but Charlie had spent much of the last day practicing at a motorcycle track in the dunes outside Cairo, preparing for an emergency like this.

The irony was that, at the moment, she still had to get to the desert. Normally, it wasn't very hard to find sand in Egypt. Less than 3 percent of its 377,000 square miles was fertile; only the narrow strip along the Nile River. There wasn't a single forest in the entire country. Almost all of it was desert. And yet, right now, there was only one patch of sand close to Charlie: the Giza Pyramid Complex.

Every night, there was a light show at the pyramids, so the gates were still open, allowing ticketed visitors inside. The display was just beginning as Charlie came up the road, but there was still a line of cars waiting to get in, tourists who were late because of the traffic and upset that they were missing the show. Charlie sped up the exit lane, which was completely empty, given that no one was leaving, and then shot through the entry gate. Only a few seconds later, the other two motorcyclists roared through behind her.

The security guards stationed at the gate yelled after them, shaking their fists, and a few ran for their cars to pursue them, but in the time that it took, Charlie and her pursuers had already sped off into the darkness.

Just beyond the entry gate, the Great Sphinx loomed in the dark, like a giant beast crouched in the sand. Charlie hurtled past it into the pyramid complex and finally found herself on a deserted road. She opened up the throttle and raced through the night.

The complex encompassed far more than just the pyramids, including several cemeteries, tombs, and temples. It was over a square mile in size, although the pyramids were understandably the biggest attractions, literally and metaphorically. To begin with, they were staggeringly old; when they had been built, nearly five thousand years before, woolly mammoths had still walked the earth. Even in Cleopatra's time, they were ancient history. In fact, Cleopatra had lived five hundred years closer to the modern age than she had to the construction of the pyramids.

Of the three main pyramids, the Pyramid of Khufu was the oldest and the largest. Designed as a tomb for a pharaoh, it was estimated to have been built from over 2.3 million blocks of limestone and granite, some of which weighed more than eighty tons. At nearly five hundred feet in height, it had been the tallest man-made structure on earth for nearly four thousand years. It was easily large enough to fit St. Peter's Cathedral inside, with room for a few other great cathedrals to spare. The largest stones had been quarried in Aswan, which was over eight hundred miles away. No one knew for sure how the stones had been delivered to the site—or how the pyramids had been constructed—although some estimates figured that up to forty thousand workers might have been involved.

Now the pyramids were lit up with colored floodlights and lasers as Charlie streaked past them, glowing brightly under the dark night sky. The music and the recorded performances of the show—which, oddly, were in English, to appeal to the greatest number of visitors—were directed toward the tourists gathered by the front gates, but the noise still echoed across the dunes.

Since the pyramids were the highlight of the program, all the lights were focused on them. The rest of the complex was dark—or as dark as things got near a metropolis of twenty million people. Charlie raced along the narrow road that passed between the pyramids of Khufu and Khafre, and then, shortly after rounding a curve by the smaller pyramid of King Menkaure, she suddenly turned off her lights and veered into the sand.

She dropped back on the throttle so the sudden change to the soft surface wouldn't send her flying over the handlebars. The motorcycle wobbled in the loose sand, but her practice paid off. The knobby-treaded tires found purchase and she sped off across the dunes, hoping that her pursuers wouldn't notice and would continue along the road. After all, who would be foolish enough to venture across the sand at night?

Sure enough, the first pursuer fell for her trick and shot right past the point where she'd left the road, speeding onward.

But the second pursuer was wise to her. They *almost* kept going on the road but suddenly skidded to a stop, then pulled a tight U-turn and came back, searching for signs of Charlie. It didn't take long until they spotted the telltale tire treads in the sand, indicating what Charlie had done—and where she was heading. Then they resumed the chase, following her trail through the desert.

Charlie cursed under her breath. Now that her gambit had failed, she was at a serious disadvantage. She was an amateur motorcyclist, going over tricky terrain in the dark—and her tread marks were leaving a path directly to her. She had run out of backup plans. Now she would have to wing it.

Even worse, her pursuer was catching up. Not only were they a better rider, but they didn't have to exercise as much caution on the shifting sands. Charlie had to be wary of obstacles that might come up quickly in the dark, whereas her pursuer simply had to follow her tracks.

Which gave Charlie an idea.

Ahead of her was a wide sweep of desert where nothing appeared to have ever been built. It might have looked the same since the days of Khufu. A large section of it had been roped off by archaeologists looking for relics buried by the sand over time. Several tall metal stakes jutted out of the ground, and a long cordon ringed them. Signs in English and Arabic ordered KEEP CLEAR: RESEARCH AREA. Just beyond it, the landscape dropped away and the dunes pitched down sharply.

Charlie saw the numbers.

She turned up the throttle all the way, then sprang off her motorcycle just before it picked up speed. The soft sand cushioned her landing while her cycle continued onward, staying upright long enough to reach the steep descent. Then it dropped over the lip and tumbled down the side of the dune.

Charlie quickly snatched one of the stakes out of the ground.

The second motorcycle roared past her in the night, following the trail her own cycle had left, her pursuer probably thinking that Charlie had wiped out badly and would be unable to escape.

Charlie heaved the metal stake into the spokes of the motorcycle's front wheel, jamming it. The motorcycle cartwheeled into the air and crashed down in the sand twenty feet away.

Charlie knew she ought to run right then, but she hesitated, wanting to make sure that her pursuer wasn't badly hurt by the accident.

Only, she saw no sign of them. The motorcycle had no rider.

Charlie sighed, realizing she had been tricked. Whoever was chasing Charlie had leapt off the motorcycle before reaching her, knowing it would provide a distraction as it passed. She had exhausted her last option to escape. Her opponent knew her too well, which led her to believe it could be only one person.

She turned around. Sure enough, the motorcyclist stood behind her, silhouetted against the brightly lit Pyramid of Khufu. Charlie could make out the stocky, muscular shape of his body.

He was aiming a gun at her.

Charlie raised her hands in surrender. "Hey, Dante," she said. "Long time no see."

"Hello, Charlie." The motorcyclist pulled off his helmet—and Charlie gasped.

The man facing her wasn't her half brother, Agent Dante Garcia from the CIA. It was Isaac Semel . . . from the Israeli Mossad.

SIX

Cairo, Egypt

R amses Shah was feeding his snakes when he heard that his son had been attacked.

The snakes were Egyptian cobras, although back in antiquity, they had been known as asps. Cleopatra was said to have committed suicide by allowing one to bite her, although Ramses suspected that was merely a myth. The snakes had been revered by the pharaohs and were used as symbols of royalty. Their venom was notoriously deadly; in ancient times, criminals were executed with it.

Ramses found it practical. Like his father and grandfather, he was a ruthless businessman. He had taken what was already an impressive shipping business and built it into an international conglomerate. And when you ran a company that big, you made enemies.

Ramses liked to deal with those people the old-fashioned way. Egyptian cobras weren't as famous as their cousins, king cobras, but they looked quite similar, with hoods that could flare out when the snakes were threatened. Ramses found them beautiful. He owned ten, which he kept separately in enormous glass tanks in a special room of his home. It was like his own personal reptile house at a zoo.

The cobra venom worked by attacking the victim's nervous system. It prevented the nerve signals from being transmitted. First, the muscles would stop working, paralyzing the victim, and then the heart and lungs would cease to function, so the victim would die of suffocation. Snake venom was a toxin, meaning that it usually needed to be injected into the bloodstream (which snakes did with their fangs)—as opposed to a poison, which was lethal when consumed. However, an effective poison could still be made from the venom.

To get the venom from the cobras, you had to milk them. That involved grabbing the snake behind the head, then getting it to bite down on the edge of a special glass vial. The vial had a rubber cap that would stimulate the snake to release its venom, as though it were biting its prey. Obviously, this was an extremely risky activity. Ramses could have hired a professional to handle it—but he enjoyed doing it himself. It gave him an adrenaline rush and a sense of power over nature.

He enjoyed feeding his snakes as well. He loved to

watch the natural battle for survival play out—although, at his home, the snakes always won. He had just placed a rat into the tank that held his biggest cobra, Akhenaton, when the phone rang.

Akhenaton, coiled at the far end of the tank, instantly sensed food. The snake began to unspool itself. All eight and a half feet of its body was suddenly in motion.

Ramses ignored the phone the first time it rang, not wanting to miss this. But then it rang again. And again. Which indicated there was trouble.

Even though the rat had been bred in a store and never faced danger in its life, something primal kicked in. The rodent tensed in fear, knowing danger was close.

Ramses answered the phone gruffly. "There had better be a good reason you are bothering me this late . . ."

"There is," came the reply. It was Dawud, the head of Ahmet's security, a man who Ramses had hired himself. "Ahmet was attacked in his home tonight."

Ramses was surprised by his own reaction. He wasn't concerned at all. Instead, he felt disappointment, as though somehow Ahmet must have brought this on himself. Ahmet was impulsive and careless, always getting into trouble.

In the tank, Akhenaton flicked his forked tongue. Snakes actually used their tongues to smell, collecting tiny particles from the air, then moving them to the Jacobson's organs, which were located in the roofs of their mouths. Akhenaton certainly knew that food was close.

"What happened?" Ramses asked.

"He was knocked unconscious. Chloroform."

"A robbery?"

"Not that we can tell. Nothing seems to be missing."

"Then why . . . ?"

"We don't know. There doesn't appear to be any reason for the attack at all."

Akhenaton was now on the hunt. Even though his tank was large, it didn't take the snake long to cross it, slithering through the rocky landscape, bearing down on the rat. The rodent was frozen in fear, trembling. There was no place for it to run.

"When did this happen?" Even as he spoke, Ramses's eyes were locked on the snake.

"Half an hour ago. He was having a party . . ."

"Again?"

"Yes. Ahmet went to his office during it—and that's where the attack occurred. It looks like he was caught by surprise."

Akhenaton came upon the rat and suddenly stopped, watching it with his small, black eyes. The hood of his neck flared, but the snake himself stayed otherwise still.

Ramses asked, "Do you know who attacked him?"

Dawud replied haltingly, embarrassment in his voice.

"It . . . Er . . . From what we can tell . . . It was a young woman."

Akhenaton struck. It was so fast, it was almost hard to see, even though Ramses's eyes were riveted to the scene. One moment, the snake was two feet away from the rat, and the next, its fangs were deep in the body of its prey. The rat gave a startled squeak, but that was all it could manage. The cobra coiled around the rat's body, holding it tight while the life faded from its eyes.

Ramses was so stunned by Dawud's last comment, he felt like he had been struck by a snake himself. Ahmet might have been foolish, but he was tough and strong. "A young woman knocked my son unconscious? Just one woman?"

"Yes."

"And how is it that you know this?"

"My men and I saw her leaving the office . . ."

"And you didn't stop her?"

"We tried. But the condo was very crowded because of the party and . . ." Dawud trailed off, too embarrassed to finish the sentence.

Ramses understood what had happened. "She got away."

He didn't say anything for a few moments after that. He made Dawud wait through the uncomfortable silence, knowing that he had failed and that his boss deserved to be livid at him.

The rat stopped moving. Akhenaton removed his fangs from its body, then unhinged his jaw and began to consume the rodent head first.

Like all snakes, cobras swallowed their prey whole. This often meant having to eat something much larger than their heads. It was a laborious process. For Akhenaton to work his jaws around a rat this large, it might take up to half an hour.

"Where are you now?" Ramses asked Dawud.

"In Ahmet's bedroom. We moved him here after we found him. My men stopped the party and sent everyone home."

"Go to the office and turn on the video on your phone. I want to see where the attack took place."

"All right." It didn't take long for Dawud to get to the office; it was right next to Ahmet's bedroom. When Dawud switched to video, Ramses had the bodyguard walk him through the scene of the crime, showing him where Ahmet's body had been splayed out, where the rag with the chloroform had been found . . .

"Wait," Ramses said. "What's that behind you?"

Dawud paused in the middle of a sentence, then looked behind him, at the stone tablet mounted on the wall, close to where Ahmet had been attacked. "It's just an old stone with some carving on it."

"Not the stone," Ramses said impatiently. "What's that

I see on it? There's something red. Is that blood?"

The camera bobbled as Dawud went to inspect the tablet. The red mark was at the very bottom of the stone. "No sir. It appears to be chalk."

"Chalk?"

"Oh," Dawud said suddenly. The camera bobbled some more as the bodyguard moved across the office again. Then it focused on something on the desk. The red stick of graphite Charlie had used lay there, still partially wrapped in tissues. One of the caterers had seen Charlie drop it as she fled through the kitchen and given it to Dawud later while the party guests were being cleared out. At the time, Dawud had been confused as to what its purpose might be. Now he held it up so that Ramses could see it, feeling embarrassed for his failure to notice the red mark on the stone tablet and connect everything. "This was left behind. I'm not sure what it is . . ."

"I do. Show me the tablet on the wall again. So I can have a better look at it." Ramses thought he knew which artifact it was but wanted to make sure.

Dawud brought the camera back to the stone again, confirming Ramses's worst fears.

Cleopatra's tablet.

Ramses leaned against Akhenaton's glass tank, oblivious to the drama taking place inside. He had forgotten all about the snake. Instead, his eyes were locked on the image of the stone relic.

He hadn't thought about it in years. Maybe even a decade. He knew the story behind it, of course. How his grandfather had foolishly paid a band of thieves to steal it from some noted archaeologists, thinking it held a message from Cleopatra. And yet it had all been for naught. If the tablet had ever held a message, it was either partly missing or indecipherable. The tablet was useless, possibly even a fake, and not very attractive to look at. It was dull and crude, which was why Ramses hadn't cared when Ahmet asked if he could decorate his home with it.

But now someone had taken a rubbing of the tablet. A young woman capable of incapacitating his son and escaping all his bodyguards. Who could she be? How had she found out where the tablet was kept? And was it possible she knew something about it that Ramses did not?

"Sir?" Dawud asked. "Are you still there?"

"Hmmm?" Ramses realized that it had been well over a minute since he had last spoken. He had been lost in thought. Now he snapped back to reality. "Have you reviewed the security camera footage from the condo? Not just the office but *everywhere*."

"My men are working on that right now, trying to determine the identity of the woman."

"I want to see it myself. Download everything to a hard drive and bring it over here right away."

"But sir . . ."

"I don't want any excuses. Just do it." Ramses hung up angrily, frustrated at the incompetence of Dawud and the other bodyguards, frustrated at himself for allowing Ahmet to have the tablet, frustrated at his grandfather for failing to ever find what might have been encoded in the stone.

It was only now that he realized he had never even asked how Ahmet was doing.

The thought passed quickly. Ramses was more concerned about the tablet—and the young woman who had dared to break into his son's home. He needed to learn who she was, track her down, and do whatever was necessary to discover what she knew about the tablet.

And then he would do to her exactly what Akhenaton had done to his prey. He would make sure the life was drained from her body.

If Cleopatra's tablet truly did lead to something important, Ramses Shah wasn't about to share it with anyone else.

SEVEN

The Sinai Desert

saac Semel held up the rubbing that he had found while searching Charlie Thorne. "What is this?"

"It's a rubbing," Charlie replied.

"I can see that it's a rubbing. I would like to know what it's from."

"It's an ancient Roman take-out menu. This is the first recorded case in history of anyone putting Canadian bacon on pizza. It's priceless."

"This is no time for jokes, Charlotte."

Charlie bristled. She hated her full name. But then, she was quite sure Semel knew that and was trying to get a rise out of her. "I tell you what. I'll answer your questions if you answer mine."

Semel sighed heavily, then sat down, facing Charlie. "I know you're extremely smart. So it should be obvious to you that you're in no position to make demands."

Charlie was well aware that her situation was dire. She was currently in the back of a dimly lit panel van, surrounded by four Mossad agents with one more in the driver's seat, passing through the heart of the Sinai desert on the way to Israel. Charlie's hands were bound behind her back with zip ties, and she sat on a hard wooden bench against one wall of the van. She had gotten a great deal of sand in her clothes back at the pyramid complex, and it itched terribly.

The Mossad was the branch of Israel's intelligence community responsible for covert operations and anti-terrorism. Charlie had first encountered Semel four months earlier while hunting for Pandora in Jerusalem. The Mossad had attempted to obtain Pandora too, making the understandable claim that it was in Israel's best interests to keep it out of the hands of their enemies. They had been formidable adversaries, even tracking Charlie to Pandora's ultimate hiding place.

Semel was in his early sixties but as fit and powerful as a man in his twenties. The only part of him that showed his true age were his eyes, which betrayed a great deal of wisdom.

"How's your arm?" Charlie asked.

Back in Jerusalem, Dante had been forced to shoot Semel. At the mention of it, the Mossad agent reflexively touched the spot on his bicep where he had been wounded. "It has healed."

"Good. How did you know I was in Egypt?"

Despite what he had just said about Charlie's demands, Semel answered the question anyhow. Because the answer made him and his team look good. "It is in the interest of Israel for us to keep a close eye on Egypt. We monitor who is coming into this country. And of course, we've been looking for *you*. My men suspected that perhaps you didn't die after all. We were quite pleased to see that we were correct. We spotted you the moment you arrived at Cairo International and have been watching you for the past two weeks."

Charlie showed a flicker of surprise, despite her best attempts not to.

Semel grinned proudly. "You're upset at yourself for not noticing us. Don't be. My agents are the best in the world. No one sees us."

"And now you're taking me back to Israel?"

"Yes."

"You don't think it's going to look weird, bringing a girl my age across the border?"

"It's *our* border. When I tell them we're Mossad, they won't ask any questions."

Charlie nodded understanding, working out the math in her head. It had taken them nearly an hour to get out of the Giza pyramid complex, as the security guards there had mounted a search for the trespassers. They'd had to slink through the dunes and cut a hole in the back fence, where the panel van had met them. Then the van had worked its way through a great deal of traffic before finally reaching open highway. There were no windows in the back of the van, but Charlie was pretty sure of the route they were taking. She had spent enough time looking over maps of Egypt to know there was only one road from Cairo to Israel, a highway that cut straight through the heart of the Sinai Desert to Eilat, at the northern tip of the Gulf of Aqaba on the Red Sea.

Without traffic, the trip was approximately five hours. Charlie guessed that the Mossad had no intentions of stopping en route. Nor would they drop their guard. Even as Semel spoke, the three other agents around him kept their attention riveted on her.

Charlie had learned martial arts well enough to get the drop on a dumb bodyguard, but she was no expert. She probably couldn't even beat an old warhorse like Semel, let alone all the younger agents around him. And even if she *could* take them out . . . what then? She would be surrounded by desert, where the daily temperatures in June maxed out at over a hundred degrees. Which meant she was trapped. For once in her life, Charlie had no plan.

Semel grinned, seeing the concern in her eyes. He held up the rubbing once again. "I will ask only one more time: What is this?"

"You're not interested in Pandora anymore?" Charlie asked.

"Of course we are. We're extremely interested in finding out what you have locked away up here." Semel reached across the van and tapped Charlie on the head, indicating that he was fully aware she had the equation memorized. "But we were also intrigued by your presence here in Egypt. Four months ago, you only escaped Israel thanks to a bit of luck and a great amount of your money . . ."

"That wasn't luck," Charlie told him. "I outwitted you."

Semel ignored her and continued speaking. "And all of a sudden, instead of lying low someplace secluded and safe, you're sneaking back into this part of the world under an assumed name. I'd like to know why." Semel pointed to the rubbing. "What is so important about this that you would go through so much trouble and expense to get it?"

Charlie had run out of ways to stall. And she was sure that Semel would know if she was lying. But then, she realized, her only chance of escape was to be honest. The truth about what Cleopatra had etched in the tablet might just convince the Mossad to remain in Egypt, rather than taking her back to Israel, where they would certainly put her under lock and key until she coughed up Pandora.

Plus, she needed more time to examine the rubbing. Since she had first entered Ahmet Shah's office, she'd barely had a moment to focus on it. Now she was eager to take another look and see if she could decode the message that Cleopatra had left behind.

So she met Semel's gaze and told him what the tablet really was:

The first clue to finding the greatest treasure of the Egyptian Empire.

EIGHT

Semel stared into Charlie's eyes for a few seconds, assessing whether or not she was telling the truth. Then he said, "And what would this treasure be, exactly?"

"I'm not sure," Charlie admitted. "But whatever it is, it's pretty important. The person who left that clue was Cleopatra."

Semel's eyes widened in surprise. "*The* Cleopatra?"

"Well, to be honest, there wasn't only *one* Cleopatra. There were six. But I'm talking about the last one. The one who went down in history. Although, weirdly, historians refer to her as Cleopatra the Seventh, even though she was sixth. Obviously, someone lost count somewhere along the way. The Ptolemy family tree could be awfully confusing. They thought their royal blood was sacred, so to keep it pure, a lot of close relatives married each other. Cleopatra's parents were cousins and her grand-parents were brother and sister. Which meant she only had one set of great-grandparents instead of four. One of her ancestors, Ptolemy the Eighth, actually married his own daughter, which made his original wife—who he was still married to—his own mother-in-law. Which must have made Mother's Day *really* confusing."

Semel frowned at the thought of this. "Really?"

"Oh yeah. The Ptolemies were so messed up, they make *my* family look well adjusted. Not only did they all marry one another, but then they went to war with their siblings for control of the empire. Cleopatra had two brothers and two sisters and, eventually, she had each of them bumped off. Strangest of all, Cleo and her fam-ily weren't even Egyptian. They were from Macedonia, which was part of the Grecian Empire, and claimed to be direct descendants of Alexander the Great. The Ptol-emies were filthy rich and basically bought the rulership of Egypt."

Semel gave Charlie a skeptical look. "I never heard that."

"Lots of people haven't," Charlie told him. "But it's true. Look it up if you want. Back then, Egypt had a thing for Alexander the Great. After all, the guy had built Alex-andria, which at that time was the most important city in Egypt, if not the entire Western world. It was like New

York, London, and Tokyo all rolled up into one. Very cosmopolitan. Although the predominant culture was Greek rather than Egyptian. And it was a huge center of knowledge and learning. The Library of Alexandria was one of the largest repositories of knowledge in the world— until it burned down. Which was a huge tragedy for all of humanity . . ."

"Was the treasure hidden there?" Semel asked impatiently.

"Calm down," Charlie told him. "I'm getting to that. I just have to make sure you know your history first." She started to say something, then changed her mind and asked, "What do you know about Cleopatra?"

"She was the queen of Egypt," Semel replied. "And she had affairs with Julius Caesar and Mark Antony."

"Yeah, that's what I figured." Charlie made no attempt to hide her disappointment. "You left out a few things. Such as: She ruled Egypt for twenty-two years, which was about ten times longer than Julius Caesar managed to rule Rome. She was very likely the most educated woman of her time, if not all of Western history up to that point. She commanded an army and a navy and oversaw the most powerful economy in the Mediterranean. She managed to keep the Roman army at bay for over two decades. And her people respected her. Under Cleopatra's reign, Egypt prospered and there was never a major revolt. But all that most people know about her is her love life—which, by the way, wasn't a couple of affairs. They were *relationships*. She loved both Caesar and Antony and they seem to have loved her, too. In fact, it was Antony's love for her that probably doomed them both—and maybe even all of Egypt."

"How's that?" Semel asked.

"When Julius Caesar was assassinated, it was unclear who should succeed him as emperor of Rome. His true heir, by birth, should have been his only son, Caesarion, who was his child with Cleopatra. However, Caesarion was much too young to lead the empire, so there was a lot of warring and conflict for a while. Eventually, two of Caesar's generals, Octavian and Mark Antony, laid claim to the throne and divided power. To seal the deal, Antony married Octavian's sister, who, because there was a real dearth of creativity in those days, was named Octavia. But Antony was madly in love with Cleopatra, who he'd started seeing after Caesar died. Antony stuck with his political marriage to Octavia for a few years, but eventually ditched her and got back together with Cleo—which is when the trouble started.

"Octavian was probably already planning to fight Antony for the control of Rome, but now he used Antony's relationship with Cleo against him. He started a propaganda war, claiming that Cleo was an exotic temptress from a distant land who wanted to take control of Rome.

Antony and Cleo ended up going to war with Octavian—and they lost. Really, really badly. Rome took over Egypt, which officially ended the Egyptian Empire, and Antony and Cleo committed suicide rather than becoming prisoners of Octavian. However, Cleo had a plan to get even, which is where *that* comes in." Charlie pointed to the scroll of paper in Semel's hands.

Semel looked at the rubbing again, this time with more reverence. "Caesarion," he said, reading the second word from the tablet. "This was a message for him?"

"From his mother. It was found in the ruins of a temple of Isis on the banks of the Red Sea. Not too far from where we are right now, I'll bet. Cleopatra had a real Isis thing going. Isis was probably the most important goddess in Egyptian mythology, the goddess of life and magic, and the protector of women and children. Cleopatra sometimes claimed to be Isis in the flesh, and a lot of Egyptians believed it. The story goes that Cleo feared she and Mark Antony were losing the war against Octavian and figured she needed to protect the *real* heir to Rome, her son with Julius Caesar. So before the final battle, she sent Caesarion out to the temple with one of his tutors to hide him from Octavian. Unfortunately, things didn't quite go as planned."

"Octavian had Caesarion killed," Semel said. It was only a guess, but he was sure of the answer.

"Yes. So Caesarion either never got that message, or he didn't have a chance to follow up on it."

Semel gave Charlie's rubbing a closer look. "And you think this tells Caesarion how to find this treasure of Egypt?"

"That's my best guess."

"So that he could use it to reclaim the throne?"

"Yes. Money was power back then, just as it is now. That's how Egypt was able to hold off the Roman Empire for so long; Egypt was rich and Rome needed money. Cleopatra's family had bought the throne once before. They could do it again. But, of course, Cleopatra had to hide her treasure to make sure that it didn't end up in Octavian's hands."

"So where is it? And what is it?"

"I don't know," Charlie replied.

"Well, good luck finding it with *this*." Semel pointed dismissively to the rubbing. "Either part of it is missing or it doesn't make any sense."

"You can read Latin?" Charlie asked him.

"Not as well as I used to. I learned it back in school. But I know enough to recognize that this isn't coherent."

"Can I see it?" Charlie asked. "I haven't really had the time to take a good look with Ahmet Shah's bodyguards and the Mossad chasing me and all."

"Be my guest." Semel held up the rubbing for Charlie

to see—although he still kept it away from her, as though worried that she might do something to it if given the chance, even with her hands bound behind her.

In the dim light of the van, Charlie scrutinized the rubbing. This was the first time she'd been able to care-fully examine it.

Semel was correct. It didn't make any sense.

The rubbing itself looked like this:

It was impossible to translate in full. Much of the message was missing; all that was left was a series of sentence fragments. Charlie was disappointed but not surprised. When the tablet had been found decades earlier, it was common for archaeological sites to be poorly excavated—if they hadn't already been pillaged by looters. There was a long history of Egyptian antiquities being treated badly: The tombs of pharaohs had been raided and graffiti had been carved into the pyramids since well before Cleopatra's reign. Sadly, even in modern times, the theft of ancient artifacts was common. It was extremely likely that whoever had found the tablet had failed to remove the entire artifact properly. Or perhaps they had broken the tablet into pieces on purpose, intending to sell each one to a different buyer. Or maybe the tablet had already been broken when it was discovered; after all, nothing was permanent. Temples collapsed, land eroded, rocks crumbled . . .

Charlie suddenly found herself drawn to the crack down the center of the tablet, now indicated as a white line through the red graphite of her rubbing. Something struck her as unusual. She leaned forward, peering at the paper intently. "Does anyone have a flashlight? The lighting in here is crummy."

Semel looked to one of his agents, who quickly produced a flashlight and shone it on the rubbing.

With the additional light, Charlie was able to see what was strange about the tablet. The rubbing enhanced the texture of the stone, emphasizing what might not have been obvious if Charlie had been looking at the real thing. Which meant that she could now see something that anyone viewing the original stone might have missed.

"What is it?" Semel asked, sensing her excitement.

"The grain of the stone in both halves of this tablet is different," Charlie observed. "This is limestone, which is a sedimentary rock. It forms when sand and other sediments accumulate on the seafloor over millions of years. So there's a great deal of variation in what different pieces are made of, even if a lot of it looks exactly the same. To the naked eye, this appeared to be a single piece of stone that had cracked in half. But it's not. It's two different pieces that were fitted together to *look* like one broken piece."

Semel gave her a dubious glance. "Are you sure? Creating that would require exceptional masonry skills . . ."

"Which were very common back in Cleopatra's day. Being a mason was an exalted position. Masons built the pyramids, the sphinx, the palaces, the temples . . ."

"But what would be the point of making a tablet that looked like it had been cracked?" Semel asked.

"It means that the *crack* is what's important," Charlie replied. "It's not random. The words weren't carved into a stone that broke. They were carved onto the break itself. See what happens if you only read the words that the crack passes through."

Semel traced his finger down the crack, reading: *"Ut potestatum nostrarum fontem et originem invenias gloriam quare quinquaginta naves atrae profectae sunt et quo unum velum atrum rediit."* With each word, the anticipation built in his voice.

Charlie translated: "To recover the source of our wealth, seek glory where fifty black ships left and one black sail returned."

"It definitely sounds like a message from Cleopatra to her son." Semel looked at Charlie with newfound respect, although it was quickly replaced by frustration. "But now we have a new problem: figuring out what she meant. What does she mean by 'seek glory'? And what is all this about black ships and black sails?"

"It's only one black sail," Charlie corrected. "Which is important."

Semel's eyes widened in surprise. "You know what Cleopatra means?"

"Of course. It's obvious . . . if you know your ancient history."

Semel gaped at the girl, at once annoyed at her cockiness and impressed by her intelligence. How could she possibly have already solved such a cryptic clue? But before Semel could ask Charlie to explain, the road in front of the van suddenly lit up.

There was a roadblock on the highway. A dozen klieg lights were aimed directly at them, shining through the front windshield so brightly, it seemed as though it was suddenly midday. The powerful glare temporarily blinded the driver, who swerved wildly.

And then the shooting started.

NINE

The snipers were aiming at the tires of the van, and they were extremely accurate. All four tires were blown out within seconds. The van careened and nearly toppled but somehow managed to stay upright, sliding to a stop sideways across the highway, its headlights aimed into the vast emptiness of the Sinai Desert.

The Mossad agents all reached for their guns, ready for a fight, until a voice rang out through the air, someone speaking over a bullhorn. They spoke in Hebrew, clearly aware of the nationality of the people in the van. "This is the Mukhabarat. We know you are Mossad. You are in violation of Egyptian law by operating within the borders of this country without permission."

The Mukhabarat was the Egyptian intelligence service, Egypt's equivalent of the Mossad.

Semel cursed, then ordered his team, "Hands off your weapons."

His agents immediately obeyed his orders, although they were clearly upset by their situation.

"You have thirty seconds to exit the van with your hands up," the Mukhabarat agent continued. "If you do not comply, we will interpret that as a sign of aggression and respond accordingly."

Semel rolled up the rubbing of Cleopatra's tablet and tucked it under his jacket. Then he snapped a large knife from his belt and leaned toward Charlie, who flinched in fear.

"Relax. I'm not going to hurt you." Semel spun Charlie around, then sliced through the zip ties binding her wrists. "The last thing I need is for the Mukhabarat to think we're forcing a tween girl over the border against her will."

"Yeah, it'd really suck if they knew the truth," Charlie said sarcastically.

Semel gave her a hard stare. "If you don't like how I'm treating you, wait until the Mukhabarat gets their hands on you. They're thugs. You'd be wise to keep your comments to yourself."

"You now have fifteen seconds left!" the Mukhabarat agent announced, then began to count down. "Fourteen! Thirteen!"

"Let's go," Semel told his agents, trying to hide the resignation in his voice.

They threw open the doors and emerged onto the highway, their hands high above their heads. Charlie followed their lead.

It was difficult to see due to the blinding lights, but Charlie could make out the shapes of two trucks parked sideways on the highway ahead, barricading it, with several more sedans behind. In front of the trucks, kneeling beneath the lights, a dozen Mukhabarat agents had guns pointed at them.

In the distance, beyond the barricade, road flares were laid out on the pavement, sparking red flames, signaling to any cars that the highway was closed.

Behind Charlie, on the opposite side of the hobbled van, more Mukhabarat agents appeared from the night along the shoulder of the highway, guns drawn. They laid out more flares to stop any traffic that might be coming from Cairo.

To the sides of the highway, there was only desert and night sky.

It was surprisingly chilly. Cold night winds whipped through the desert, blowing sand across the road. Charlie, only wearing her party dress, found herself shivering.

A man strode forward from the barricade, silhouetted against the lights. "Hello, Isaac," he said to Semel with what sounded to Charlie like knowingly fake friendliness. "It's been a while."

"Hello, Anwar," Semel replied. His face betrayed nothing. Charlie couldn't tell if Semel was pleased to see the Mukhabarat agent. Or upset. Or somewhere in between.

Anwar stopped a few yards away, keeping a safe distance from them but close enough that Charlie could now make out his features. He looked like an Egyptian version of Semel: an older man, weathered by years in the desert but still in good shape. His hair was obviously dyed, so black it blended into the night. His eyes immediately fell upon Charlie, although he continued speaking to Semel. "She looks awfully young for a Mossad agent."

"True. But we can use that to our advantage. We're here to bust a child-trafficking ring . . ."

"Don't bother lying to me," Anwar said angrily. Then he looked back over his shoulder and yelled, "Is this her?"

"It is," came the reply.

Charlie knew the voice. It immediately brought a smile to her face. "Hey, Dante," she said. "I guess the Mossad weren't the only ones keeping an eye on me."

Her half brother stepped out of the darkness and stood by Anwar. Dante was handsome and powerfully built. He wore jeans, a polo shirt, and a windbreaker to protect him against the nighttime cold. Charlie could see the bulge of his shoulder holster beneath it. He gave Charlie a smug grin and said, "You're not quite as stealthy as you think."

"Where's your girlfriend?" Charlie asked.

Dante's smile faded and he turned red. "Milana's not my girlfriend. And she's in the car." He stuck a thumb over his shoulder, indicating one of the sedans on the highway.

Charlie waved toward it cheerfully. "Hey, Milana!" she called out.

Dante grew even more embarrassed. He now looked like a high school senior whose parents had forced him to bring his little sister to a party.

Meanwhile, Anwar was facing down Semel. Charlie sensed the two men had a long history. There was a great deal of tension in the air.

"You and your team stay right where you are," Anwar told Semel. "Let the girl come forward. Try anything funny and we'll shoot. Understand?"

Semel nodded agreement. His expression remained cool and calm, but Charlie could tell that he was angry.

Charlie said, "Mr. Semel has something of mine that he took from me. Can I take it back?"

"What is it?" Anwar asked.

"Just a drawing I did. But I worked really hard on it."

"Go ahead," Anwar said. "Carefully. And hold it where I can see it."

Charlie unzipped Semel's jacket and removed the rubbing. "Just so you know," she whispered to him, "I had nothing to do with this ambush. I'm as surprised by it as you are." Then she turned around and held the rubbing up in the air, letting Anwar confirm that it was simply a piece of paper. "This is it!"

She walked across the no-man's-land in the middle of the highway, between the Mossad and the Mukhabarat.

Dante came out to meet her. Although he was doing his best to be professional, it was evident that he was concerned about Charlie.

"Are you all right?" he asked her. "Did they hurt you?"

"No," she replied, then shivered as another gust of wind swept through the desert. "Although I'm very cold."

Dante immediately took off his windbreaker, even though he was only wearing the thin polo shirt beneath it, and draped it over Charlie's shoulders. Then, keeping his arm around her protectively, he steered her back toward the barricade. He paused as they came alongside Anwar. "Thank you for helping me find her."

"Of course, my friend," Anwar replied with genuine warmth. "Thank *you* for tipping me off that the Mossad was operating here." He then turned his attention to Charlie. "Would you mind showing me your drawing?"

"Sure," Charlie said, and then unrolled the rubbing for Anwar to see.

Anwar looked it over, obviously concerned that it might have been something important, perhaps an ancient papyrus scroll that Charlie had swiped. He appeared pleased to see that it was only a rubbing on a piece of paper, although also confused as to what it might be from. "Where did you make this?" he asked.

"I visited the Egyptian Museum in Cairo today," Charlie replied. "There's a whole room where you can do rubbings of fake artifacts. Like a real archaeologist!" Charlie was doing her best to act like a kid her age, maybe even one a bit younger, playing up her innocence for Anwar. There was really such a room at the museum. She had seen it while visiting. In fact, she had even swiped that very piece of paper and the red graphite stick from that room, after seeing how perfect they were for rubbings.

Anwar considered the rubbing a bit longer, then flashed a smile at Charlie. "It's very nice. I sincerely apologize for any trouble you might have encountered in Egypt." With that, his eyes shifted toward Isaac Semel and narrowed.

"I appreciate your help," Charlie said. "You have a lovely country."

"Thanks," Anwar replied. "I try my best to keep it that way." He waved Charlie and Dante onward.

The two of them slipped past the row of klieg lights. It took a few moments for their eyes to adjust to the darkness. Beyond the Mukhabarat's roadblock, a long line of vehicles was now backed up on the highway. Much of the traffic was old, rusted buses, shuttling people who couldn't afford cars across the desert.

Dante led Charlie toward a rental sedan that was parked among the Mukhabarat's cars.

The familiar shape of Milana Moon leaned against it.

Milana was a tough and exceptionally capable agent with a softer side that she only showed to a few close confidantes. It had taken her a long time to warm up to Charlie, but now she genuinely cared about the girl. She smiled with relief as Charlie approached. "Looks like you got yourself into some trouble, as usual."

"I was just about to escape them on my own before you arrived," Charlie replied. "Did you do something with your hair?"

"Yes!" Milana exclaimed. "Right before we came to Egypt."

"It looks great," Charlie told her.

"Thanks," Milana said, then gave Dante a sharp look. "I'm glad *someone* noticed."

Dante groaned and rolled his eyes. "This is why I hate going on missions with my little sister."

"You're the one who dragged me into all this," Charlie reminded him. "If it wasn't for you, I'd still be living a normal, carefree life right now." As she reached the car,

Charlie glanced back toward the standoff in the middle of the highway. She was too far away to hear the conversation between Anwar and Semel, but she could tell it was strained. "No one's going to get killed here, are they?"

"No," Dante said confidently. "But the Mossad really overstepped their bounds, and Anwar's not going to let them off easy. Although no one wants an international incident either. The Mukhabarat will probably cuff them, drive them to the Israeli border, and make some threats about what will happen if something like this ever occurs again." He unlocked the rental car and they all got inside, Dante in the driver's seat, Milana next to him, and Charlie in the back.

They couldn't go anywhere right away because the highway was blocked, but they could talk freely in the car, away from the Mukhabarat agents, and they were shielded from the wind.

"How'd you know I was in Egypt?" Charlie asked.

Dante said, "We know you hacked the CIA to get Einstein's files and the list of historical figures who hid their discoveries. Cleopatra was a brilliant woman who wasn't given enough respect for her brains. We figured you'd feel a kinship with her—and might come looking for whatever she had found."

"So you told the Mukhabarat to keep an eye out for me?"

"Actually, we used a mole at the Mossad." Dante grinned proudly. "They keep a closer eye on Egypt than the Mukhabarat does. Now, what's this art project of yours *really* about?" He pointed toward the rubbing in Charlie's hands.

Charlie considered denying that the rubbing was a clue, but she knew that Dante and Milana wouldn't believe her. Plus, she needed their help.

It was hard being on her own. Now the Mukhabarat, the Mossad, and the CIA were on her case—and for all she knew, there could be others as well. With all those complications, Charlie wouldn't be able to track down Cleopatra's treasure solo.

Even more importantly, she was lonely. Charlie had always been a social person. Lying low and keeping to herself was no fun at all. Even though Dante could be a pain in the rear sometimes, and Milana often kept to herself, Charlie was glad to see them.

And yet there was one thing Charlie had to discuss before Cleopatra. "I can see you guys are dating now. There's a tiny bit of Milana's lipstick on your cheek, Dante."

Dante reflexively glanced in the rearview mirror, only to find that his cheeks were clean. Then he grimaced, realizing that Charlie had tricked him.

"Ha!" Charlie cried. "I wasn't really sure before, but

you just confirmed it! Milana's not even wearing lipstick, you dummy."

Milana gave Dante a disappointed look, although there was amusement in it. "Some spy you are."

"When did this start?" Charlie asked excitedly. "Was it back in Peru?"

"We are not talking about this," Dante said. "I want to know what you've discovered about Cleopatra. If you don't cooperate, I can hand you right over to the Mukhabarat. I'm sure they'd love to know what you've really been up to."

"You're bluffing," Charlie said. "You would never do that."

"I'm starting to give it serious consideration."

"I tell you what," Charlie said. "If you tell me about your first kiss, I'll tell you whatever you want to know about Cleopatra."

"No!" Dante snapped. "You're in no position to make demands like that. I'm not telling you—"

"It was in Peru," Milana said, interrupting him. "At the eco-lodge. Dante took the initiative. It was very sweet. Now, what the heck does this clue mean?"

Charlie grinned, pleased by what Milana had shared, then met her end of the bargain. "It's a message Cleopatra left for her son Caesarion. Most of the writing is only there to mislead you. The really important words are the ones that follow the crack: 'To recover the source of our wealth, find glory where fifty black ships left and one black sail returned.'"

Dante and Milana looked at her expectantly. "So . . . ?" Dante asked. "Do you know what that means?"

"Of course," Charlie said.

"Where is this telling us to go?" Milana pressed. "Is it somewhere close to here?"

"Sorry, no," Charlie replied. "We need to travel quite a bit farther than that."

TEN

Ramses Shah had many connections. He had close friends in politics, in law enforcement—and in intelligence.

Eventually, he found someone with the information he needed.

Her name was Zara Gamal, and she was a data analyst with high-level clearance. It was late at night by the time Ramses tracked her down, but she took the call anyhow, because when someone as powerful and important as Ramses Shah called, you answered.

Ramses had already put his own security team on the case rather than the morons who worked for his son. In fact, he had fired each and every one of the men who'd been at Ahmet's party that night, including Dawud. Ramses's personal team had gone over the security footage from Ahmet's condo and pulled some still frames of the young woman who had taken a rubbing of Cleopatra's tablet.

The woman had been very smart, originally keeping her head down, so that the security camera in the office couldn't record her face directly—but once Ahmet surprised her, she hadn't been able to continue that behavior. Especially when she had attacked Ahmet and knocked him out. (Ramses had watched with bitter disappointment how easily his son had been rendered unconscious by a person half his size—and a woman, no less.) For a few seconds, the young woman, while clinging to Ahmet's back and chloroforming him, had provided a direct view of her face for the camera. Ramses's security team had taken those frames and enhanced them to produce a clear photograph of the woman they were looking for.

Now Ramses sat at the desk of his home office and relayed the story of the events at Ahmet's condo to Zara, although he altered one fact: He claimed the young woman had actually stolen a priceless artifact. The Mukhabarat might not be as motivated to help him find someone who had merely taken a rubbing of a tablet—and as far as Ramses was concerned, the less the Mukhabarat knew about Cleopatra's coded message, the better.

"What time tonight was this?" Zara asked, intrigued.

"Around eight thirty. Why? Have you heard anything about it?"

"One of our senior agents, Anwar Zafadi, ran an operation in collaboration with the CIA tonight. The CIA knew that a Mossad cell was working illegally in Egypt, transporting a girl through the Sinai to Israel. They recovered the girl about an hour ago."

Ramses's pulse raced with excitement. "Is she still in your custody?"

"She never was. She's an American citizen. So they handed her off to the CIA. As far as Zafadi was concerned, the real prize was getting to bust the Israelis."

"Did the Mukhabarat take any photos of her?"

"You know I can't send intel from an operation to you."

"You don't have to. I'll just send *you* a photo, and all you have to do is confirm if it's the same person."

There were a few seconds of silence while Zara considered that. Then she said, "I guess that'd be all right."

"I'm forwarding you the photo right now."

A few more seconds passed while Zara compared the photos. Then: "It's the same person."

"You're sure?"

"Not one hundred percent but close enough."

"Do you know where she is now?"

"Personally? No. She's in the hands of the CIA."

"A senior Mukhabarat agent wouldn't just hand over the girl and let the CIA walk away," Ramses said. "Zafadi must have put a tail on them."

"If he did, I wouldn't be able to share that information with you," Zara told him, although her tone indicated that maybe she was only saying this because she had to protect herself from anyone who might be eavesdropping.

Sure enough, even as she spoke, Ramses received a text. It wasn't from Zara's phone directly, which could be traced back to her, but from a random number, which meant she was using a phone the Mukhabarat didn't know about.

Aircraft #NC3378B.

"Thanks anyhow," Ramses said. "Your cooperation will not be forgotten."

He hung up on Zara, then called Omar Jobrani, the head of his security team, and told him to track the flight plan of an aircraft with registration number NC3378B.

Five minutes later, Omar called Ramses back. The plane was a private jet, owned by the Stonehenge Security Corporation, which Omar suspected was a front for the CIA. It had departed from the private terminal at Cairo International Airport twenty minutes before. But it hadn't filed a flight plan.

"Can we figure out where they're going?" Ramses asked.

"It's possible. There are ways."

"Then do it. And Omar?"

"Yes?"

"Have my jet ready as soon as possible. Wherever the CIA lands, I want to be right behind them."

ELEVEN

Somewhere over the Mediterranean Sea

T his is a nicer jet than the last one they gave you," Charlie observed. "That one smelled like old cheese."

The jet was small but had been well cared for. Milana Moon was flying, although she kept the cockpit door open so she could hear what Charlie and Dante were saying. Charlie and Dante were seated on opposite sides of a small table near the rear of the plane, where Charlie had laid out an array of snacks from the tiny kitchenette. She popped a handful of M&Ms into her mouth, then chased them down with a gulp of Dr Pepper.

"After all that sugar, you're not going to be able to sleep tonight," Dante warned her.

"I need some energy, or I'm gonna pass out right now," Charlie told him, then made a show of eating more M&Ms. "It's been a really long day." She waved to the interior of the jet. "Someone at the CIA must be really proud of the work you're doing."

Dante shrugged noncommittally. He had only learned earlier that day that Jamilla Carter had been forced out, which was upsetting news. Even though Charlie had ultimately escaped, Carter had been pleased with Dante's performance overall. His unorthodox plan to recruit Charlie had finally led the CIA to Pandora after generations of agents had failed. He and Milana had kept the equation out of the hands of their enemies and learned how to crack Einstein's secret code. That had earned them an unusual degree of autonomy in the search for more hidden discoveries. But now that Carter was gone, Dante worried this operation might soon come to an end.

Therefore, he had wasted no time relaying the good news to Arthur Zell's office: He had located Charlie Thorne once again, and she was cooperating with him to locate another treasure, this one hidden by Cleopatra. They had already solved one clue and were following it to the next location.

Zell had yet to respond.

Dante had not shared what the next location was because he didn't know. Charlie had stubbornly refused to tell him until they were in the air. "For safety precautions," she had explained. "The fewer people who know where we're going, the less chance we have of someone following us. Just head northwest and I'll give you the rest of the info on the way."

Dante hadn't bothered to argue. But now he was losing his patience. "Okay, kiddo. We've done everything you requested. Want to tell me where we're heading?"

"You haven't figured it out yet? Didn't you do any research on Cleopatra for this mission?"

"Of course."

"Well, it obviously wasn't enough." Charlie flashed an obnoxious grin, her teeth flecked with tiny bits of M&M. "You remember what the clue was, right?"

Dante gave Charlie a sharp look, annoyed at her for questioning his memory. "'To recover the source of our wealth, find glory where fifty black ships left and one black sail returned.'"

"Very good. Now, Cleopatra wasn't trying to be cryptic here. She desperately wanted Caesarion to find the treasure she had hidden. She had probably tipped him off to what the trick to reading the tablet would be, then left a clue that he would clearly understand. So all you have to do is consider what would have been common knowledge in Cleo's time."

"Naval history?" Dante guessed.

"No. Homer."

Dante looked at her quizzically. "You mean, the guy who wrote the *Iliad* and the *Odyssey*?"

"Right."

"That was common knowledge in Egypt?"

"It was a fundamental part of any classical education. Back then, Homer was treated the way that Shakespeare is now. I mean, why is Shakespeare taught in school these days, even though he lived over four centuries ago?"

"Because he was the greatest playwright who ever lived."

"Says who? It's not like the people of the world ever voted on that." Charlie polished off her bag of M&Ms, then tore into another. "The British decided that we should all know Shakespeare. Back when their empire spanned the planet, they wanted all their subjects to think that British culture was the finest in the world. Therefore, the greatest writer of all time ought to be British. So they started telling the children of Canada and India and Hong Kong that Shakespeare was the top of the heap, even though his plays were kind of hit-or-miss and *The Taming of the Shrew* is totally sexist. Plus, in *Antony and Cleopatra*, he did more to paint Cleo as some exotic vixen than anyone else in history."

"And the ancient Greeks did the same thing with Homer that the British did with Shakespeare?" Dante concluded.

"Exactly." Charlie took another swig of soda. "They declared Homer was the end-all-be-all of literature, and even though their empire had gone into decline by Cleopatra's time, a traditional Greek education was still in vogue for the children of the rich and powerful all throughout the Western world. Julius Caesar had one, even though he was Roman. And Cleopatra and everyone in her family got one. Unlike some cultures, the Egyptians didn't have an issue with teaching women. Cleo got a serious education. The Library of Alexandria was literally in her backyard. She had the finest tutors in the world. Greek was the first language she learned—and Homer was mandatory. Schoolkids were taught that he wasn't a man; he was a god. They had to start memorizing the *Iliad* before they even learned to read. By the time Cleopatra was a teenager, she would have known the entire text backward and forward—and the same was true for Caesarion."

"Well done," Dante said, making it clear he was impressed; everyone liked being flattered, even Charlie Thorne. "So then, this clue references something in Homer?"

"Yes. You know the story of the *Iliad*, right?"

"Of course. It's an epic poem about the Trojan War, focusing on the siege of Troy by the Greeks."

"Right. According to Homer, the war started when this Trojan troublemaker named Paris stole a woman named Helen from her husband, Menelaus, who was the king of Sparta. Now, Helen was supposed to be a major catch; every king around had tried to win her affection. One of them was Menestheus, the king of Athens, but even though he lost Helen to Menelaus, there weren't any hard feelings. When war was declared, Menestheus stepped up. The *Iliad* says no one was better than him at arranging chariots and troops for battle—and that he sent fifty black ships to Troy."

"Cleopatra said to look where the fifty black ships left!" Milana called from the cockpit. "So we're heading to Athens?"

"Yes!" Charlie called back.

"Consider it done." Milana quickly adjusted their heading.

Out the window, far below the jet, Charlie could see a large, oblong island outlined by the lights of its coastal towns. Crete. It appeared to rotate slightly as they veered from northwest to north, heading toward Greece.

"Hold on now," Dante said, sounding slightly concerned. "You're basing this whole decision about Athens on this 'fifty black ships' thing? No offense, but that sounds a little weak. Didn't lots of cities send ships to Troy?"

"That's a valid question," Charlie admitted. "But there's more to the clue. The part about the one black sail returning. And that not only confirms Cleopatra means

Athens, but it also tells us *where* in Athens to look."

Dante grew excited once more. "Because of something else Homer said?"

"No. This time, you have to know your Greek mythology—which would have been something else Cleopatra was well versed in. Do you remember who Theseus was?"

Dante took a moment to search his memory. "He was the guy who defeated the Minotaur."

"Right. Somewhere down there." Charlie pointed out the window at the island of Crete. "Although Theseus was from Athens. In fact, he's the mythical hero-king of the city. His father, Aegeus, was king before him. Aegeus was a good dad, and so he was really worried when Theseus went off to deal with the Minotaur. So they came up with a plan to keep Aegeus informed; if all went well, Theseus would fly a white sail on his ship on his return to Athens, but if he died, his men would fly a black sail. Well, Theseus might have been a great warrior, but he was kind of an idiot when it came to planning ahead. He defeated the Minotaur but totally forgot about the sails. He flew the black one instead of the white one. When Aegeus saw it, he was so upset, he threw himself into the ocean and drowned. That's why the Aegean Sea is named after him."

Dante beamed, proud of his half sister. "That's good work. Definitely sounds like Athens is the place. I know

Cleopatra went there sometime late in her reign . . ."

"Yes. In 32 BC. She was the first of the Ptolemies to ever visit, although her family had been very generous to Athens for hundreds of years. They had donated food and military assistance and buildings. Cleo spent an entire summer there, which was plenty of time to hide another clue . . ."

"Where?" Dante asked pointedly. "You said it had something to do with the black sail . . ."

"Many versions of the Theseus myth say that when Aegeus leapt into the sea, he did it from the Acropolis."

"The Acropolis?" Dante repeated. "But that's nowhere near the sea. No one could jump from there into the ocean."

"And Theseus was on his way back from fighting a cannibalistic half man–half bull that lived in a giant maze," Charlie reminded him. "Whoever came up with these myths wasn't really focused on making sense. Plus, there's one more clue from Cleo's tablet leading us to the Acropolis and telling us what to look for there."

Dante gave a sigh of fake exasperation. "What do I need to know to translate this part? Sanskrit? Hieroglyphics? Ancient Persian basket weaving?"

"Only a little Greek." Charlie popped the last M&M into her mouth. "Because Cleopatra's name comes from that language, not Egyptian. 'Kleos' and 'Patros' means 'Glory of the Father.'"

"Glory," Dante echoed. "The clue says to find glory where the black ships left and the black sail returned. So Cleopatra doesn't mean actual glory. She means . . . herself?"

"Right. Cleo had a problem when she came to Athens. The Athenians were nuts for Mark Antony's ex-wife, Octavia. They revered her as a goddess. There were statues of her everywhere. So Cleo went on a charm offensive. She spread a lot of money around. And it worked. The Athenians shifted their allegiances and even erected statues of Cleopatra and Mark Antony right in the heart of the city—in the Acropolis."

"So if we find the statue of Cleopatra, we find the next clue?"

"Theoretically," Charlie agreed, although there was hesitation in her voice.

"Wait," Milana said from the cockpit, sensing what the issue was. "The statue can't possibly still be in the Acropolis. It's been over two thousand years since Cleopatra was there. The Acropolis has been looted a hundred times since then."

"That's true," Charlie conceded.

Dante gave her a dubious look. "If the statue isn't there anymore, how are we supposed to find it?"

"It might be tricky," Charlie warned. "But I know someone who can help."

TWELVE

The Sinai Desert
Halfway between Cairo and Eilat, Israel

The Humvee carrying Isaac Semel and the other three Mossad agents pulled off the highway in the middle of the desert. Isaac could tell because the feel of the road changed. The highway this far from the city was in poor condition, cracked and pocked with potholes, but it was still much smoother than the desert road, which was rutted like a washboard.

This was a bad sign. It indicated that, instead of taking him and his men directly to the Israeli border, the Mukhabarat was making a detour.

Still, Semel showed no response. He continued pretending to be asleep.

He had been doing this for over an hour now, letting the Mukhabarat think he was snoozing so they would drop their guard and relax around him. He suspected his fellow agents were doing the same thing, as he hadn't heard a peep out of them—although it was possible that they had truly nodded off.

The four of them were handcuffed and blindfolded in the back of the Humvee, which was being driven by two of the Mukhabarat agents from the highway blockade that had caught Semel by surprise. Semel was still upset about the ambush; once again, he had allowed Dante Garcia to take Charlie Thorne away from him and blamed himself for the failure. But it did him no good to dwell on it. He needed to be calm and collected, not angry. So he focused on his breathing, keeping his heart rate low, and stayed alert for anything the Mukhabarat agents might say.

The two of them were cautious; they didn't discuss anything of a secure nature. However, the agent in the passenger seat did communicate with other people at times, and though Semel could only hear one side of the conversation, he was still able to deduce two things.

First, he could tell the agent was using a radio rather than a phone, indicating that he was talking to someone close by, which meant they were being accompanied by another vehicle carrying other agents. Semel presumed that Anwar Zafadi was in that vehicle, calling the shots.

Second, there was some discussion about Cairo International Airport and a private terminal. Semel figured that the Mukhabarat had put a tail on the CIA, and that Dante Garcia had left the country with Charlie Thorne.

The Humvee was old and in dire need of a tune-up. The shocks were gone, and the vehicle jounced wildly over the desert road, jostling Semel and his fellow agents about. It became pointless to pretend that they were dozing; no one could sleep through such turbulence.

"Where are you taking us?" Semel asked in Arabic.

"Eilat," the agent in the passenger seat replied.

"I'm not an idiot," Semel said. "I know we've left the highway. Where are we going?"

"You'll find out soon enough," the agent told him.

In truth, it was another twenty minutes before the Humvee came to a stop. Once the engine shut off, Semel could hear other voices, men outside, including Anwar Zafadi. Zafadi shouted, "Get them out!" and then, sure enough, the back of the Humvee opened and Semel and his agents were yanked out of the vehicle.

Semel's blindfold was knocked slightly askew, allowing him to see a tiny bit of his surroundings. They were out in the middle of nowhere, far from any city lights. The sky was dark, but Semel didn't need time for his eyes to adjust, as they had been closed for the past hour. He could make out the silhouettes of several men and, behind them, great monoliths of jagged rock. Even this far from civilization, litter was strewn on the ground; plastic water bottles and junk food wrappers. Semel also caught the glint of metal; shell casings from spent ammunition. Semel presumed this was a training ground for the Mukhabarat and maybe the Egyptian army as well.

He was forced to his knees in the dirt, as were his men. They were lined up in a row, facing off into the distance.

"Isaac," Anwar said, "you made a big mistake, coming into my country like this. That girl must have been very important for you to take such a risk. Who is she?"

"I don't know," Semel replied. "My orders were only to extract her. I wasn't told anything else."

Someone clubbed him on the back of the head with the butt of a rifle. Not hard enough to knock him unconscious but close. He saw stars, felt blinding pain, and fell forward into the dirt.

"Don't lie to me, Isaac." Anwar didn't sound angry. There was pleasure in his voice, as though he was enjoying this. "You wouldn't have come on this mission without knowing what was at stake. And you obviously knew the Americans. So I will ask one more time: Who is the girl?"

Hands grabbed Isaac, lifted him from the dirt, and set him back on his knees. He was still dizzy from the blow, but he could sense that the agent who had clubbed him before was beside him, ready to club him again.

And then he wasn't.

A shot rang out in the night. The Mukhabarat agent yelped in pain, spun, and fell.

Semel could see that the agent was still alive, just hit in the meat of his leg, where he would be incapacitated. Now he writhed in the dirt, clutching his wound and screaming.

Two more shots were fired. Two more agents dropped, wounded in the exact same spot in their legs.

Panic set in among the other Mukhabarat agents. They fled, looking for cover, although there was nowhere to hide.

Only Anwar stayed put, realizing there was no point in running.

Semel grinned at him. "You honestly didn't think I'd come on a mission like this without backup, did you?"

Anwar removed his own gun from its holster and aimed it at Semel's head. "Order your sniper to stop or I'll—"

Another shot rang out. And then Anwar was down on the ground, struck in the leg as well. His gun tumbled from his grasp.

Semel snapped to his feet and kicked the weapon away before Anwar could grab it again. Then he flashed a smug smile at the fallen Mukhabarat agent. "My team has been following you for the last hour. You've just led them into the perfect spot for an ambush. They're now stationed in the rocks around us and, as you can tell, they have one heck of a sniper with them. He just hit you and your men cleanly from over a hundred yards away in the middle of the night. If he wanted to hit you anywhere else, he could do it. You understand that, right?"

"Yes," Anwar said through gritted teeth.

"Good. Because now it's time for *you* to answer some questions. Where has the CIA taken the girl?"

PART TWO
THE
TREASURY

In time we hate that which we often fear.

—WILLIAM SHAKESPEARE,

Antony and Cleopatra

THIRTEEN

Athens, Greece

Athens is one of the oldest cities on earth, with a recorded history dating to 1,400 years before Cleopatra's time, although there is evidence of human settlement going back at least another five thousand years before that. It is often considered the cradle of Western civilization and the birthplace of democracy, a city that nurtured the arts, science, and philosophy. It was famed for its architecture, its theater, its academies of learning, and of course, the Olympic games. However, after being conquered by the Turks in the 1400s, Athens went into a long period of decline; a few centuries later, the once-great city had dwindled to a population of only four thousand people. Most of its buildings fell into disrepair; shepherds grazed their flocks around the ruins.

Then, in the 1840s, the Greeks rebelled against the

Turks in the Greek War of Independence. Afterward, Athens was once again chosen as the capital city of Greece. The population rebounded, and today, almost a third of all Greeks live in the metropolitan area. Now, as was the case in the ancient times, the focal point of the city is the Acropolis.

During the golden age of Athens, the Acropolis was the religious and financial center of the city. Set atop a 500-foot-tall mountain, it was home to several temples, although the most famous and impressive was the Parthenon. Completed in 438 BC, the Parthenon was designed to showcase the power, wealth, and artistic skill of Athens. The finest masons were recruited from around the world, and the great marble building was designed with expertise that remains astonishing today. The exterior was originally decorated with intricately detailed friezes, while the interior was filled with sculptures, most notably a massive representation of Athena, carved from ivory and gold.

Even though the Parthenon was a temple, it also served as the treasury for the city. Unfortunately, Athens's wealth was also its undoing. The city was sacked multiple times over the centuries—by the Spartans, the Visigoths, the Ottomans, and many others—and as its fortunes declined, so did those of the Parthenon. The building was looted of its renowned art. It was converted into a church and then a mosque. The worst blow came in 1687. The Turks used the Parthenon to store ammunition, which exploded during an enemy bombardment, destroying much of the building. Today, virtually none of the original decorations remain on the Parthenon. Many have been taken to museums around the world (often without the permission of the Greeks) while the rest is housed in the Acropolis Museum in Athens.

This was where Charlie, Dante, and Milana were headed the next morning, having scored a few hours' rest in a nearby hotel. The museum was located at the base of the mountain that the Acropolis sat on, with the Parthenon looming above it. They were hoping to meet with Dr. Learka Karathinasis, who was a senior archaeologist at the museum.

Dr. Karathinasis was the aunt of Eva Karathinasis, one of Charlie's closest friends from college. Thanks to Charlie's extreme intelligence, she had been admitted to several universities at the age of eleven. She had selected the University of Colorado, although this had far less to do with its strong astrophysics program than its location. Charlie's primary reason for going to college was to get away from her parents, who had only cared about her great IQ if they could make money off it. The University of Colorado had plenty of hiking, mountain biking, kayaking, rock climbing, and skiing close by—although Charlie still needed a car to get to it. Which was where Eva had come in.

Eva was also more interested in goofing off than attending classes. More importantly, she was one of the few students who talked to Charlie like she was an equal rather than a child—or a freak of nature who could help them with their homework. Eva also knew a lot about things that Charlie had never given much thought to, like pop music and political protests. Charlie had always enjoyed their time together, and she missed Eva a lot. The single worst thing about being saddled with Pandora was that it was now impossible for her to have a normal life and friends. Since the day Dante had showed up and dragged Charlie into the hunt for Pandora, she had been forced to cut off all contact with Eva. Eva didn't even know what had happened to her; Charlie had ditched her in the middle of a ski trip and disappeared from her life without any explanation at all.

Charlie had never met Dr. Karathinasis, but Eva had spoken highly of her, claiming she was brilliant and possibly the friendliest person on earth. So, first thing in the morning, Charlie had called the Acropolis Museum and left a message for her, saying that she was a friend of Eva's and that she was in town and hoping they could meet up. (She'd had to use Dante's phone, as she didn't have one of her own; she only used cheap burner phones to avoid being tracked, and the last of those was back in Cairo.) Then, Charlie headed to the museum with Dante and Milana anyhow, figuring it was better to wait there for Dr. Karathinasis to return her call, because they could do some research themselves in the meantime.

Although they had to make a stop on the way. Charlie desperately needed new clothes.

Dante and Milana had stashed extra clothing on the plane, while Charlie was still wearing her party dress from the night before. It was impractical, it made her stand out, it was terribly wrinkled because she had slept in it—and she still couldn't dislodge all the sand she had gotten in it.

There were plenty of places to purchase clothes on the way from their hotel to the museum; their route took them directly through a tourist district, along a pedestrian street lined with souvenir stores, coffee shops, and outdoor cafés. Most of the boutiques only sold casual tourist clothing, but that was fine with Charlie. The day was already warm and promised to get a lot hotter, and she wanted to look like a tourist to blend in. So she bought a T-shirt, shorts, baseball cap, and cheap sneakers, then left the party dress hanging in the changing room for anyone who wanted it; she had no more use for it.

The CIA paid for everything. While Milana was handling that, Charlie stopped at the jewelry counter to check out some local trinkets. She was examining some earrings studded with low-quality gemstones when Dante came up beside her.

"Here, try this on," he said, and then snapped a metal bracelet around her wrist.

Charlie was so surprised that Dante was suggesting a piece of jewelry for her that it took her a moment to realize what he was up to. The bracelet was a chain of metal links with a thick circular clasp. It made a strange noise as it locked, as though something electronic inside it had engaged.

Charlie instantly tried to take it off but found that she couldn't. She glared at her half brother angrily. "This is a tracking bracelet?"

"We can't take any chance that you'll ditch us again," Dante explained.

"What makes you think I'd do that?"

"You've already done it twice. Once in California and again in the Amazon . . ."

"I didn't ditch you in the Amazon. I got kidnapped . . ."

"And then went on your merry way after you escaped."

Charlie had no response to that, because it was the truth.

Milana finished paying and left the store. Dante and

Charlie followed her, heading toward the museum along the crowded pedestrian street.

The street wrapped around the base of the mountain upon which the Acropolis sat. They were at the eastern end, so they couldn't see the Parthenon yet, but they did have a good view of the incredible feat of engineering that had made the construction of the site possible.

The original mountaintop had been too small and uneven to build the Acropolis. So the Athenians had made the mountain bigger, building retaining walls around its upper flanks and then filling them in with hundreds of tons of dirt and rock. In this way, they had created an artificial mesa with a wide, flat plain at the top, strong enough to support the huge buildings of the Acropolis. From the base, it looked like a fortress, with the walls perched high up on the jagged, rocky flanks of the mountain. The walls weren't exactly beautiful, built from rough-hewn stone, but they were certainly impressive; it had been over 2,500 years since their construction and still, they stood firm.

Dante told Charlie, "The CIA is obviously interested in what Cleopatra hid, which is why we haven't run you right back to America. But our primary objective in all this is still Pandora. In the Amazon, you promised to give it to us if we helped you. I met all of your demands. I didn't tell the CIA—or anyone at all—what we *really* found down there. Even though it made it look like that mission was a failure. Which made Milana and me look bad, and yet you took off without telling us anything. This time, I expect you to hold up your end of the bargain."

"I *will*," Charlie said, even though she was trying to figure out a way not to. While she trusted Dante to try to keep Pandora from being misused, that wasn't the case for the entire US government. Once she shared the equation, Charlie was certain that, sooner or later—probably sooner—it would be used to make weapons. If the US government didn't do it, it wouldn't be long before the equation got leaked to someone who would. "You don't need *this*." Charlie jangled the tracking bracelet. "I'm not going to run again."

"Let's just consider that an insurance policy," Dante said.

Charlie looked to Milana for help. "You're okay with this?"

"It was *my* idea," Milana replied.

Charlie gave her a look of betrayal. "Really?"

"In fact, I suggested tagging you on our previous missions. Your brother was the one who balked at it."

Charlie tugged on the bracelet, seeing if there was any give to it.

"That won't come off without the key," Dante told her. "And it's made of a steel alloy. You can't cut it and you can't break it."

"We'll see about that," Charlie said.

They rounded a corner and found themselves facing the southern flank of the Acropolis. Now they could see the Parthenon, perched high above at the top of another great retaining wall. At the base of the mountain beneath it were the ruins of more temples and an amphitheater, and below all that was the Acropolis Museum itself.

The museum was extremely modern, providing a strong contrast to the artifacts it displayed. It had been built during a burst of urban renovation for the hundredth modern Olympic games in 2004, which had also included a new subway system, highway network, and international airport. The museum's location had turned out to be above some ancient city ruins—which wasn't really surprising, since almost every place in Athens was built above ancient ruins. The architects had come up with an ingenious solution to protect and display the area: The museum was built on pillars, so that its first floor was actually two stories above the ground. Tourists could still visit the ruins via a series of catwalks below the museum—or even look down on them from inside the museum through thick glass floors. Because of this design, the museum's main entrance had to be accessed by a wide bridge.

As they headed for the doors, Dante's phone rang. He checked the caller ID and smiled. "It's Dr. Karathinasis. Looks like it's time for us to get to work."

FOURTEEN

Washington, DC

Arthur Zell couldn't sleep.

Some of it was the excitement of his job. Some of it was fear.

As the new director of the CIA, he had been briefed on an enormous amount of classified information in a very short period of time. Only days before, he had been blissfully unaware of how many threats to democracy there were. Now he knew.

And yet the one that nagged at him most was Pandora and Charlie Thorne.

Unlike Jamilla Carter, Zell did not live in the Virginia suburbs, near CIA headquarters. Instead, he had an apartment right in Washington, DC. His wife and two daughters still lived back in Nebraska, his home state. Zell flew home to see them on weekends and during breaks between congressional sessions, but that was going to change; his new job required he be in Washington full-time, which meant his family would have to move here. The apartment's location had made sense for a congressman, as it was located close to the Capitol, although he was thinking that he would still keep it. He liked the liveliness of the city, as opposed to the quiet of the suburbs. Even now at three a.m., the city was stirring. He stood at his windows and looked down on the streets, watching cars and pedestrians pass.

It was his duty to protect them.

Zell had never met Charlie Thorne. He only knew her from her files, but his daughters were close to her age. As far as he was concerned, there was nothing as unpredictable as a teenage girl. Although he loved his daughters dearly, he couldn't imagine trusting them with something as powerful and deadly as Pandora. The burden of being the only person on earth who knew the equation must have been incredible.

Zell was also concerned by the recent series of mission updates from Dante Garcia. Carter had originally given Garcia carte blanche to track down Charlie Thorne, letting him communicate with her only when he wanted to, through an archaic system of dead drops, as if it was still the Cold War. That had changed after the business in South America, where the attempt to locate a discovery of Charles Darwin's had led to Charlie being abducted by the Russians. The mission had been a complete failure. Darwin's treasure hadn't been found, and Charlie had ultimately vanished once again.

As a result, Jamilla Carter had gotten the axe—and Dante had been put on a shorter leash. He was now sending daily encrypted updates via email. These had originally gone directly to Carter, but as of today, they were coming to Zell, and Zell wasn't pleased.

The mission had already gone sideways. Charlie had been captured by the Mossad, forcing Dante to recruit the Mukhabarat to spring her, which meant that both foreign intelligence services were now involved. Dante had the jump on them for the moment, but that might not last. Zell didn't want Israel or Egypt—or *anyone* besides the United States—getting their hands on Pandora. Drastic measures needed to be taken.

He had spent much of his sleepless night considering his various options. Now, as he watched the city below him, he realized which one he had to choose.

First, he called the government airfield where the CIA kept its planes and ordered a jet to be readied.

Then he called Dante Garcia.

FIFTEEN

Dante didn't answer Zell's call, because he wasn't carrying his phone.

Instead, he had given it to Charlie, who ignored the incoming call to speak to Dr. Karathinasis.

"Charlie!" the archaeologist exclaimed. "I just called Eva to ask her if she really knew you and, my goodness, she went on and on about you. She says you're the smartest person she's ever met and that she would have completely flunked her first semester if it wasn't for you . . ."

"She's exaggerating," Charlie said diplomatically. "I didn't help her that much."

"I know my niece. She's no fool, but she needs a kick in the pants when it comes to studying. So thank you. Would you like to visit the Acropolis Museum? You said you were staying close by . . ."

"We're *here*, actually," Charlie said. "We just got to the main entrance."

"Really? Stay by the front doors. I'll be right down!"

A long line of tourists was waiting to enter the museum, most of them dressed in T-shirts and shorts, the way that Charlie, Dante, and Milana were. The three of them breezed past the line and stood to the side of the main doors.

The entire wall of the first floor was glass, so they could see inside easily. It wasn't long before a woman who looked enough like Eva to be a close relative came along. Dr. Karathinasis was tall and slender with unruly hair. An official ID dangled from a lanyard around her neck. Charlie waved to her and she beamed back, then held open the exit door for them.

"Hello!" she exclaimed. "It's such a pleasure to meet all of you!"

They made quick introductions, Charlie referring to Dante and Milana as her older brother and his girlfriend, which Dante winced at but Milana appeared to be amused by.

Everyone who entered the museum had to pass through a metal detector, which was standard procedure the world over. Knowing this, Dante and Milana had left their CIA-issued weapons in the hotel safe. Dr. Karathinasis flashed her ID and spoke to one of the security guards, who allowed Charlie, Dante, and Milana to jump the line and pass through quickly.

This brought them into a wide entry foyer, where there was a ticket booth, a gift shop, some introductory videos, and sections of glass flooring to look down onto the ruins below. The art was on the upper levels, accessed via a central bank of escalators. Dr. Karathinasis led the way to them. "What brings you to Athens?" she asked. "Vacation?"

"Research, actually," Milana said, following the plan that she, Charlie, and Dante had concocted the night before. "I'm doing my PhD in anthropology at Penn, studying the cult of Isis in other cultures around the Mediterranean at the time of Cleopatra. As I'm sure you know, Cleopatra was seen as the embodiment of the goddess not only in Egypt but also amongst sects in Athens and Rome. I was hoping that you—or someone else here—might be able to share some information about the statue of Cleopatra that used to be in the Acropolis . . ."

"Oh!" Dr. Karathinasis said with genuine excitement. "That sounds like a fascinating area of study. Although sadly, that statue of Cleopatra has been lost for centuries, which is unfortunately the case with so much of the art here."

"I'd heard that," Milana said. "However, I was hoping that someone might at least have an idea as to where the statue *was*. Even knowing its position in the temple, especially relative to that of the statue of Athena, would give some indication of how important the Athenians considered Cleopatra to be."

Dr. Karathinasis considered that thoughtfully, then nodded. "I might be able to help with that."

They arrived at the second floor of the museum. Here, dozens of statues from the Acropolis were arranged around the exterior, while the conservation laboratories were housed in the center. Dr. Karathinasis waved her ID in front of a lab door to unlock it, then led them inside.

The lab was relatively up-to-date and modern, given that the museum itself wasn't very old. Conservators worked at computer stations around the edges, while the middle of the room was dominated by a horizontal interactive flat-screen table. The screen was rectangular and had the exact same proportions as the Parthenon itself, which was evident as it was currently displaying an enormous aerial photo of the Parthenon.

Dr. Karathinasis explained, "This is a project we've been developing for some time, using information compiled by all of our conservators and archaeologists. It allows us to see the Parthenon as it was throughout its history. For example, when it was first built." She tapped some icons on the screen, and the photo was replaced by a computer simulation of the Parthenon from the beginning of its lifetime, in 438 BC. Once again, the view was from above, but even from this angle, amazing details leapt out. The Parthenon had originally had two rooms inside, the western one slightly smaller than the eastern, and the floor was laid with an arresting black-and-white pattern.

"This was the treasury," Dr. Karathinasis said, indicating the smaller room.

Dante whistled appreciatively. "That's as big as Scrooge McDuck's vault. They must have had some serious money."

"They did—at first," Dr. Karathinasis agreed, then pointed to a large object directly beside the treasury, in what would have been the very center of the Parthenon. "Now, this is the statue of Athena, although I can get you a much better look at it." She tapped some more icons, and the view quickly rotated to ground-level.

The degree of detail was incredible. Staring at the screen, Charlie felt as though she was looking at photos that had been taken inside the Parthenon 2,500 years before. They were looking directly at the statue of Athena, which towered over the digital humans in the room, at least fifty feet tall by Charlie's guess. It depicted a woman dressed as a great warrior, with traditional Greek armor, a war helmet, a spear, and a shield. In one hand, she held a human-size statue of Nike, the goddess of victory. On the breastplate of her armor was the head of Medusa. Athena's body was sculpted from ivory, so her skin was blinding white, while her armor was made of gold.

Dr. Karathinasis said, "Obviously, this is only a guess as to what the statue actually looked like, but everything you see here is our best approximation based on the research of our staff. The golden armor didn't last long. Even Phidias, who sculpted it, suggested that it could be melted down in case funds were needed—which is exactly what happened. A leader of Athens named Lachares used it to pay his troops around 296 BC, so if we look at the statue then . . ." She tapped a few more icons, and the scene switched slightly, showing the statue without its armor.

Milana asked, "Can you show us where the statue of Cleopatra was?"

"Well, I can show you where we *think* it was. Although there's a good chance the presumed location is correct. Our researchers have pored over thousands of documents from antiquity." Dr. Karathinasis opened a small search window on the screen and entered "statue of Cleopatra." The screen's display shifted once again. The great statue of Athena was now clad in bronze. And to the side was a smaller but still impressive statue of a woman on a pedestal.

"That's Cleopatra?" Dante asked.

"It appears so," Dr. Karathinasis replied.

"She's right beside Athena!" Charlie exclaimed. "That must mean the Greeks thought she was awfully important."

"Yes—although it's also possible that Cleopatra paid handsomely to have a place of honor." Dr. Karathinasis zoomed in on the sculpture. "Again, we can only guess as to what this really looked like. Perhaps it would have been an idealized female form, like the statue of Athena, rather than an exact likeness—although I believe that this representation is more realistic, based upon the few images of Cleopatra that we have."

On the screen, the statue of Cleopatra was dressed as the goddess Isis, wearing a draped dress and a diadem, a thin jeweled crown that Charlie knew was extremely important to the queen. Unlike the statue of Athena, which depicted a young woman without a single flaw or blemish, the statue of Cleopatra showed a middle-aged woman with a thin nose and a protruding chin, her hair braided and knotted in a bun.

Dante asked, "What images is this based on?"

"Coins, mostly," Dr. Karathinasis replied. "Those are the best likenesses of Cleopatra that we have."

Charlie had spent an hour that morning with Milana, getting her up to speed on Cleopatra so that she would sound knowledgeable about the subject for this exact discussion. Now Milana explained, "Cleopatra oversaw some major advances in the use of coins. Like the idea of stamping a denomination on them. Before Cleopatra, a coin's value was determined by its weight, which meant every merchant needed a scale, and scales weren't always accurate. But with denominations, coins were simply worth what Cleopatra said they were worth. It revolutionized money. We still use the same system today. Cleopatra also oversaw the minting of the coins, so chances are, she had approval over the artwork. Which is why we feel that the images of her on the coins are probably good representations of what she really looked like."

Dante squinted at the statue. "I know I'm going to catch heck for this, but . . . she's not very attractive. I thought she was famed for her beauty."

Charlie, Milana, and Dr. Karathinasis narrowed their eyes at him, although Charlie beat the others to a response. "In her time, Cleopatra was famed for her intelligence, her leadership, and her diplomacy. It wasn't until long after she was dead that people started to say that she must have been beautiful. Mostly men. They found it easier to believe that Julius Caesar and Mark Antony had fallen for her because of her looks rather than her brains."

Dante held up his hands in surrender. "I was just asking. For the record, I'm all for a woman being respected for her brains." He shot a quick glance at Milana. "Although I also happen to think you're really beautiful."

Milana flashed him a smile, then asked Dr. Karathinasis, "So, there's nothing left of this statue at all? Not even the pedestal?"

"No. It's all been gone for centuries."

"Is there any chance that we could visit this location in the Parthenon?"

Dr. Karathinasis frowned. "We're really not supposed to take guests up there. The whole building is under renovation. It's a giant construction site."

Charlie shared a look of concern with Dante and Milana. They had known the statue was no longer in the Parthenon—but Charlie had figured that the real place to search for a clue would be where the statue had *been*. "Cleopatra had seen enough statues get knocked down to know there wasn't much chance of hers staying up for long," Charlie had explained to both of them earlier in the day. "She'd toppled plenty herself. In which case, the safest place to hide something wouldn't be on a statue itself but in the ground beneath it."

Getting into the Parthenon was imperative. They knew they could break into the site at night, but that would be risky. They had really hoped to be invited in as guests. So Charlie employed one of the greatest weapons she had at her disposal: guilt.

"I guess that makes sense," she said, sounding as sad as she could. "But isn't there some way in? Eva told me that you've brought her into the ruins before—and she's only your niece, not a graduate student who's come all the way here from the United States, hoping to do some important research for her thesis . . ."

Dr. Karathinasis cracked. "Oh, all right. But only because you're such good friends of Eva's. And you'll all have to follow the safety regulations. If one of you gets hurt, I'll end up in serious trouble."

"Of course!" Milana said enthusiastically. "I promise we won't cause any problems for you. When could we go?"

"Soon," Dr. Karathinasis said. "We just have to wait for one thing."

"What's that?" Milana asked.

There was a knock at the door of the lab.

"You're about to find out," Dr. Karathinasis said, grinning. Then she flung open the door to reveal someone who caught Charlie completely by surprise.

Eva Karathinasis.

SIXTEEN

Ramses Shah had to fork over a lot of money to find out where the CIA had gone with the girl.

First, he had to pay off an air traffic controller at the private terminal of Cairo International. By the time Ramses and his men were able to get through traffic to the airport, the CIA jet had already been in the air for over an hour. The air traffic controller had been tracking the jet the entire time and reported that it had just filed a change of flight plan to land at Athens International.

Ramses then footed the bill for his own private jet to fly to Athens. Along with Ahmet, who he needed to positively ID the girl, he brought three of his best men: Omar—his head of security, Baako—a clever ex-soldier, and a mountain of muscle named Lembris.

In Athens, he spread a lot of money around the private terminal, getting information. He learned that the jet he was seeking was still there, parked out on the tarmac after being refueled. He also learned that there had been only three people aboard: a man, a woman—who had been the pilot—and a teenager. He flashed the photo he had of the girl and got confirmation that she was the one on the plane.

The man who ran the taxi stand reported that he had put those same three people in a cab to the King George Hotel, so Ramses and his men took two cars there and slipped some cash to every person on duty. No one had seen those three people check in. Ramses wasn't surprised; the King George was too fancy for the CIA to spring for. Obviously, the people he was tracking were using precautions, taking a cab one place but staying at another.

Still, Ramses figured maybe they were at a hotel nearby. So he sent his men out to pound the pavement, showing the photo of the girl at all the hotels within walking distance, while he checked into the King George himself and got some sleep.

Sure enough, one of his men got a hit. Baako found a cheap tourist trap a few blocks away where the night clerk recognized the girl in the photo. By this point, it was two thirty in the morning. Baako was wise enough not to disturb Ramses's sleep with the information. Instead, he paid off the clerk to call him if he saw any of the three people leaving the hotel, then posted himself down on the corner.

Ramses was already showered, dressed, and having room service for breakfast the next morning when the call came in. The CIA was on the move.

Ramses told Baako to stay on them, then called Ahmet's room to make sure he was awake and ready to go. They headed out with Omar and Lembris, hired a car, and met up with Baako, who was now stationed outside the Acropolis Museum.

So when the CIA left the museum a few minutes later, Ramses Shah was watching.

There were now five people: three women, the girl, and the one guy.

Even from a distance, Ramses could recognize the girl from the photo. But still, it made sense to check. "Is that the girl who knocked you out last night?" he asked Ahmet.

"Yes," Ahmet said, teeth clenched angrily. "That's her."

"Want us to take them out?" Lembris asked.

"Not yet," Ramses said, even though it would have been easy for his men to do it.

The CIA agents probably weren't armed. The museum had security. The CIA couldn't have passed through with any weapons.

Ramses's men had weapons. But as far as Ramses was concerned, there was no point in coming all this way just to take out the CIA.

He wanted to know what they were after. Within hours of making the rubbing in Ahmet's condo, the girl and the CIA had made a beeline for the Acropolis. They certainly seemed to be onto something.

So for now, Ramses would let them keep doing the work.

And when that was done, he and his men would strike.

SEVENTEEN

Eva was a problem.

Charlie was torn. She was delighted to see her friend again—but she also knew this was not the time for a reunion. Whenever something of great value was at stake, things could get dangerous.

It turned out, Eva was spending the summer in Greece with her aunt. When Charlie had called Dr. Karathinasis and said she was a friend of Eva's, Dr. Karathinasis had immediately called Eva, who had flipped out when she heard Charlie was in town. She had begged her aunt to meet with Charlie right away but to not spill the beans that Eva was there. Eva wanted her appearance to be a surprise for Charlie. Which had certainly been the case.

Now, as they headed to the Parthenon, Eva insisted on tagging along. Charlie kept suggesting that she and Eva could meet later to catch up, but Eva stubbornly refused. After all, Charlie had a lot to answer for, given how she had vanished from Eva's life without a trace four months earlier.

"What happened to you?" Eva pressed. "You just took off on the ski run, and no one ever heard from you again!"

"I had some trouble with the law," Charlie said, which was the truth. But then she lied about what that trouble was. "I told you I didn't get along with my parents, right? Well, I left home without permission to attend college, and they weren't happy about it. So they sent these goons after me to drag me back home."

"And you couldn't call me to say what happened? We were worried sick about you! We thought maybe you'd skied into a ravine and broken your neck. We called the ski patrol and the police and everyone. They combed the backcountry for two days looking for you!"

"I'm sorry," Charlie said, and she really meant it. "But the guys that grabbed me took my phone and wouldn't let me make any calls. They were total jerks. And then, when they finally delivered me back to my parents, well . . . I was really unhappy. I hated being back there, and I missed college, and I guess I thought that talking to you would only make things worse for me. I know that was wrong, but . . ." Charlie pretended to grow teary, hoping to play on Eva's sympathies.

It worked. Eva's annoyance at Charlie changed to

concern. "Oh gosh. I'm so sorry about all that. It must have been terrible."

"It was." Charlie felt awful about lying to Eva, just as she had about ditching her on the ski slopes, but there was no way she could tell the truth. "Luckily, things are much better now. Dante and Milana have been looking after me, and they've been amazing." She flashed them a coy smile.

"That's great," Eva said. "Although . . . I have to admit, I don't remember you ever mentioning that you had a brother."

"Half brother," Charlie corrected. "And we were estranged. But that was really because of our parents. Now that we've gotten to know each other, we're really getting along well. I'd be happy to tell you all about it later, if you wanted to meet for lunch or something . . ."

"No way," Eva said. "I've waited long enough to see you again. You're stuck with me today."

The walk from the museum to the Parthenon wasn't long, but it was steep. First, they had to follow a road uphill to the parking area, and now they were climbing a great flight of marble stairs that led to the ruins of an ancient grand entrance. There was little shade and the day was already hot; the steps were baking in the heat and radiating it back up again, so Charlie could feel it through her shoes. Even though everyone was in good shape, the ascent still wasn't easy.

"Why would they have built the Acropolis all the way up here?" Dante asked, hoping to change the subject away from Charlie's strange disappearance. "I mean, it would have been far more accessible if they built it down there, right?" He pointed to a flat, tree-dotted park below them to the north.

Dr. Karathinasis said, "The Acropolis was designed for maximum impact, not convenience. "The Athenians wanted everyone who visited it to be struck with awe. And by all accounts, that was the case. This entrance would have been far more dramatic back in its day, although even that paled to *this* . . ."

They passed through the remains of the monumental gateway at the top of the steps and found themselves looking at the Parthenon. Even though the building was in ruins, it was still stunning.

It stood at the edge of the great mesa of rock, high above Athens. Beyond it, there was only clear blue sky. The city lay far below, its white buildings shimmering in the sunlight. Beyond it was the Aegean Sea.

Hundreds of tourists were gathered around the Parthenon, taking photos or staring in wonder.

There was another security checkpoint after the ancient gateway, to ensure that no one was carrying any weapons. Once they had passed through it, Dr. Karathinasis led the group toward the Parthenon, crossing slabs of stone that were polished smooth by the footsteps of a hundred generations of humans. It occurred to Charlie that Cleopatra herself had probably walked over this same ground, as had Julius Caesar, Alexander the Great, Sophocles, Socrates, and hundreds of other famous people from history.

Dr. Karathinasis said, "Obviously, the Parthenon would have looked even more impressive back in Cleopatra's day. The temple was covered with statues and other art, all of which were brightly painted. Now all we can see are the bare bones of the building, although even those are impressive."

An enormous restoration project was underway. Much of the western end of the Parthenon was wrapped in scaffolding, and a crane had been erected inside the building, although, at the moment, no one appeared to be doing any work.

"Where are all the workers?" Milana asked.

Dr. Karathinasis sighed. "Some days they are here, but often they are not. Who knows why? This is a very long-term project. It may be decades before it is done."

She brought everyone to the southern side of the Parthenon, where there were fewer tourists. Here, the path followed the very edge of the man-made mesa. A thick, waist-high stone border provided some protection, but Charlie could easily lean over it and look down at the steep, five-story retaining wall below her. At its base were the jagged, rocky cliffs of the mountain, which gave way to a gentler slope that ran through the ruins of yet another temple, and then down into the modern-day city.

On the other side of the path sat the Parthenon. To prevent tourists from getting too close to the ancient temple, there was only a single, thin cordon of rope that passed through a series of metal posts, and a single security guard on patrol. Dr. Karathinasis led her guests over the rope, flashing her badge to the guard so he recognized this was official business, and then took them up the ancient steps and into the Parthenon itself.

On their way, they encountered a few ramshackle, temporary buildings that were part of the renovation: masonry shops, storage sheds, and a supervisor's office. The area around them was strewn with large chunks of marble, sacks of concrete, and other construction debris. Then the group passed between the towering columns of the Parthenon and found themselves inside the great building itself—or, at least, what remained of it.

Dr. Karathinasis noted, "Every inch of this building was sculpted in meticulous detail. The floor is slightly higher in the center than it is at the edges, so that rainwater will run out of the building instead of pooling inside. To account for that slight tilt in the floor, each column is curved—although it is so subtle, you can't even detect it with the naked eye. All of this was done without the aid of any of our modern machinery. Only picks, chisels, and hand drills."

"I can't believe I'm standing here," Milana said. Even though she was only pretending to be a PhD student, her enthusiasm sounded real to Charlie. "This is incredible."

Not much was left of the interior walls of the Parthenon, only a few remnants of the treasury. The group walked toward the center of the building. Dr. Karathinasis stopped close to where the statue of Athena had stood and dramatically pointed to the floor. "According to my colleagues, this is where the statue of Cleopatra would have been."

They were now in the heart of the restoration area. The iron struts, wooden planks, and dangling ropes of the scaffolding surrounded them, shielding them from the view of all the other tourists. The floor was thick with stone dust. It felt as though they were in the middle of a construction site, not an ancient wonder of the world. Charlie grew concerned; now that she was here, the idea that Cleopatra might have hidden something that remained undisturbed for two thousand years suddenly seemed like a pipe dream.

And yet Charlie still needed to do her best to find it.

"The statue was located exactly where you're standing?" Charlie asked Dr. Karathinasis.

The doctor checked her phone, where she had inputted the presumed coordinates, then shifted two feet to her left. "It was right here."

"And how tall was it?"

"Assuming classical standards of human dimension and a pedestal of about two to three feet, then approximately eight to nine feet from top to bottom."

Charlie positioned herself a few feet away from Dr. Karathinasis, at the point where she figured she would have stood to observe the statue, had it still been there. Then she tried to imagine that area as it had been when Cleopatra visited, twenty centuries before. The Parthenon would have been a very public place at that time, the center of Athens's society. Thousands of people would have passed through it every day. So where could you hide something and be assured that it wouldn't be accidentally discovered—or moved?

Charlie looked down at her feet. If Caesarion had come to find glory, as his mother had suggested, then he would have been standing right there.

Charlie dragged her foot through the dust, revealing the ancient marble floor underneath. The white stone was perfectly smooth, expertly carved by the finest masons in ancient Greece. In Cleopatra's time, this floor probably would have been kept spotless, as befitted a temple, rather than covered with dust.

But now that it *was* covered with dust, Charlie could see a slight imperfection in the marble.

She dropped to her knees and carefully wiped more of the dust away. Most came off easily, sliding across the smooth stone, but a little of it stayed put, caught in tiny ruts so shallow that they would have been almost invisible if the stone was clean.

There was a pattern carved in the floor.

Charlie looked up to the others, grinning widely.

"I think we're in the right place," she said.

EIGHTEEN

Mossad headquarters
Tel Aviv

saac Semel was in a foul mood. He had been traveling nonstop for most of the night, following the long, dusty highway from the abandoned training zone in the middle of the Sinai Desert to Eilat, and then heading north through Israel to Tel Aviv. He was filthy and tired, but instead of being at home, showered and in bed, he was in the office of his commander, Yitzhak Levin, getting chewed out.

"We knew that Charlie Thorne had entered Egypt two weeks ago," Levin said. When he was angry, he paced around his office like a caged animal. "Two weeks! If you had just taken her then, as you were ordered, we would have Pandora by now!"

"We don't know that for sure. The CIA was aware of her presence in Egypt as well. They still might have got the jump on us."

Levin glowered. He was older than Semel but remained fit and muscular. With his thick-set, stocky build and his bald head, he looked vaguely like a fire hydrant. Through the window behind him, Semel could see the towers of downtown Tel Aviv and the blue waters of the Mediterranean Sea. "So, your defense is that the CIA would have bested you no matter what?"

"They could make an alliance with the Mukhabarat. I couldn't."

"The point remains the same: Rather than bringing the girl back here, you squandered valuable time."

"I don't consider that to be the case at all."

"And why is that?"

"Because she was obviously on the hunt for something. I figured it might be important."

"She's a thirteen-year-old girl, Isaac! For all you know, she could have been hunting for a bargain on clothes."

"She's not a normal girl and you know it. The first time I met her, she was looking for the most powerful equation known to mankind. And she found it—with clues uncovered right here in our own country—after decades of Mossad agents had failed. So I figured that this time, she might be after something important again."

"But now, since the CIA ambushed you, you have no idea what it was."

"On the contrary, I have an extremely good idea. Only, instead of going after Charlie to find out for sure, I'm stuck in this office, defending my actions."

"I'm your superior!" Levin exploded. "It's my right to question your actions!"

Semel didn't flinch. Instead, he said, "I know where she went."

"Where?" Levin demanded, still too angry to ask calmly.

"The Mukhabarat had some of its agents tail the CIA after they left us in the Sinai. The CIA had a private jet waiting for them in Cairo. According to the flight plan, they went to Athens. But my guess is, they won't be there long."

Levin stopped pacing, intrigued. "You're positive that's where they've gone?"

"Not one hundred percent, but I think it's worth following up on."

"And this new object Thorne is looking for. Do you think it could be something else along the lines of Pandora?"

"It's the source of all the power of the Egyptian Empire. So yes, I'd say that would be pretty significant."

Levin gave Semel a curt nod. "All right then. Assemble a team and get to Athens."

"Yes sir." Semel snapped to his feet and started for the door.

"Oh, and Isaac?"

"Yes sir?"

"Don't let her slip through your fingers this time."

"I won't, sir. I promise."

NINETEEN

The Parthenon
Athens

L ook," Charlie said proudly, pointing to the floor of the Parthenon.

There, delicately etched into the marble, was the word *KLEOS*.

"Glory," Dr. Karathinasis translated, amazed.

"We came here to 'find glory,'" Milana said with a smile. "Looks like we've done it. Only . . . what now?"

"I'm working on it." Charlie brushed more dust away from the marble floor, so she could see it better. Everyone else gathered around her to look down upon the stone.

The five letters were carved in simple block script but with a delicacy that indicated a master craftsman had done the work. Each was only two inches high, and they weren't etched very deeply into the marble. Once the dust was swept away, they were almost imperceptible.

If Charlie hadn't known to look for them, she probably would never have noticed them.

She ran her hands over each letter, feeling for anything she might not be able to see, and noticed a slight shift when she touched the *O*. She knelt closer, inspecting the round piece of marble in the center of the circle. "I think this piece comes out," she announced. "I need something to pry it loose. Like a chisel."

"I'll check the workshops!" Eva exclaimed, and raced back the way they had come.

"I'll look this way," Dante said, and disappeared into the maze of scaffolding.

"Wait!" Dr. Karathinasis called after them. "We can't start chipping away at the Parthenon! Not without permission from the director of antiquities!"

"Relax!" Eva yelled back. "We're not going to damage anything! Besides, this place is in ruins anyhow!" She pointed to the collapsed building around her, then disappeared through a line of broken columns.

Dr. Karathinasis helplessly watched her go, then turned to Milana, suspicious. "I thought you only wanted to locate the position of the statue of Cleopatra. No one said anything about excavating . . ."

"We aren't going to excavate much." Milana placed a reassuring hand on Dr. Karathinasis's arm. "I know I wasn't completely honest with you, but if Charlie is right, the item we're looking for was concealed here by Cleopatra herself."

Despite her concerns, Dr. Karathinasis was intrigued. "You think Cleopatra left something *here*? In the Parthenon? Something that hasn't been discovered for over two thousand years?"

"That's our guess."

"What is it?"

"I don't know. But we assume it's important."

Dr. Karathinasis wavered, torn between the thrill of discovery and her concern for breaking the rules. After a few moments, she shook her head. "I'm sorry, but I can't allow any excavation of this site without going through the proper channels. Otherwise, we're no better than the looters . . ."

That was as far as she got. Her eyelids suddenly drooped and she slumped into Milana's arms. Milana gently laid her down on the dusty floor of the Parthenon.

"You drugged her?" Charlie asked.

Milana held up the hand she had placed on Dr. Karathinasis's arm, revealing the small dart she had subtly pricked the archaeologist with. "She seemed like she was about to make a fuss. And we don't need any attention right now. "What's the chance your friend will understand what I've done?"

"Pretty good, I think. Eva's not so big on following the

rules herself." Charlie glanced in the direction Eva had gone. She couldn't see the workshops through all the scaffolding but figured her friend must be still searching them for tools.

Dante came running back, clutching a hammer and chisel. "I found these in a toolbox . . ." He trailed off as he noticed the prone body of Dr. Karathinasis. "Was she about to cause trouble?"

"Afraid so," Milana said.

Dante frowned, as though he were disappointed things had come to this, then knelt over the marble floor with Charlie. "We better make this quick."

"It will be." Charlie snatched the tools from his hand. "I know what I'm doing." She set the tapered blade of the chisel along the edge of the O in *KLEOS*, at what she had already determined was the weakest point. Then she gave the handle of the chisel a solid whack with the hammer.

The crack rang through the Parthenon.

A perfect circle of marble popped out of the center of the O and skittered away, revealing a small hole in the floor beneath it.

It was only half an inch deep, which was more than enough room to hold what had been hidden beneath it:

A single coin.

Dante quickly plucked it out and held it up for everyone to see. It sparkled in the sunlight.

"Think this is gold?" he asked.

"It's bronze," Milana said knowingly. "Which makes sense. Cleopatra introduced the metal for coins during her reign."

She and Charlie crowded around Dante to get a better look at the coin. It was the size of a quarter but twice as thick. One side depicted a snake in a circle, eating its own tail, while the other side showed a picture of a temple, along with the words "Julius I."

The craftsmanship was exquisite. The coin was beautifully designed and perfectly round.

"This doesn't look like it was printed in mass," Charlie observed. "Coins like that weren't so well made. In fact, a lot were kind of misshaped. But this looks like it was minted specially."

"But what does any of it mean?" Milana pointed to the inscription, "Julius I." "I assume this is a reference to Caesar?"

"It couldn't be," Dante said. "No one becomes a 'Julius I' until there's a 'Julius II.' There was no other Julius who led Rome—and even if there had been, that wouldn't have happened until well after Cleopatra's time."

Charlie looked to him, impressed. "Ooh. Nice deduction."

Dante grinned, despite himself.

Milana said, "If 'Julius I' doesn't mean Caesar, then what does it mean?"

"It's a date!" Dante exclaimed. "Julius wasn't just a person! It was also a month! July was named after Caesar!"

"That's true . . . ," Charlie agreed, although she didn't sound as excited about this line of thought.

"So then, this would be from July in Year One?" Milana asked.

"No," Charlie said. "Cleopatra died thirty years before then—and even if she had still been alive, she wouldn't have called it 'Year One.' The calendar wasn't changed to having BC and AD until hundreds of years later."

"Could it just mean the first of July, then?" Milana suggested.

"Maybe," Dante said. "But why would you put a date on a coin without adding the year?"

Charlie peered closer at the coin. "Hey. I think there's something written around the edge of this."

Sure enough, it looked as though there were letters engraved into the thick, curved edge of the coin, between its two faces. But before Dante could show them to Charlie, they were interrupted.

Four men emerged from the scaffolding on all sides, surrounding them.

One was Ahmet Shah, and another looked like an older, meaner version of him, so Charlie figured it must be his father, Ramses. The other two men were big and imposing and were obviously there as muscle.

Since everyone had to pass through a metal detector to get into the Acropolis, the men didn't have guns, but they had found makeshift weapons around the construction site.

Ahmet and the goons carried wrenches and crowbars, which they clutched menacingly. Ramses only held a phone. They kept their distance, remaining several feet away, too far for Charlie, Dante, and Milana to attack but close enough to keep them hemmed in.

Dante and Milana quickly scanned their surroundings, looking for anything they could use as a weapon. There wasn't much, although Dante noticed a piece of broken masonry close by that he could at least hurl at someone. As he reached for it, Ramses said, "Take one more step and the girl dies."

The tone of his voice was ominous enough to stop Dante in his tracks. Dante pointed to Charlie and asked, "You mean her?"

"No," Ramses replied. "The other girl. Her friend." He held up his phone, displaying the screen to Charlie, Dante, and Milana, then came closer so they could see.

He was on a video call. It displayed Lembris, the Shahs' most imposing thug, who had captured Eva. From their surroundings, it looked to Charlie like Lembris was holding Eva inside one of the workshops, where he must have caught her by surprise when she had gone to find a chisel. Lembris stood behind Eva, pressing a crowbar against the front of her neck. Eva was crying.

"If I give the word, he crushes her windpipe," Ramses said, then extended his hand. "The coin, please."

Dante glowered at him.

Charlie felt a burning hatred toward the man but also horror and guilt, knowing that Eva was only in this mess because of her.

"Quickly," Ramses ordered.

Dante saw he had no choice. He tossed Cleopatra's coin to Ramses, who caught it, then looked it over. Charlie saw the man's eyes light up in excitement, then cloud in confusion. He shifted his gaze to Charlie.

"You broke into my son's home," he said. It was a statement, not a question. "Somehow you translated the inscription on the tablet in his office. And that's what led you here. To *this*." He held up the coin.

"That's right," Charlie admitted.

"I thought that tablet was a piece of junk," Ramses said. "A hoax. But my grandfather didn't. He spent his whole life trying to understand what it said. He thought it led to a treasure of some sort. Does it?"

"I'm not sure," Charlie replied.

"I doubt that. You're obviously very smart. Smart enough to understand this: Your friend's life is hanging by a thread—and it's under my control. If you don't want her to die, you're going to tell me everything you know about this treasure. So start talking."

TWENTY

Charlie's mind raced, analyzing every aspect of her situation.

Dante and Milana were excellent fighters, but at the moment, Ramses and his men had leverage over them. Charlie didn't know Ramses well, but she was quite sure he wasn't bluffing about Eva. Even if his henchman didn't kill her, he could certainly cause her serious pain, or break her neck and paralyze her. Charlie wasn't about to let that happen.

However, she also couldn't tell Ramses everything she knew. If she did that, there was a good chance Ramses and his men would kill her, Dante, Milana, and Eva anyhow, just to get rid of the competition.

Charlie had to figure out a way to get the jump on them.

But while she was working that out, Ramses wanted her to talk. So she talked.

"The trick to deciphering the tablet involves the crack in it," she said.

"What crack?" Ramses asked.

"There's a crack down the middle," Charlie answered. "It looks like the tablet has been broken, but it hasn't. The crack was always there. The words on either side of it don't mean anything. It's only the words down the crack that matter."

Ramses gave her a look of begrudging respect, impressed that she had figured this out when no one else had. "And what do these words say?"

"'To recover the source of our power, find glory where fifty black ships left and one black sail returned.' Now, the way I solved this was—"

"I don't care how you solved it. Obviously, it led you here, to this coin. What I want to know is, what's the source of power that Cleopatra's talking about?"

Charlie hesitated. She had been hoping to stall for a few more minutes by explaining how she had solved Cleopatra's clue, giving herself time to come up with a plan. But Ramses either was too wise to let her do this— or too dumb to care.

She cast a quick glance around her, looking for anything she could use to her advantage. Scaffolding surrounded her, up to four stories of it in many places, rickety constructions of thin metal struts supporting long wooden platforms. Charlie could guess what might be lying on the platforms—mortar, masonry, various tools— although the only thing she could see for sure was a power drill, its electrical cord dangling over the side like a jungle vine. . . .

Ramses recognized she was stalling and grew angry. He lifted the phone to his ear and spoke to Lembris in Arabic. "Hurt her."

Eva's scream rang out through the phone.

"No!" Charlie yelled. "I'll tell you what the treasure is!"

"*Qaf*," Ramses said into the phone. *Stop*.

Eva stopped screaming, but she was crying harder now.

Charlie said, "I wasn't stalling. I hesitated because I'm not completely sure what the treasure is. It's only a guess."

"Tell me," Ramses ordered.

"It's the Library of Alexandria," Charlie said.

Ramses looked at her curiously. "The entire library?"

"Well, no. Not the building. But what was *inside* the building. All the scrolls. Or the really important ones, at least."

"Scrolls?" Ramses scoffed, unimpressed. "Cleopatra's code said the treasure was the key to her power."

"Knowledge *is* power," Charlie stated. "And the Library of Alexandria was the greatest accumulation of knowledge in the ancient world. They didn't have books back then, but they had scrolls. At its height, the library was rumored to have up to forty thousand of them."

"It also burned down," Ramses reminded her. "Thanks to Caesar."

"He didn't burn *everything*," Charlie said. "Cleopatra saved much of it. And so did her teachers. The library was already in decline by Cleopatra's time. In fact, her entire empire was crumbling, thanks to the rulers who came before her. Cleo had some ancestors who were real tyrants, and tyrants often feel threatened by knowledge. So scholars had been secretly removing important scrolls from the library for a hundred years before Cleo's reign. Meanwhile, Rome became a bigger and bigger threat. The scholars of Alexandria wanted to protect the library from them, too. By the time Cleopatra came along, many of the scrolls had already been spirited away. Cleo's tutors recognized that she was a brilliant woman who appreciated the value of knowledge and would respect what they had done. They let her in on the secret location of the scrolls, which she tried to pass down to Caesarion."

"How do you know this?" Ramses asked, suspicious but somewhat impressed as well.

"I read a lot," Charlie said. "And the rumors of the library being moved come up now and again . . ."

"No. I mean, how do you know Cleopatra means the

library at all? She didn't mention it in the inscription on the tablet."

"The coin," Charlie said.

Ramses looked at the coin in his hand. "There is nothing about a library on here."

"Yes there is," Charlie told him. "The image of the snake, eating its own tail. It's an ancient symbol. The Egyptians called it 'Ouroboros,' while the Greeks called it 'Zhunbei zhandou.' It signifies knowledge and was used to mark the entrance to great libraries all over the world."

Up until this point, much of what Charlie had been saying was true. However, the part about the scrolls of the library being hidden somewhere was only a rumor she had heard—and the Greek name she had given for the image of the snake was an outright lie. In fact, she hadn't even spoken in Greek. She had spoken in Mandarin Chinese, which she knew both Dante and Milana understood. She was hoping that wasn't the case with Ramses Shah or any of his men, because what she had just said was, "Get ready to fight."

She looked directly at Dante and Milana as she said the words, watching their reactions closely. Both nodded very slightly to her, indicating they had received her message and were prepared.

Ramses turned the coin over in his hand, considering it thoughtfully. "So the markings on this coin tell you where these remaining scrolls are all hidden?"

"In theory," Charlie replied. "I didn't have much time to look at it before you showed up. In fact, there's still some words on the edge that I didn't even get a chance to see."

Ramses turned the coin sideways, noting that Charlie was right. "There are."

"What do they say?"

"Magnum Opus." Ramses smiled, his excitement growing. "That's Latin for 'a great work of art or literature.' And the Library of Alexandria would certainly be a collection of great works."

Charlie grew excited upon hearing the words too, although for an entirely different reason. The term "Magnum Opus" had another meaning from antiquity. A very important meaning that Ramses Shah, thankfully, didn't seem to know.

Ramses looked to Charlie curiously now. "I am very impressed by your thinking. You're quite a clever young woman. How old are you?"

"Thirteen," Charlie said. "As of yesterday."

Ramses reacted with astonishment, then looked to Ahmet with disgust. "You got your butt kicked by a thirteen-year-old girl?"

"She caught me by surprise," Ahmet said defensively. "And she cheated."

Ramses tossed the coin to his son. "Get this back to

the hotel. Keep it safe. It's the key to a fortune."

This order was in Arabic, but Charlie understood it perfectly. She also understood what Ramses was thinking: The ancient scrolls from the Library of Alexandria would have been worth millions. Ideally, they should have been public property, given to research institutions and museums, but a collector of stolen antiquities like Ramses was certainly thinking of what they would be worth on the black market.

Ahmet began to leave the Parthenon with the coin.

Charlie grew even more concerned about her situation. The coin was the key to uncovering Cleopatra's next clue, and even with Charlie's near-photographic memory, she wasn't sure she had seen enough to solve the puzzle. She still had no idea what "Julius I" meant, or if there were other clues hidden on the coin that she hadn't been able to see yet.

"Wait!" she yelled, loud enough to make Ahmet stop. "If you take that, I won't be able to figure out where the next clue is hidden!"

Ramses glared at his son, angry at him for hesitating. "Keep going!" he yelled in Arabic. "You don't listen to her! You listen to *me*!"

Ahmet nodded and hurried onward, disappearing behind the columns as he slunk out of the Parthenon.

Charlie turned her attention to Ramses. "I'm not lying. I barely got to see that coin."

"And yet, as I said, you are an extremely intelligent young woman." Ramses considered her carefully. "I think you already know exactly where that coin is telling us to go. But you are pretending like you don't to keep Ahmet from leaving with it. That coin alone is probably worth a fortune."

Charlie shook her head. "I'm telling you the truth. You must have watched us find the coin. You know we barely had any time—"

"What does the coin tell you?" Ramses demanded, holding up his phone again so that Charlie could see Eva on the screen. "I want to know now!"

"Okay!" Charlie shouted. "Don't hurt her! I'll tell you!"

Ramses grinned proudly. "I knew it. Go ahead."

Charlie had been bluffing. In truth, she had no idea where the coin was telling them to go next. Fortunately, Ramses had fallen for her charade, but now Charlie had to come up with something quickly, something that sounded realistic. Her mind spun—and then, to her relief, she had an idea that might solve many of her problems at once.

"The engraving of the temple wasn't really a temple at all," she said. "It was a map."

"A map of what?" Ramses asked, curious.

"I'm still working on that," Charlie replied. "It would really help if I could *look* at the coin again, but since you're not about to let that happen, would you mind if I drew it?"

Now Ramses grew wary. "Drew it how? Like on paper?"

"No. I can draw it right *here*." Charlie pointed to a section of the Parthenon floor coated with even more dust than the rest. It was directly under some scaffolding where concrete appeared to have been mixed, and the concrete dust had rained down from above. Charlie didn't wait for Ramses to agree. She quickly walked there, knelt, and started drawing in the dust with her finger before Ramses could protest.

As it was, she had his attention. He came and looked over her shoulder as she drew.

While Charlie had many talents, artistic skill wasn't one of them. But then, she didn't really want her drawing to be accurate. Instead, she wanted it to be abstract and confusing to lure Ramses in.

It worked. "What is this supposed to be?" Ramses asked.

"The columns of the temple on the coin weren't really columns," Charlie lied. "I *think* they're supposed to represent streets. The streets of ancient Alexandria. And there was a convergence point of the columns here." She poked her finger into the deepest pile of cement dust, covertly grabbing a handful.

As she did, she glanced at Dante and Milana again, making sure they were paying close attention to her, then gave them a subtle nod, letting them know the time was right for a counterattack.

Cement was made of a combination of stone, sand, and trace amounts of metals like iron and aluminum. A handful of it in a person's eyes would temporarily blind them. Ramses was now within close range, and he was distracted by Charlie's drawing. He had lowered his phone to his side and seemed to have forgotten all about Eva and the henchman threatening to kill her.

Ramses said, "But we don't even know where Alexandria was. Its location has been lost. So what good does it do to know where that point in the city is?"

Charlie stood, still clutching her handful of dust. "I'll admit, that *is* a problem. But there are archaeologists at the University of Cairo who think they know where the city was located, and if we can combine their work with this map, then we could—"

Ramses suddenly lashed out, catching her wrist with his hand. He glared at her and squeezed her arm tightly. "Open your hand," he ordered.

Charlie grimaced, then complied, dropping the handful of dust.

"You couldn't possibly think I'd be stupid enough to fall for that trick, could you?" Ramses scowled.

"Of course not," Charlie said confidently. "Which is why I planned *this*."

Charlie had another reason for luring Ramses to this spot. While Ramses was distracted by her hand with the dust, she reached behind his back and yanked on the electrical cord that dangled like a vine from the scaffolding above. The power drill attached to it tumbled off the scaffolding and landed squarely on Ramses's head. Having seen the numbers in her mind, Charlie had maneuvered him into exactly the right place. The heavy drill struck Ramses hard, and he dropped like a stone. His cell phone clattered across the marble floor.

Instantly, Dante and Milana were in motion. Both of Ramses's thugs stayed to fight, which was a bad decision. Dante and Milana were extremely skilled martial artists—although at the moment, they were unarmed, while their assailants had a wrench and a crowbar.

Ramses was severely dazed but not quite unconscious. He started to order Lembris to hurt Eva, but Charlie quickly clamped her hand over his mouth, shoving the good amount of dust she still had into Ramses's throat, silencing him.

She didn't grab the phone and turn it off, because she feared doing either of those things would alert Lembris that something was wrong. Instead, she left Ramses coughing and gagging, kicked the phone out of his reach, and ran for the workshop where Eva was being held.

Ramses hadn't been looking directly into the camera for the past minute, so Charlie figured she might have a little bit of time before Lembris realized something was truly wrong. Maybe just enough to get the jump on him.

Nearby, Milana had squared off against Omar. He was an adept fighter, but Milana was better. She quickly disarmed him, then jabbed him with the sedative she had used on Dr. Karathinasis. This was the last dose she had, and it was just enough to incapacitate the big man. It worked quickly. Omar wobbled on his feet, then toppled to the ground.

Meanwhile, Dante still had his hands full. His opponent, Baako, was even bigger than Omar and more skilled a fighter, swinging his crowbar again and again. Dante had grabbed a piece of wood to parry the attacks but was still at a disadvantage. He saw Milana look to him, then yelled, "Go! I'm fine!"

So Milana ran, quickly catching up to Charlie as they fled from the Parthenon.

"Where's Eva?" Milana asked.

Charlie pointed to the workshop she presumed Eva was being held in, judging from the construction of the building she had seen in the video.

"Leave this to me," Milana said.

"But . . . ," Charlie began.

"I can handle this!" Milana said sharply. "Go get the coin!"

Charlie knew better than to argue. Milana was right; she was far more capable of rescuing Eva than Charlie. And if Ahmet got away with the coin, then they had a big problem.

While Milana ran for the workshop, Charlie quickly scanned the Acropolis for Ahmet. She spotted him far beyond the entry gate, already well on his way down the ancient steps that led to the parking lot.

Ahmet had a massive head start. Charlie was fast but not *that* fast.

Although she had an idea about how to catch up to him. It was crazy and dangerous, but she didn't see that she had any other options. If she didn't take a big risk, the coin—and the key to finding Cleopatra's treasure—would be gone.

TWENTY-ONE

Dante faced off against Baako, dodging again and again as the crowbar swung past him. He needed to get close to defeat his opponent, but Baako had long arms and an even longer reach with the crowbar. If Dante mistimed things and got hit in the face, his skull would be bashed in.

As Dante fought, he noticed Ramses off to his side, struggling to get to his phone. The man was still dazed from the drill that had dropped on his head and could barely speak, thanks to the cement dust Charlie had shoved down his throat, but still, even a whisper to his goon in the workshop would be the end of Eva.

Dante dodged the crowbar one last time, ducked away from Baako, then sprinted toward Ramses and dropped on him, using a piledriver from his wrestling days. He drove the Egyptian's head down into the marble floor, knocking him out for good.

But he had turned his back on Baako. Dante heard

something whistling through the air toward him. He curled into a ball, wrapping his arms over his head, and felt the crowbar clang off his shoulder. Pain shot through him, but he could tell no bones were broken. Then he glanced back and found the thug bearing down on him.

His shoulder aching, Dante rolled away, sprang to his feet, and met Baako head-on.

In the workshop, Lembris was just beginning to suspect that something was wrong with Ramses. He was still holding the crowbar to Eva's throat while shouting into his phone, asking what was going on, when Milana burst through the door and caught him by surprise.

Milana was much smaller than Lembris, but she was strong for her size, lithe and agile. Before Lembris could think to strangle Eva, Milana had whipped a hammer off the tool bench and flung it at his head. Lembris reflexively raised his arms to protect himself, letting Eva go.

Eva scrambled away, gasping for breath, her throat red and bruised. Lembris reached for her again, but Eva was quick and athletic herself and dodged his grasp.

"Get out of here!" Milana ordered, and Eva didn't question her. She fled from the workshop, leaving Milana to face Lembris.

Milana heaved a sigh of relief. She had saved Charlie's friend.

Now she had to save herself.

There was a much faster way out of the Acropolis than the stairs. But it happened to be extremely dangerous.

Charlie ran to the low stone railing that formed the top of the retaining wall. Below her, the wall went down fifty feet, and below that were several stories of rocky cliff. A fall from this height would be fatal.

To the west, Ahmet was more than halfway down the marble steps at the entrance to the Acropolis.

Charlie eased over the railing and started climbing down the wall.

A little girl who was watching her screamed in fear.

"Don't worry!" Charlie yelled to her. "I'm okay!"

She hoped that would turn out to be true.

Charlie was an adept rock climber, and the wall was rough-hewn enough to offer plenty of good hand- and footholds. But one of the cardinal rules of rock climbing was to not rush. Especially while heading down an unfamiliar route. When you climbed *up*, you had a good look at every hold before you used it. You could assess how solid it was. When you were climbing down, you just had to guess.

So, for her safety, Charlie should have been completely

focused on her climb. But she wasn't. She also had to keep an eye on Ahmet, tracking his progress.

He was almost to the parking lot.

The wall had been baking in the summer sun all morning, and the stones were hot to the touch. Every now and then, Charlie had to remove a hand and shake it in the air to cool her fingers off again. But she kept working her way down, down, down.

Ahmet reached the parking lot. A car was waiting for him there, a black sedan that he had probably arrived in.

Charlie made it to the bottom of the wall and found herself atop the natural cliff that formed the base of the mountain. There was a large bulge of rock at the top, which the retaining wall sat upon. It gave Charlie a place to stand and rest her arms for a few seconds, but it was also a problem, because the rest of the cliff was hidden beneath the bulge. Charlie couldn't see what lay in store for her. She just had to hope she could handle it.

The black sedan pulled out of the parking lot and sped down the road along the southern side of the Acropolis. Its route would take Ahmet right past the cliff Charlie was descending.

Only, Charlie still had a good way to go.

She quickly started climbing down, working her way past the bulge. For the first twenty feet, it was actually pretty easy going and she could move quickly, but then she hit a snag.

She reached the part that she hadn't been able to see.

The bottom of the bulge was a large overhang, like the eave of a very big house. It jutted out ten feet. There was no way Charlie could get to the cliff wall below it.

She had hit a dead end. There were only two options:

Climb back up.

Or jump.

Charlie judged the distance to the ground below her. It was about thirty feet, and the landing would be tricky: a steep slope that angled down through some ruins to the road.

The black sedan with Ahmet was speeding along that very same road.

Climbing back up would take far too much time. The sedan with Ahmet would be gone within a minute.

Charlie looked down at the slope below her and saw the numbers.

Then she jumped.

Baako slammed into Dante, driving him backward into the scaffolding so hard that all four stories of it trembled. Cement dust rained down upon them from above.

Dante scored a few quick blows, but Baako was built

as solid as any opponent he had ever faced. It was like punching one of the marble columns of the Parthenon. Plus, the scaffolding was quivering like it was about to collapse; it appeared that whoever had erected it hadn't done a very good job. So Dante whirled away before Baako could strike back.

Baako came after him.

Dante found the crowbar that Baako had thrown at him, lying amidst some rubble, then snatched it up and wielded it like a club.

Baako kept coming, unfazed, as though getting hit by a crowbar was no big deal.

Dante took a swing with it.

Baako sidestepped, surprisingly nimble for someone so big.

The crowbar went wide of him and struck one of the supporting struts for the scaffolding, knocking it free. The vibration of the strike radiated up Dante's arm and into his wounded shoulder, causing a shock of pain that made him drop his weapon.

Baako laughed. "You missed," he said.

"I wasn't aiming for you," Dante replied.

And then the scaffolding, weakened by the loss of the support strut, fell apart. The lowest wooden platform, along with all the masonry that was on top of it, dropped on Baako, knocking him down, after which the platforms from the levels above came down on him too.

Baako lay unconscious beneath it all.

Dante limped out of the Parthenon, aching everywhere, wondering where Milana and Charlie had gone.

In the workshop, Milana battled Lembris. Not only was the man big, but there were potential weapons everywhere: hammers, chisels, chunks of masonry. Lembris was grabbing anything he could find and hurling it at her. Milana couldn't even run, because that would mean turning her back on the onslaught. Instead, she had grabbed the lid of a trash can and was using it as a makeshift shield, letting every object clang off it as she backed toward the door.

She noticed a pile of circular-saw blades lying on a worktable, grabbed one, and whipped it at Lembris like a frisbee. Its teeth scored his arm as it flew past, making him yelp in pain and pause his assault.

Milana took advantage of the moment, attacking while Lembris's guard was down. She flung the trash-can lid at him, catching him in the face with it, and by the time Lembris had recovered from that, he found Milana coming right at him. She sprang into the air and delivered a roundhouse kick to his head that sent him flying backward. He hit the far wall of the workshop and crashed right through it, thudding into the dirt outside.

Milana armed herself with a pair of hammers and stormed toward him, fire in her eyes. "You want more of this?" she asked menacingly. "Because I've got plenty more to give."

Lembris scrambled to his feet—and ran. He fled down the pedestrian path toward the exit of the Acropolis as fast as he could go.

Milana dropped the hammers and exited the shop, coming upon Dante, who sighed with relief upon seeing that she was all right.

"How's Eva?" he asked.

"Fine," Milana said, wondering where the girl had run off to.

"And where's Charlie?"

"She went after the coin."

There was a sudden chorus of shouts from far below them, at the base of the mountain. It sounded like there was trouble.

"Charlie," Dante said knowingly, and they both ran to the railing to see what was going on.

Charlie had landed on her feet on the steep slope at the base of the cliff, although her momentum carried her forward. Rather than fight it, she went with it, tucking into a ball, rolling once, and coming up on her feet again. Then she ran like heck down the hill.

The most direct path to the road took her straight through the archaeological site she had seen from above, a lesser-known ruin called the Temple of Asclepius. A dig was underway, and the archaeologists and their assistants shouted as Charlie ran right through their work.

"Sorry!" Charlie yelled to them in Greek as she passed. "Archaeological emergency!"

She angled downward through the remnants of an old amphitheater built into the hillside and found herself almost back at the Acropolis Museum again. She could see the car with Ahmet coming down the road and chose the right vector to intercept it.

Unfortunately, even with the slope of the hill, she wasn't quite fast enough to get there. The sedan shot past mere seconds before she arrived.

Nearby, a woman heading to the museum was climbing off her Vespa scooter.

Charlie leapt onto it, gunned the ignition, and— despite the woman's startled cries—sped after Ahmet Shah.

TWENTY-TWO

Ahmet had seen the girl running down the hill toward his car.

He couldn't believe his eyes. Only minutes before, the girl had been up in the Parthenon, surrounded by his father and his father's best enforcers, and now somehow she was here at the bottom of the mountain, coming straight for him. It didn't seem possible.

Through the rear windshield, he watched as the girl commandeered a Vespa and chased after him. She sped down the road behind them, getting closer and closer.

"There's a girl behind us on a red scooter," Ahmet told the driver. "Do whatever it takes to lose her."

"But there's traffic . . . ," the driver began.

"If you get away, my father will take care of all your traffic violations. But if she catches us, he will have your head."

The driver knew Ramses Shah's reputation well enough to fear him. "All right," he said.

The narrow road they were on intersected with a grand six-lane boulevard, one of the major arteries of Athens. The light was changing to red. The driver punched the gas, weaving around a car that had stopped and hurtling through the intersection just before traffic started coming the other way. A bus missed their rear bumper by inches.

Now there were three lanes of traffic in between them and the girl.

Ahmet wondered if it would be enough to stop her.

Charlie knew she couldn't safely cross the three lanes of traffic. Thankfully, a scooter was more versatile than a car. She made a sudden left and veered up onto the sidewalk, racing alongside the boulevard, slaloming through pedestrians, who shouted angrily at her as she passed.

She kept one eye on the people ahead of her and the other on Ahmet's black sedan. The boulevard arced around yet another archaeological site—Athens was full of them—this one the remains of the Temple of Olympian Zeus. The temple had taken over six hundred years to build and had at one point been the largest in Greece, although it was pillaged by barbarians less than a hundred years after its completion. All that remained were 13 of its original 104 columns—but the park that surrounded the site was as large as the Acropolis complex. The entrance was marked, just as it had been in ancient times, by the Arch of Hadrian, which stood on the street corner ahead.

The great boulevard curved around the arch. Charlie watched the black sedan fly through the bend and speed away.

Ahead of Charlie, a crosswalk spanned the boulevard, leading from the sidewalk she was riding on to the arch. A throng of tourists was waiting at the corner, indicating that the light was about to change. Charlie gunned her engine and arrived just as the pedestrians started to cross. She wove through them and leapt onto the far sidewalk, swerving around the arch.

The sedan had gained a lot of ground, but it had to stick to the road. Charlie had a shortcut. She shot straight through the grounds of the Temple of Zeus, dodging sidewalk artists selling caricatures, locals walking their dogs, entrepreneurial kids hawking cold water, and tourists busily snapping selfies.

Charlie was so focused on the obstacles ahead of her, she barely had a moment to glance at the grand remaining columns of the Temple of Zeus. She made a mental note that one day, it would be nice to spend some quality time at an ancient monument instead of only seeing it in the midst of a chase.

Then she zoomed out the far side of the park and

dropped back onto the boulevard not far behind the black sedan.

At Ahmet's urging, the driver tried to shake Charlie again. He floored the gas and zigzagged wildly through traffic. Other cars swerved to avoid him, the drivers pounding their horns angrily. Twice, the sedan forced cars to crash behind it, which caused immediate backups in traffic. Still, Charlie managed to stay close, weaving through the wreckage, using her math skills to evaluate the gaps between cars. In short order, they raced past the National Garden, the presidential palace, and the two-thousand-year-old marble stadium that had hosted both the ancient Olympics and the modern games.

Then, just beyond the stadium, they suddenly came upon a traffic jam. All three lanes on their side of the boulevard were blocked by hundreds of cars stacked bumper-to-bumper, going nowhere. Ahmet's driver took evasive action, veering onto a smaller street, trying to cut through an intersection before the light turned red, but he was too late. A bus was already coming through. It clipped the rear of the sedan, sending it into a spin, and then careened into oncoming traffic, setting off a chain reaction of minor accidents. Metal crumpled. Headlights shattered. Horns blared.

Charlie jumped a curb to avoid being flattened by a taxi, only to find a group of schoolchildren in her path.

She nailed the brakes and skidded into a bush, coming to a sudden stop that flung her over the handlebars. Fortunately, the bush broke her fall, preventing any injury beyond a lot of scratches. She fought her way out of it and found the children all staring at her in surprise.

"Learn a lesson from this," she told them in Greek. "Always wear a helmet." Then she looked across the intersection. It was now a sea of wrecked cars, the bus stranded in the midst of it like an island, blocking her view of Ahmet's sedan.

Her scooter was so deep in the bush, she couldn't pull it out, and besides, there was no way she could ride through all the wrecked cars anyhow. Instead, she ran over them. She clambered atop a stalled pickup truck and then crossed the intersection by leaping from one vehicle to the next, running across hoods, trunks, and roofs, until she rounded the bus.

The black sedan had crashed into a lamppost at the far side of the intersection, knocking it loose from its setting. As Charlie watched, the post toppled like a tree, crashing down onto the car and flattening the roof.

The passenger door hung open, revealing the interior of the sedan. It was empty. Ahmet Shah was gone.

Dante charged down the steps of the Acropolis. He had left Milana behind to deal with everything back there: the unconscious bodies of Ramses Shah, Omar, Baako, and Dr. Karathinasis, and tracking down Eva as well. It was too much for one person to handle, but Dante had no choice: He had to find Charlie.

He glanced at the screen of his phone, which displayed her location, thanks to the tracking bracelet he had put on her wrist. Impossibly, it showed her already a mile away. He had no idea how she had gotten so far so fast; for all he knew, Charlie was clinging to the roof of Ahmet's getaway car as it raced down the highway. Charlie might have been brilliant, but that had sometimes proved to be her undoing. She was overconfident in her ability to solve problems, which made her impetuous and prone to making rash decisions. And when something like Pandora— or the greatest treasure of Egypt—was at stake, she was willing to take bigger risks than usual.

There was a taxi station in the parking lot. Dante leapt into the first car and gave the driver the location that Charlie was at, according to his phone. "The Lyceum of Aristotle! As fast as you can! I'll pay for your speeding tickets."

"Okay," the driver agreed, looking excited by the prospect, and then peeled out of the parking lot.

Dante checked his phone again. Charlie was no longer moving as fast as she had been only a minute earlier. That indicated she was now probably on foot. And yet she was still several minutes away.

Dante hoped he could reach her before she got herself into any more serious trouble.

Ahmet had been holding Cleopatra's coin in his hand when his driver had wrecked the car. He had been trying to commit the thing to memory, just in case things went wrong. He knew that he shouldn't be afraid of the girl pursuing him—after all, she was barely a teenager—but she had gotten the jump on him once before, and if he failed again, his father would probably disown him out of embarrassment.

Ahmet didn't even know where to begin in trying to make sense of the markings on the coin. He guessed that the drawing of the temple was pointing him to an actual temple, but he had no idea where on earth that might be. And the inscriptions "Julius I" and "Magnum Opus" meant nothing to him. . . .

Suddenly there was a screech of tires, and his body seemed to be getting pulled in every direction at once. His car had been hit and was spinning—and then, just as abruptly, it stopped. When the sedan rammed into the lamppost, Ahmet was thrown forward so hard that he felt as though his seat belt would cut him in two. The airbags inflated instantly, filling the air with white powder and the smell of burnt paper.

It took Ahmet a few seconds to realize what had happened, and then panic set in. He was no longer moving—and he no longer had the coin. It had flown from his hand during the wreck.

He pounded on the airbag to deflate it, then desperately looked around the footwell of the car.

There! The coin was down by his left toe. He bent to grab it and pain shot through his body. He was aching all over from the wreck. But he couldn't sit still. Not with the girl after him. Ahmet flung open his door and fled down the street.

He quickly came upon the ruins of the Lyceum of Aristotle, the school where the great Greek scholar had taught his students everything from philosophy to zoology to politics. Now it was little more than the excavated foundations of ancient buildings and piles of rubble. Ahmet glanced back the way he had come. To his surprise, he saw the girl. Somehow she had made it through all the wrecked cars and was still coming after him. Ahmet quickly clambered over the fence around the Lyceum and dashed into the ruins.

Charlie caught a glimpse of Ahmet as he disappeared over the fence, then raced after him. She was tired after her climb down the Acropolis wall and the pursuit through Athens, but she willed herself to press onward. She jumped the fence and followed Ahmet through the ruins.

Even though Charlie was in the middle of a chase, she still noticed the signs stating what had been there two thousand years before and was struck by a moment of awe. Aristotle's teachings had been the basis for much of Western science. He had made landmark strides in many disciplines (although he also made mistakes, such as promoting the idea that flies and mice could spontaneously generate from rotting meat). Aristotle had been the private tutor of Alexander the Great, Cleopatra's ancestor, establishing the principles of her classical education. So, in a sense, Cleopatra's brilliance had its roots in this very location.

Charlie was getting winded now, her strength running low, but Ahmet appeared to be having the same issue. He was hurting from his car crash, breathing heavily and staggering as he ran.

So Charlie was gaining on him. She wasn't far behind when he ran out the opposite side of the archaeological site and into the modern-day city again. They passed through a gate and suddenly returned to the noisy, crowded bustle of Athens. They were a good distance from the main tourist area now, so there were no cafés or souvenir shops. Instead, there were apartment buildings, grocery stores, and fast-food restaurants.

Ahmet foolishly cast a glance backward to see how far Charlie was behind him, rather than watching where he was going, and crashed into a garbage can. He tumbled over it, landed hard on the sidewalk, and felt something snap in his ankle. The garbage can clattered into the street, spilling fast-food wrappers and soda cans.

And Cleopatra's coin flew from Ahmet's grasp.

In his hurry to flee from Charlie, Ahmet had never put the coin safely in his pocket. He had forgotten that he was even carrying it. Now it bounced along the curb and rolled away.

It was heading right for a sewer grating.

Charlie leapt over Ahmet's sprawled-out body and sprinted down the sidewalk after the coin, using every bit of strength she had left, knowing that if the coin dropped through the grating, it would likely be gone forever.

The coin kept rolling, closing in on the sewer.

Charlie grabbed it at the last second, with only an inch to spare. Her momentum carried her a few more feet and then she stumbled, falling and rolling to a stop in front of an auto body shop.

She lay there for a bit, right on the sidewalk, clutching the coin tightly, exhausted but relieved.

Down the sidewalk, Ahmet was in even worse shape than she was. He appeared to have broken an ankle during his fall, and the storekeeper whose shop he had collapsed in front of was yelling at him about the spilled garbage.

Charlie realized this was the first time she had actually

held the coin since she had discovered it. Still lying on the sidewalk, she finally took a close look at the object that had caused her so much trouble.

She noted the Ouroboros, the "Magnum Opus" inscription, the etching of the temple, and the "Julius I" that had been so confusing.

And suddenly she realized what it meant.

"Oh," she said as a few things fell into place. Not only did she understand the clue, but she even knew where she needed to go next.

"Ma'am?" a man asked her in Greek. "Are you all right?"

Charlie pulled her attention from the coin. A young mechanic from the garage was standing over her, staring at her with concern.

"I'm fine," Charlie replied in Greek. "Actually, I'm *great*." She struggled back to her feet, tired and aching.

The mechanic watched her, concerned. "Are you sure you're okay?"

"Absolutely." Charlie mustered the biggest smile she could, given everything that had happened recently. Then she tucked Cleopatra's coin into her pocket and felt the clink of Dante's tracking bracelet on her wrist. "Any chance you have some bolt cutters at this garage?"

TWENTY-THREE

When Dante Garcia finally arrived at the location of Charlie's tracking bracelet, Charlie was nowhere to be found. The clasp containing the tracking chip was lying in the gutter, not far from where Ahmet Shah was still seated on the curb, waiting for an ambulance.

Thanks to his broken ankle, Ahmet was in terrible pain and had no desire to get into more trouble with the CIA. The moment Dante flashed his badge, Ahmet started talking. He explained how Charlie had recovered the coin from him, made a quick stop at the auto shop, and then taken off. He hadn't been able to follow her with his bum ankle and had no idea where she had gone.

So Dante was in a foul mood when he returned to the hotel room. Milana was waiting for him there.

Dante tossed her the remains of the bracelet. "She gave us the slip. Again."

Milana examined the clasp, surprised. The metal links on both sides of it had been ripped apart. "I thought this was supposed to be unbreakable."

"It *was*. But Charlie figured out how to break it anyhow. She used a combination of battery acid and heavy machinery from a local auto mechanic. Then she left it where she knew I'd find it, just to rub it in my face."

"You don't know that for sure . . ."

"Yes I do. Because I know Charlie. She could have tossed that tracker into the back of a cab or put it on a subway car and had me chasing it all day. But she left it in the gutter, right out in the open. I'm guessing she also wanted me to find Ahmet Shah, so he could tell me she took the coin—and our only lead to this treasure." Dante sank into a chair and placed his head in his hands.

"Did you get anything else from Ahmet?" Milana asked.

"A bit. He said the Mukhabarat tipped them off that we were coming here. Which means the Egyptians are probably sniffing around here for us too. But he didn't know much more than that. He said his father was the one to talk to. Did you get anything out of Ramses?"

"I didn't have a chance. Someone had called the

police, and they were all over the Parthenon. I had to split before I got wrapped up in anything."

Dante nodded understanding. If the Greeks learned that the CIA had removed an artifact from an archaeological site without permission, there would be an international incident. The theft of artifacts, particularly where the Parthenon was concerned, was an understandably sore spot with the Greeks. For example, in the early 1800s a Scottish diplomat named Lord Elgin had removed over fifty marble panels from the Parthenon and shipped them to the British Museum in London. Lord Elgin had claimed to be protecting the art, but the Greeks insisted that the sculptures had really been looted; over two hundred years later, the issue was still a point of contention between the countries.

"I tried to find Eva," Milana continued, "but she was with the police as well, reporting what had happened. I took off before she saw me. She seemed to be all right, though. . . ." She trailed off, watching Dante, carefully assessing his body language. "What else is wrong?"

"You mean, besides the fact that Charlie's gone with our only lead to the treasure?"

"Yes. I can see something is eating at you."

Dante sighed heavily. "Arthur Zell has been calling. Over and over. He's on his way here to meet with us."

"Oh," Milana said, concerned. "Right now?"

"He's already on a jet. I've listened to his messages but I haven't called him back yet. Because I have nothing but bad news to give him." Dante shook his head sadly. "This operation was already on thin ice after we lost Charlie in the Amazon. The only thing that saved us was Jamilla Carter's faith in us. But when Zell hears that Charlie's given us the slip again, he's definitely going to pull the plug on this mission."

Milana perched on the arm of Dante's chair and ran her fingers through his hair, knowing it relaxed him. "Then we just have to find Charlie before Zell gets here. We must still have a few hours. . . ."

"Find her how? She could be *anywhere* in this city— or on her way to another country by now. She's smart and she has plenty of money at her disposal. I was hoping that, maybe, she would have come back here, but obviously that was just wishful thinking. Let's face it, we're in bad shape."

"That doesn't mean we should give up."

As Milana spoke, Dante's phone began buzzing. The caller ID showed a phone number with a 757 area code, which meant it was coming from the CIA. Most likely Zell, being routed through the switchboard.

"I might as well answer it," Dante said, and sighed

again. "Why wait to give him the bad news?"

"Hold on . . . ," Milana said.

"The more I put him off, the more upset he's going to be." Dante answered the phone. "Agent Garcia speaking."

"Dante, this is Director Zell. I've been trying to reach you all morning."

"Yes sir, I know. I'm sorry I didn't get back to you. I've been in the middle of something."

"I figured as much. But if you have the time, I'd like to be briefed on your progress so far . . ."

"Of course." Dante steeled his nerves, preparing to deliver the truth.

Milana tensed as well.

There were footsteps in the hall outside their room. They stopped in front of the door.

"Give me a minute," Dante said to Zell, then muted his phone.

Milana took her gun from her holster and quietly moved to the side of the door, ready to ambush whoever came through.

"It's just me," Charlie said from the other side. "Don't shoot me."

Then she unlocked the door and stepped inside.

Dante was overcome by different emotions. He was thrilled and relieved to see that Charlie had returned—

and he was livid at her for ditching him. Relief won out. "Where have you been?" he asked.

"Getting *this*." Charlie triumphantly held up Cleopatra's coin. "And then I was starving, so I got some lunch. Action sequences take a lot out of you. I must have burned like five thousand calories . . ."

"You went to get lunch?" Dante said heatedly. "We've been worried sick about you! Why did you take your tracking bracelet off?"

"Because I'm not a pet," Charlie said. "I'm a member of this team. You don't need to put a collar on me."

Dante fumed at her response, because he knew she was being defiant just to do it. If anything, her behavior had proven that his putting a tracker on her was justified. But before he could argue, Milana held up a hand, signaling him to be calm, and said, "Dante, you still have Zell on hold."

"The director's on the phone?" Charlie asked. "Tell him 'hi' for me." She grabbed a soda out of the minibar and popped the cap off.

"He's on his way to Athens right now to meet with us." Dante began to unmute his phone.

"That's not a good idea," Charlie said. "We're not going to be here much longer."

Dante froze, his thumb poised over the phone. "We're not?"

"No." Charlie flashed him a smug grin. "I figured out the next clue."

"What does it say?" Milana asked.

"That Zell ought to meet us in Rome. Because that's where we're going next."

TWENTY-FOUR

Tel Aviv, Israel

The Israelis weren't the only ones who could run operations in another country.

While the Mossad had agents operating inside Egypt, the Mukhabarat had agents operating inside Israel. In fact, they even had a mole inside Mossad headquarters.

The mole was a young woman named Ellie Kallner. On the face of things, she appeared to be the perfect Mossad agent, born and raised in Israel, an excellent student in school, and an outstanding soldier during her mandatory two years of military service. Her background had been carefully vetted before her Mossad recruitment. But Ellie had a weakness: Her grandfather, who lived in the United States, was very sick, and his health insurance didn't cover all of his bills. That meant her grandparents were desperate for money; without it, her grandfather couldn't afford the treatments he needed to survive.

The Mukhabarat had money.

Ellie had been slowly cultivated by a Mukhabarat field agent operating in Tel Aviv, another woman who had first approached Ellie as a friend. Her name was Yifat. It had been six months before Ellie learned the truth, and while she felt angry at first, the fact was, she would do anything to help her grandfather. Besides, the Mukhabarat never asked her to directly betray her country; it had been a long time since Egypt and Israel were actively at war. All the Mukhabarat wanted was the occasional piece of information. Sometimes months went by between asks.

But they wanted something now.

Ellie had seen the telltale chalk mark on the sidewalk in front of her apartment building as she left for work that morning. If someone had drawn a hopscotch board that had the numbers jumbled in a specific way, that meant Yifat wanted to meet for lunch.

Ellie followed the usual routine. She walked down to the beach, which was only a few blocks from Mossad headquarters, grabbed a sandwich at a take-out café, and sat down at a prearranged spot along the seawall to eat it.

It was a good place to meet, as the location was a popular lunch spot. Hundreds of other people were lined up along the seawall, some in business attire, some in more casual clothes. It was a hot summer day, and everyone was relishing the breeze off the Mediterranean Sea. The beach was crowded with sunbathers, volleyball players, and boogie boarders. A few of the businesspeople had even taken off their shoes, rolled up their pant cuffs, and waded ankle-deep into the surf.

Yifat came along and sat close to Ellie on the seawall. She wore sunglasses and a sunhat, like many other people out that day, and she only had an iced tea in her hand, indicating that she wouldn't be staying for long. If she really needed to talk, then she would have had her own lunch. A copy of *Haaretz*, the Tel Aviv newspaper, was tucked under her arm. She set it down on the seawall beside her and looked out at the sea rather than at Ellie.

Ellie didn't look at Yifat either. She continued to stare at the sea as well.

"Zafadi needs a favor," Yifat said. There was no point in making small talk.

"No kidding," Ellie replied. "What is it?"

"Isaac Semel has a team on its way to Greece right now. All we want is updates on their progress."

Ellie paused midbite, caught by surprise. She knew who Semel was, of course. Everyone at the Mossad knew Semel. She didn't know what he was up to—only members of his hand-selected team would know that—although she had heard office rumors that he had only returned from a mission in Egypt that morning. "Don't you already have people working on this? I heard Semel was on his way to Greece because of something he learned from *you*."

"The Mukhabarat doesn't have the flexibility that the Mossad does. We couldn't mobilize a team as fast as you." Yifat didn't tell Ellie the full story, which was that Ramses Shah had gone after Charlie Thorne himself—and that he had failed.

Even so, Ellie knew something must have gone wrong where the Egyptians were concerned. If they were bringing her into this, they were grasping at straws. She asked, "You know I'm not on Semel's team, right? So finding out what he's doing is a tall order."

"We know. But still, it would be in your interest to give us anything you can. Your grandfather's interest too. You know where to find me." Yifat hopped off the seawall and continued down the beach. Throughout the entire conversation, she hadn't made eye contact with Ellie once.

Yifat left her copy of *Haaretz*. Ellie picked up the newspaper and opened it, like she was reading it. But in truth, she was checking to see if there was an envelope full of cash inside.

There was, although it wasn't nearly as thick as Ellie had hoped. The Mukhabarat wasn't going to pay her in full until she delivered the information they wanted.

Ellie sighed and stood. She still had more than half her lunch left, but she was no longer hungry. Spying on her own people always made her stomach queasy. She would never have considered it for a second if her grandfather wasn't sick.

Ellie tucked the envelope into her purse, gave the rest of her lunch to a homeless man, dropped the newspaper in a recycling bin, and went right back to the office, intending to find out what Isaac Semel was doing in Greece.

TWENTY-FIVE

Athens, Greece

"Why are we going to Rome?" Dante asked.

He had posed the question several times already, but Charlie had put off answering, telling him she would provide more details on the way.

They had quickly checked out of the hotel and were now in a cab heading to the airport, racing along the outskirts of Athens. Charlie and Dante were in the back seat, while Milana was in the front. The highway skirted the flank of a mountain, and the great, white city was spread out below them.

Charlie asked, "Do you know what happened from Thursday, September third, until Wednesday, September thirteenth, in 1752?"

"I don't care," Dante told her. "I want to know why we're going to Rome."

"I'm trying to explain it. Do you know what happened on those eleven days?"

"Nothing," Milana answered. "Those days didn't exist."

Charlie looked to her, impressed. "That's right."

Dante frowned, confused. "Wait. Eleven days just didn't happen?"

"They had to be cut out of the calendar," Charlie explained. "Because the history of human calendars is a mess. We take our calendar for granted now, but it took centuries of work to figure everything out. A lot of mistakes got made. Although that makes sense, because our planet wasn't designed to fit perfectly into a calendar. The orbit of the earth isn't exactly three hundred and sixty-five days. It's three hundred and sixty-five and a quarter, more or less. That's why we need leap days every four years. But no one realized that for a really long time. The Julian calendar, which was set up by good old Julius Caesar, didn't have leap years. In fact, it only had three hundred and fifty-five days, although the Romans tried to make up for that by inserting extra days into the year. That didn't work very well, though, and after a few centuries, everything was way off and Easter was falling in the middle of winter. So the calendar had to be rejiggered a few times. The final tweak was to lop off eleven extra days that no one knew what to do with. In 1752, the calendar went right from September second to September fourteenth. A lot of people were angry about it. They didn't understand what was going on. Some actually thought their lives were going to be eleven days shorter. There were riots. And, to make matters worse, the calendar wasn't changed at the same time everywhere. Only Britain and its colonies changed it in 1752. France, Italy, Spain, and Portugal had already changed it back in 1582, while Turkey didn't get around to fully adopting the new calendar until 1927. So, for most of human history, the date could have been different depending on what country you were in."

"That's very interesting," Dante said, meaning it. Then he held up Cleopatra's coin, which he had been examining for the last few minutes. "But how does it tie into this?"

"I'm getting to that. My point is, we think of the calendar as being this static thing, like it's been the same for thousands of years, but that hasn't been true at all. Like, Cleopatra didn't think she was born in 60 BC. There *was* no BC. BC and AD weren't invented until nearly five hundred years after Cleo died. Before that, almost every culture had its own calendar, and none of them agreed on much. What we have now is a mishmash of several calendars, which is why half our days of the week are named after Norse gods, like Wodin's Day and Thor's Day, and the other half are named after Greek and Roman gods, like Saturn's Day and Mars's Day, which somehow became Tuesday. But most of what we got was handed down to us by the Romans, and frankly, their calendar was a disaster."

"How so?" Milana asked without turning around. Her eyes were locked on the rearview mirror, keeping a constant watch to see if anyone was following them.

"First of all, they only had ten months," Charlie explained, "and each had thirty or thirty-one days—which obviously only adds up to about three hundred and five days. The remaining fifty days just got dumped into an unorganized winter, and as I said, that still wasn't the right number of days for a solar year. Then the weeks all had eight days, but just to make everything as confusing as possible, the Romans counted everything inclusively, so they called the eighth day the ninth day. *Then*, they didn't number the days of the month in order. They counted toward special days and then away from them, so instead of saying things like, 'It's March eighth,' they'd say 'It's six days before the Ides.' Honestly, it's hard to imagine how they ever got anything done.

"Well, Julius Caesar realized this was a problem and instituted reforms, which resulted in the Julian calendar. One of the biggest changes was to create two extra months instead of just having fifty random days floating around. But rather than tacking those months onto the end of the year, the Romans jammed them into the middle of summer—and then kept the names of all the other months the same anyhow, which is why the name of our ninth month, September, actually means 'seventh month,' our tenth month, October, means 'eighth month,' our eleventh month, November, means 'ninth month,' and our twelfth month, December, means 'tenth month.'"

"And that's how July and August came about?" Dante asked.

"More or less," Charlie said. "Although they weren't given those names right away. That was really a political move. Mark Antony was the one who decided to name a month after Julius Caesar to honor him. And then, when Octavian defeated Antony, he decided he wanted a month named after him too. He became Augustus Caesar, and the month he grabbed became August. Although August was originally shorter than July. Octavian didn't like that, so he stole some days from February and added them to August. That's why February only has twenty-eight days." Charlie rolled her eyes. "Politics."

Staring at Cleopatra's coin, Dante suddenly understood where Charlie was going. "So the date on this coin doesn't mean the first of July. It means the *first* July."

"Exactly!" Charlie confirmed.

"When was the first July?" Milana asked.

"In what we now call 46 BC," Charlie replied. "And we know where Cleopatra was then: in Rome with Mark Antony."

Dante pointed to the temple on the back of the coin, under the "Julius I" inscription. "Then this temple is in Rome? That's what she's directing us to?"

"That's what I assume," Charlie answered.

"Which temple?" Milana asked.

"Well, it's a little hard to say for sure, because the engraving on the coin isn't that detailed, but I'm betting that this is the Temple of Venus Genetrix. It looks about right. Also, Venus was kind of the Isis of Rome. And Julius Caesar put a statue of Cleopatra in that temple. We found that coin where a statue of Cleo used to be. If the clues are following the same pattern, then we'll find the next one at the site of a statue too."

Dante and Milana shared a look. Once again, both were impressed by Charlie's logic and her breadth of knowledge.

Dante asked, "Where in Rome is this temple?"

Charlie didn't answer. She was staring out the window of the cab. They were leaving Athens behind, and she was getting her last glimpse of the Acropolis in the distance.

She had been forced to leave Eva back there. Once again, she had abandoned her friend and disappeared. Milana had filled her in, letting her know that Eva was safe, but Charlie still felt terribly guilty about everything that had happened.

She had been with Eva less than half an hour before her life had ended up in danger. They had barely even had a chance to talk. Charlie had learned almost nothing about what Eva had been doing over the last few months. She had hoped there would be time for them to hang out for a few hours, maybe even grab a meal together, but sadly, that had proven not to be the case.

Charlie had lied to Dante and Milana about what she had done after getting the tracker off her wrist. She hadn't only gone to get lunch. She had called Eva, wanting to apologize for everything—and to explain what was really going on. She had found one of the few remaining pay phones left in Athens and dialed Eva's cell number from memory.

But Eva hadn't answered. The call had gone through to voicemail. Maybe Eva didn't want to answer a call from a random number in Athens. Or maybe she was busy talking to the police. Whatever the case, Charlie wasn't sure how to explain everything in a message—and she thought it might be dangerous to leave a recording of it anyhow. So all she said was, "Eva, it's Charlie. I'm sorry. I have to go again. Hopefully, someday, I'll be able to explain everything to you."

Now, staring at the city of Athens, knowing Eva was

out there somewhere, probably still hurt and upset, Charlie wondered if she would ever get a chance to make amends.

"Charlie," Dante said sternly, breaking her thoughts.

She turned back to him from the window. "Yes?"

"Where in Rome is the Temple of Venus Genetics?"

Charlie cracked a smile. "Not Genetics. *Genetrix*. It's in the Roman Forum. Or, what's left of it. The buildings from Cleopatra's time in Rome didn't hold up as well as the Parthenon did."

They passed into a long tunnel through a mountain, and Athens disappeared behind them.

"In fact," Charlie went on, "the buildings that we think of as being really old in Rome—like the Colosseum—weren't even built until over a hundred years after Cleopatra lived. And almost all of these are in ruins. The oldest building that's still standing, the Pantheon, wasn't even finished until about 200 AD. So the Temple of Venus Genetrix is long gone. Except for a tiny bit of it."

"Oh," Milana said. She had brought up a photo of the temple on her phone. "I recognize this. And you're right, there's almost nothing left." She held her phone out to Dante.

All that remained of the temple were three columns with a lintel across the top of them. They looked like a Roman numeral three: III.

"I recognize this too," Dante said. "It's right in the middle of the city."

"Yes," Charlie agreed. "Those columns probably aren't even part of the original temple. The city only erected them to give tourists something to look at."

Milana squinted at the photo. The area around the columns wasn't nearly as well tended as the Acropolis. The floor was no longer there, and whatever remained was overgrown with grass. "If Cleopatra left something here, it might not be easy to find it."

"No," Charlie conceded. "But I'm hoping our discovery from the Acropolis might help. Maybe Cleopatra used a similar technique to hide whatever she left behind."

Dante added, "And hopefully, instead of leading us to yet another clue, it will actually lead us to the Library of Alexandria."

"Oh, I doubt that," Charlie said.

Dante looked to her curiously. "You think there'll only be another clue?"

"I don't know for sure, but we're not looking for the Library of Alexandria at all."

"But you told Ramses Shah . . . ," Dante began.

"You wouldn't expect me to tell our enemies the truth now, would you?" Charlie asked, flashing a devious grin.

Milana gave her a look that was at once surprised and

impressed. "So . . . if Cleopatra's secret wasn't the scrolls from the library, what is it?"

"Something way more powerful and important," Charlie said.

TWENTY-SIX

Greek airspace
Near Athens

The Mossad jet was preparing to land at Athens International when the pilot heard the control tower mention a familiar aircraft registration number. The jet was coming in low over the Aegean Sea. Below them, hundreds of Greek islands studded the crystal-blue water.

Isaac Semel was aboard the jet, along with three of his top agents. The pilot was also Mossad, an ex–fighter pilot from the Israeli Air Force named Rachel Barak. Semel had told Barak to stay alert for any mention of the CIA jet's registration number.

Like most municipal airports, the one at Athens International had both commercial and private air traffic, and the control tower was responsible for handling it all. As Barak discussed her incoming landing instructions with air traffic control, she was told that the jet with the registration number she was looking for was taxiing to take off. Once it left, a commercial airliner would be next, and then she was clear to land.

Only, Barak now suspected that Semel would have no interest in landing at all.

The Mossad jet was relatively new, with a modern heads-up display that gave the position of every aircraft within twenty miles. Each was indicated by its specific registration number, so Barak could see the CIA jet clearly marked on the runway on her screen.

"Agent Semel," Barak called from the cockpit. "The CIA is on the move again."

Semel set down the files he was reading and hurried to the cockpit. By now, they were close enough to the mainland that he could see Athens laid out ahead of him, shimmering in the summer heat.

Barak quickly explained how the heads-up display worked, pointing out the CIA jet's registration number on the screen. Even as she did, the number began moving along the runway, indicating that the jet was taking off. "What do you want to do?" Barak asked.

Semel considered his options. The obvious assumption was that the CIA was on the jet and leaving Athens, so he ought to follow them. But you had to be very careful making assumptions where Charlie Thorne was concerned. He had no way to tell if she, Dante, and Milana were really on that jet; for all he knew, Charlie had hired another plane—or perhaps a boat—and they were sending the jet off as a decoy. If he followed it, it might lead them to Iceland before he discovered his mistake.

However, if he didn't follow it, and Charlie *was* on it, then he would blow a big chance to find out where she was heading next.

"Sir?" Barak prodded. "I need to know what we're doing. We're next in line to land."

Even as she spoke, she was banking over the Aegean and lowering in altitude. Athens International came into view in the distance ahead. Semel could see the CIA jet lifting off, glinting in the sun.

The commercial airliner sat at the end of the runway, ready to take off. Semel had only a few seconds to decide whether or not to abort their landing.

"Follow that plane," he told Barak.

"Yes sir." Barak radioed the control tower and said she would not be landing after all, then banked again, veering away from the airport. She couldn't follow the CIA jet directly over the runway due to the commercial jet that was about to take off. If she got in its way—or got caught in the turbulent wash of air behind it—the Mossad would be in grave danger.

But it was probably better to not stay directly behind the CIA jet anyhow. They didn't want to tip the CIA off that they were following them. They only needed to keep the jet within sight for long enough to figure out where it was heading.

And then they would get the jump on the CIA and grab Charlie Thorne.

TWENTY-SEVEN

Charlie held up the coin she had worked so hard to recover. "There are two clues on this that led me to believe the source of wealth Cleopatra is talking about isn't the Library of Alexandria: the Ouroboros and the words 'Magnum Opus.'"

They were back on the CIA jet again, heading northwest across Greece toward Rome. Charlie was devouring a gyro they had bought in the private terminal at the airport, even though she had already had lunch that day. "Car chases make me hungry," she had explained.

Dante and Milana were eating gyros too, although Milana had been forced to wait until she could activate the autopilot to really dig into her food.

"What do the clues tell you?" Dante asked, his mouth full. He'd had even less to eat that day than Charlie.

Charlie gave him a disappointed look. "Does the CIA

not require you to do any research at all before you come on these missions?"

"We researched plenty," Dante snapped. "What do the symbols mean?"

"They're both references to the philosopher's stone."

Dante coughed on his gyro, spraying a bit of tzatziki sauce across the cabin. "The philosopher's stone? The mythical ancient thing that turns lead into gold?"

"Not just lead into gold," Charlie clarified. "It was supposed to turn all sorts of base metals, like tin, zinc, and copper, into precious ones like gold or silver. And according to this coin, it wasn't mythical at all."

Dante shook his head. "No. There's no way someone could have discovered the philosopher's stone way back then. They were primitives compared to us."

"There were plenty of intelligent people two thousand years ago," Charlie said, sounding slightly offended. "And for thousands of years before that as well. The Egyptians built the pyramids back in 2,500 BC, and we still have no real idea how they did it! Eratosthenes worked out the size of the earth three hundred years before Cleopatra lived and got it exactly right. The Library at Alexandria had forty thousand scrolls filled with knowledge. The philosopher's stone was the holy grail of metallurgy for centuries, and the Egyptians knew more about that science than anyone else. So it's entirely possible that they could have figured out how to make one—and then kept it a secret. In fact, it explains a lot of unanswered questions about the Ptolemies."

"Like what?" Dante asked.

"Egypt's power derived from the fact that it was an incredibly rich country. For centuries, the Ptolemies staved off a Roman overthrow by buying them off. They literally handed over tons of gold to keep their country safe. The Egyptians were said to have had the largest stockpile of gold in the world. Well, where did it all come from?"

"They mined it," Dante answered confidently.

"By the ton?" Charlie asked skeptically. "Also, it's worth noting that the Ptolemies might have discovered the stone before they even came to Egypt. They were loaded when they showed up from Macedonia and bought their way to power. Macedonia doesn't have much gold—but it was the leading producer of lead in the ancient world. With the philosopher's stone, they could have turned all that into something much more precious."

"That's all just speculation . . . ," Dante began.

"True. Until you consider *this*." Charlie held up the coin again to display the image of the snake eating its own tail, then realized she had gotten tzatziki sauce on it and wiped it clean. "In her first message to Caesarion, Cleopatra talked about finding the source of her wealth.

I know I told Ramses and his goon squad that was meta-phorical, but it makes more sense if it was literal. And here we have definite references to the stone—which, by the way, wasn't necessarily a stone at all. Most alchemists suspected it was a chemical compound, and they called it all sorts of other things, like 'the elixir of elixirs,' 'the tincture,' 'the powder,' 'materia prima,' and my personal favorite, 'the quintessence.'"

Dante sighed and gave in. "Okay. What does this Oompa-Loompa snake mean?"

"Ouroboros," Charlie corrected. "When I told Ramses that it was a symbol for the library, that was a pile of horse patootie. It was actually a symbol for the process of altering metals. The serpent biting its tail represents immortality—and the way that everything in the universe slowly becomes something else. Any alchemist would have recognized it. Plus there's *this*." Charlie turned the coin sideways to show the words "Magnum Opus." "While the official Latin translation for this is 'great work,' alchemists used the term to refer to the process of turning the original substance into the philosopher's stone."

Dante sat back, chewing his food thoughtfully. "And you really think this could exist? That they could have turned lead into gold?"

"Why not? Lead and gold are right next to each other

on the periodic table of the elements. The only difference between them is a single proton and electron."

"Yes, but the Egyptians didn't know that. They didn't even know what a proton *was*."

"So? Making bronze from copper and tin is also a chemical process, but no one questions that the ancients were able to do that without knowing about protons. It's completely possible that they could have figured out how to transmute metals, even though we haven't. And it makes sense that they would have tried to keep it a secret. Because a tool with the power to create wealth like that is the sort of thing that wars were fought over."

"Not only in the past," Milana said from the cockpit. "People would fight wars over it *now*."

Charlie and Dante looked her way, surprised she had been listening all along.

Milana said, "In the wrong hands, the philosopher's stone could be almost as dangerous as Pandora. Someone with the unlimited ability to turn base metals into gold could flood the markets and destroy the world's economy—or use the sudden influx of wealth to fund all sorts of evil operations."

"Although, in the right hands, that wealth could be used for good," Charlie observed. "Someone with billions of dollars could fund health care for the needy—or fight climate change."

Dante gave her a leery stare. "Would this 'someone' you're referring to be you by any chance?"

Charlie said, "I've known about Pandora for a few months now, and I haven't done anything terrible with it. I think I could be trusted to use the philosopher's stone wisely."

"The point of this mission isn't to acquire the stone for ourselves," Dante informed her. "It's to get it for the United States . . ." Before Charlie could protest, he raised his voice and continued, ". . . who will not abuse its use, I promise. Furthermore, we can safeguard it from people who *would* use it for criminal purposes."

Charlie backed down, choosing not to debate the point. She had argued with Dante before about whether or not the US government could be trusted. She didn't think it could; he did. Neither of them was going to change the other's mind. And since she was now relying on the CIA to help her track down the philosopher's stone, there was little use in antagonizing her brother and Milana.

She shifted her gaze to the window and looked at the earth below her. They were crossing the mouth of the Ionian Sea, having already left Greece and now heading to Italy. Charlie was struck by how small the world had become. Back in Cleopatra's day, it had taken weeks to get from Alexandria to Rome, and the travel had to be timed to take advantage of the seasonal trade winds. Now it was only a matter of hours to go from one to the other.

And yet, despite all that had changed, the philosopher's stone would be just as powerful now as it had been in Cleopatra's time. Cleopatra would have needed to be an extremely judicious ruler to use the power of the stone wisely. Charlie wondered if Julius Caesar and Mark Antony had known of it, or if Cleopatra had kept it a secret from them. Charlie would have bet on her keeping it secret; for men who wanted to rule the world as badly as Caesar and Antony, the lure of the stone's power would have been too great. Cleopatra would never have been able to trust them with it.

"Charlie?" Dante asked. "We're in agreement on this, right? As we've seen, there are dangerous people looking for this stone too. We have your back, but I want to make sure you're not plotting any funny business."

Charlie turned to face him. "I returned to the hotel when I could have run away, didn't I?"

Dante considered that, then admitted, "Yeah, you did."

"You can trust me," Charlie said. "Now, let's go find this stone before anyone else does."

TWENTY-EIGHT

Athens, Greece

Where the heck have you been?" Ramses Shah demanded angrily when Ahmet returned to their hotel suite.

"At the hospital." Ahmet pointed to the cast on his foot. "I broke my ankle."

He had been ignoring his father's calls all afternoon, hoping it might worry Ramses and win him some sympathy.

It didn't work. As usual, the only emotion his father showed him was annoyance. Ramses didn't seem the slightest bit concerned that Ahmet had been hurt. "Why didn't you answer your phone when I called?"

"I was unconscious," Ahmet lied, then launched into the story he had worked out. There was no way he was going to tell his father that Charlie Thorne had bested him again. "The stupid driver wrecked the car. A bus hit us head-on. I woke up in the hospital. The doctors said I'm lucky to be alive."

Even this story didn't move his father. Ramses only snorted with disgust. "Do you still have the coin?"

Ahmet frowned, knowing he couldn't lie about this. "No."

"The girl got it?"

"I don't know. Like I said, I was unconscious."

"If you don't have it, then we have to assume she does." Ramses glared at Ahmet. "So that's twice she's defeated you. *A thirteen-year-old girl.* Some man you are."

"I got hit by a bus!"

"You lost the coin! I told you to keep it safe, and you failed!"

"I took some pictures of it." Ahmet brought his phone to his father to display them. They were blurry, as he had taken them in the car while it was racing through Athens, but still it was something.

Ramses looked them over but remained disdainful. "You can barely make anything out."

"You can see enough."

"It'd be better if we had the coin. But you screwed that up. Just like you screw up everything."

"It doesn't look like you did so well either," Ahmet said heatedly, pointing to Ramses and his thugs, who were gathered around the room. All of them showed signs of battle. Their clothes were torn. Their faces were mottled with bruises. Ramses was still covered with cement dust. There hadn't been time for any of them to clean up yet.

"We were fighting CIA agents, not girls," Ramses said curtly, even though this was a lie as well. The girl had gotten the best of him, too, but he wasn't about to admit that to his son. And his men knew better than to contradict him. "Plus, while you were sleeping in the hospital, we've been talking to the police all afternoon."

After Dante had knocked him unconscious, Ramses had awakened surrounded by the Athens police. The police had spent the next hour grilling Ramses and his men at the Acropolis, like they were criminals, wanting to know what everyone had been fighting about and if anything had been stolen. Ramses had lied to them, claiming to be an innocent tourist who had spotted some thieves stealing artifacts and tried to stop them, only to be waylaid.

And yet the police had kept on questioning him, like they didn't believe his story. In Cairo, it would have been different. The police would never have dared question him. But in Athens, they had acted like he was just a regular person.

So Ramses had already been angry before Ahmet returned with the news that he had failed once again. Now he was ready to explode.

His cell phone rang. It was a number he didn't recognize, but he was expecting a call like this. He snatched up the phone and answered gruffly, "Hello?"

"I got your message." It was Zara Gamal, his insider at the Mukhabarat. It sounded as though she was on a pay phone, which made sense. She wouldn't want to call Ramses from the building.

"We lost the CIA in Athens," Ramses said. "I need to know where they're going next."

There was a long pause as Zara weighed how to deal with such a request. Finally, she said, "I'm not sure that anyone at the Mukhabarat even knows that information."

"Of course someone does. So find out."

"I've already put myself at risk giving you the last information you asked for. I can't do that again . . ."

"No. What you can't do is afford to make me an enemy. If you leave me hanging here, you will severely regret it. Do I make myself clear?"

There was another long pause before Zara said, "I'll try. But I can't promise anything."

"That's not good enough. You have an hour to get me what I need." Ramses hung up, then got to his feet and stormed across the suite. "I'm taking a shower," he told Ahmet. "Why don't you make yourself useful and figure out what those markings on the coin mean?" He ducked into the bathroom and slammed the door behind him.

Ahmet sat down in the same chair his father had just vacated, seething. He hated Ramses and was embarrassed by the way he had been treated in front of the other men, but he hated himself as well. Because he *had* failed. The truth was far worse than he had let on. He really had been bested by a thirteen-year-old. He hadn't even been able to escape her in a car. The girl had pursued him through the streets and then chased him down on foot. Now she had the coin, and all he had were blurry photos of it.

Although those were better than nothing. He brought them up on his phone again and scrolled through them.

Unfortunately, the images on the coin meant nothing to him. He had no idea what any of them stood for. Just like he had never understood the stone tablet that had sat on the wall of his office for years.

Now he realized he hated the girl, too. He hated her even more than he hated his father. He hated her for being smarter than him, for outwitting him, for making him look bad over and over again.

Ahmet decided that if Zara Gamal came through and told them where the girl was, he wouldn't let her defeat him again. Instead, he would make her pay for what she had done to him. He would make her spill her guts about everything she knew—and then, just maybe, his father would be proud of him for once.

The next time he met Charlie Thorne, she would lose.

PART THREE
THE ARENA

Cleopatra made Rome feel uncouth,
insecure, and poor.
—STACY SCHIFF,
Cleopatra: A Life

TWENTY-NINE

Rome, Italy

Although Rome was well on its way to becoming the most powerful empire in the Western world during Cleopatra's lifetime, the city itself paled in comparison to Alexandria. Cleopatra's capital was well designed and carefully laid out, with a simple grid pattern of streets and classical, Greek-inspired architecture. The wealth of Egypt was on display everywhere. Alexandria's museums, academies, and gardens—and of course, its library—were the envy of the Western world. The city square was lined with thirty-foot-tall sphinxes and three-story-high statues of Cleopatra's ancestors. The streets were wide and clean; the central thoroughfare alone was a hundred feet across, wide enough for eight chariots to ride abreast. Alexandria even had a zoo with giraffes, cheetahs, and lions. The city's location along the Mediterranean was one of unparalleled beauty. The lighthouse in its harbor was one of the Seven Wonders of the Ancient World, an astounding feat of architecture and engineering.

Meanwhile, Rome was a swampy, malarial backwater. Its streets were narrow, congested, and dirty. Its iconic structures, such as the Pantheon and the Colosseum, wouldn't be built for another few centuries. Most of the buildings were poorly constructed of wood and plaster. Its renowned sewer system hadn't been built yet, and thus, its inhabitants were constantly throwing garbage and emptying chamber pots out their windows; the practice was so common that the Roman writer Juvenal remarked that a smart man only went to dinner after writing his will.

However, there were a few notable buildings in Rome, omens of the city's great future. One was Caesar's palace, a sprawling, opulent estate perched atop one of the seven hills of Rome, where Cleopatra had lived with Caesar while visiting the city for the first time. Another was the Temple of Venus Genetrix, in the Forum, which Caesar had dedicated in 46 BC as part of the festivities of his triumphant return to Rome from Egypt.

"To understand Rome, you have to understand Julius Caesar," Charlie said as she, Dante, and Milana rode through the city in a cab. "Rome was already ascendant when Caesar came along, but he made it a world power— by conquering as much of the world as he could."

Their flight from Athens had taken a little over two hours. There had been no need to get a hotel room; they had left their belongings on the jet and were heading straight from the airport to the Temple of Venus Genetrix, which was located near the center of the city. Their cab was moving slowly, as the roads were thronged with tourists. Even though night had fallen, many of Rome's outdoor tourist attractions still drew large crowds, such as the Piazza Navona, the Spanish Steps, and the Trevi Fountain. These were brightly lit with floodlights and much cooler to visit now than in the heat of the summer day. So many people were heading from one to the other that it was almost as if rivers of humans were coursing through the narrow streets. In addition, the roads were choked with merchant stalls selling souvenirs, artists hawking paintings of the monuments, caricaturists, singers, magicians, and even a man dressed as a gladiator, complete with a horse and a homemade chariot, charging a fee for photos.

Charlie said, "Caesar was one of the greatest generals of all time, although he was also really brutal. He conquered Germany and Belgium and was the first Roman to enter Britain—and he killed plenty of the people he met along the way. When he invaded Switzerland, there were nearly four hundred thousand people living there, and his army slaughtered almost half of them. And at the

Battle of Alesia, against the French, his forces are said to have massacred as many as ninety thousand people in one day. Caesar said the only reason they didn't kill more was because his soldiers were too exhausted from all the stabbing.

"Caesar's reputation even frightened a lot of his own people. Rome was a democracy, and the Senate worried that Caesar might try to make it a dictatorship. So they asked him to disband his army—and he refused. He returned to Italy with his soldiers, which immediately sparked a civil war. Caesar ended up fighting an old friend of his named Pompey—who was also his son-in-law, even though he was a lot older than Caesar. Caesar won and Pompey fled to Egypt, which as we know, had plenty of gold and power. Pompey sought help from Cleopatra's younger brother, Ptolemy the Thirteenth, but Ptolemy didn't want to make an enemy of Caesar, so he had Pompey beheaded. Then, when Caesar showed up in Egypt, Ptolemy gave him the head as a present."

The taxi finally made it through the crowds and arrived at the Piazza Venezia, which marked the center of Rome. It sat at the base of the Capitoline Hill, one of the famed Seven Hills that the ancient city had been built upon. Capitoline Hill had been the seat of the Roman government, for which reason the word "capitol" was derived from it.

"Anyhow," Charlie continued, "Caesar now found himself in the midst of another civil war, this one between Cleopatra and her brother. Both were vying to win him over, because while they had money, he had military power. Ptolemy got the upper hand at first with the whole killing-Caesar's-enemy-and-giving-him-the-head-as-a-gift thing, so Cleo made a bold move. She had herself smuggled into Caesar's chambers wrapped inside a carpet. Then she popped out and surprised him—and as you know, they hit it off.

"Caesar backed Cleo against her brother, and they clobbered his army. Ptolemy tried to flee across the Nile and drowned. Then Caesar and Cleo got married and had Caesarion. After a while, though, Caesar had to get back to Rome. With his army and Cleo's money, he was now almost invincible. On the way home, he conquered Turkey in five days, even though the Turks had twice as many soldiers as him. That's where he said the famous 'I came, I saw, I conquered' line.

"Caesar finally got back to Rome in 46 BC, having defeated most of the Western world, and he decided to throw himself the biggest party ever. He had a huge parade, he changed the calendar, he staged a fight where gladiators killed four hundred lions, and he flooded one of the chariot courses to stage a naval battle. He even had two armies of captured soldiers fight to the death for entertainment. Four thousand people were killed. That means ten times more people died at Caesar's party than at the Battle of Yorktown at the end of the American Revolution. Ancient Rome was a crazy place."

The taxi came to a stop around the back of the Capitoline Hill, right by the ruins of the Temple of Venus Genetrix, at the northern edge of what had been the Forum. Unlike the section of Rome they had just come through, the Forum was closed to tourists at night. During the day, it would have been mobbed with visitors, but now it was eerily quiet. The sidewalk was devoid of pedestrians. Even the road that skirted the ruins, the Via dei Fori Imperiali, which was always busy during the day, was now mostly unused. The few other cars on it were racing along at such high speeds that the cab driver was concerned about stopping. He pulled over only long enough for Charlie, Dante, and Milana to get out, then sped away.

A broad, tree-lined sidewalk ran along what remained of the Forum, flanked by a low railing. It was a fifteen-foot drop down into the ruins.

Charlie stood at the rail, looking at the three columns that marked where the Temple of Venus Genetrix had once stood. "On the last day of Caesar's celebration, he dedicated the temple right here. It wasn't really for religious purposes, like we think of temples now. Instead, temples were places to meet with people and get deals done, like coffee shops or restaurants today—except with more statues of gods. In a way, this one was really Caesar's office. Venus was his go-to goddess. And to honor Cleopatra, he installed a life-size gold statue of her here."

In the time of Cleopatra and Julius Caesar, the Forum had been the centerpiece of Rome, but now everything lay in ruins. It was in far worse condition than the Parthenon, even though it had been built centuries later. Except for the reconstructed columns, all that remained were the shattered foundations of the ancient buildings, with bits and pieces of carved marble scattered about haphazardly.

The only light was from the streetlamps along the Via dei Fori Imperiali, so much of the site was shrouded in darkness. Charlie knew that would make searching for whatever Cleopatra had left there difficult, but there was also an advantage to coming at night: They were less likely to be noticed.

There was no one else in sight, and no cars were coming along the road. "Let's go," Milana said, then sprang over the railing and dropped into the Forum.

Dante and Charlie followed her. They slunk through the ruins, heading toward what remained of the temple. Each carried a flashlight from the emergency kit on the jet, although they didn't use them yet, as they were trespassing and didn't want to draw attention to themselves. Without the lights, they had to move slowly and cautiously.

Twenty centuries earlier, the ground had been covered in gleaming marble; now it was carpeted with grass and weeds. Plenty of careless visitors had tossed litter into the area as well. Charlie found herself stepping around shards of broken beer bottles, crumpled coffee cups, and of course, empty plastic water bottles, which were ubiquitous wherever she went. The ruins also appeared to be home to plenty of rats and feral cats; Charlie caught glimpses of their dark forms scurrying through the weeds.

"What happened to this place?" Dante whispered. "Did invaders destroy it?"

"No," Charlie replied. "The Romans did it themselves. During the Renaissance, they looted the Forum and the Colosseum for material to build St. Peter's Basilica in Vatican City and lots of other things. Eventually, it dawned on people that maybe they ought to be preserving this area, but by that point, not much was left." She waved to the ruins around her.

Dante frowned. "Given the condition of this place, it doesn't seem very likely that anything Cleopatra left behind would still be here. I mean, even the floors are gone."

"Don't give up hope," Charlie told him, even though she was feeling the same concerns herself. She paused to assess the landscape around her. She and Dante had spent much of their flight researching the Temple of

Venus Genetrix. The CIA jet had computers and Wi-Fi, and there had been a good amount of information online, including maps of the layout of the temple and the Forum around it. Charlie had printed some of these out, which she now consulted.

Dante approached the trio of columns that represented the remains of the temple, wondering if anything was carved into them. He nearly stumbled over a feral cat that had caught a rat. The cat was big, mangy, and mean. Rather than running away, it stood its ground and hissed at Dante angrily.

Charlie considered the three columns, then looked back to her map. "Those aren't from Caesar's original temple. They're a reconstruction from a few hundred years after Caesar. Apparently, the Forum caught fire a few times and had to be rebuilt a lot. The original location was over there." She pointed farther up the Capitoline Hill.

Given the hill's importance to Rome, it wasn't particularly tall. A pedestrian walkway slowly angled up toward the peak. Charlie, Dante, and Milana followed it until they reached a point where the walkway zigzagged through a jumble of ruins: Marble columns from antiquity stood beside brick arches from buildings constructed in medieval times. Two thousand years of civilization was piled up in the same area.

A medieval wall now hid them from the main road, while the bulk of the Capitoline Hill loomed to the other side. The sounds of the city had faded, so that Charlie could almost imagine that she had time-traveled to another period in Rome's history, long before cars or streetlights existed.

To one side of the walkway, the remnants of a marble floor were partially exposed. The stones were cracked and broken. Some of them had a hint of color, indicating that the floor might have been a work of art at some point, but for now, it didn't seem that impressive. Charlie figured most people would barely give it a glance, given how many other structures were around.

She consulted her map once more, then announced, "We're here."

They were now so far from the streetlamps that it was hard to see. Since Charlie, Milana, and Dante could no longer be spotted from the road, it now felt safe to use the flashlights. They flipped them on, hopped over the walkway railing, and began examining the marble floor.

"What are we looking for exactly?" Milana asked.

"I'm not completely sure," Charlie admitted. "But I'm guessing it's similar to what we found at the Parthenon. Why bother to switch up something that works?" She paused by an ancient stone pillar. "According to the map, the golden statue of Cleopatra would have been right where I am now, so someone looking at it would have been standing—"

"Here!" Dante exclaimed, so excited that he raised his voice a bit too much. He was five feet away from Charlie, hunched over a disc of blue marble the size of a salad plate. It had been so neglected, a layer of dirt had built up on it and weeds sprouted in the gaps around its edges. Dante dropped to his knees, brushed aside the dirt, and found five familiar letters faintly etched in the disc.

KLEOS.

Once again, the center of the *O* appeared to have been carved from another stone than the rest. The blue was a slightly different shade.

This time, Charlie and her team had come prepared. In addition to his flashlight, Dante had a chisel and a small hammer. He quickly went to work, chipping at the center of the *O*. It took him a few shots before the circular piece popped free and clattered across the marble.

It came to a stop by Charlie's feet. She picked it up and immediately felt something on the underside.

While the top had been roughened by centuries of exposure to the elements, the bottom had been protected and was still smooth to the touch. Smooth enough for Charlie to feel the irregularities in it.

She turned it over.

At the same time, Dante was shining his flashlight into the hole he had uncovered. "There's nothing here," he said, frustrated.

"Yes there is," Charlie told him, holding up the marble disc to display its underside. "We found the next clue."

THIRTY

saac Semel crouched in the shadows, watching the CIA.

His instincts had been right to follow the jet from Athens. The Mossad pilot, Agent Barak, had tracked it at a distance, just far enough to stay off their radar, until they figured out it was heading to Rome, at which point Barak had slotted into the landing path behind it. The Mossad had landed at Fiumicino International Airport only two minutes after the CIA had touched down, close enough that they had been able to observe Charlie, Dante, and Milana deplaning.

The CIA agents had exercised their usual caution to make sure they weren't being tailed, but the Mossad were experts at following people without being noticed. The CIA switched taxis three times on the way into the city, but the Mossad stayed on them.

Now they were biding their time, waiting to see what the CIA was up to.

While Charlie and the others had been distracted by their search, the four members of the Mossad team had spread out silently, surrounding the area. Semel had circled around to a high point on the Capitoline Hill, from which he could observe the CIA below.

He was positioned at the edge of what had once been an enormous public latrine. The Romans had recognized that any great city center like the Forum needed a sanitary place for people to go to the bathroom. The design wasn't very different from what a person might find at a modern-day stadium: a semicircular structure with a curved outer wall providing ample room for a hundred people to relieve themselves at once. Although in ancient Rome, going to the bathroom had been a much more public affair. There were no walls between stalls—and there wouldn't have been separate bathrooms for men and women; both sexes used the same latrine. The original floor had been raised—Semel could see the remnants of what had supported it—so that water could flow beneath it. The latrine had been so well constructed that much of it was still standing, as opposed to the temples, which lay in ruins. Semel wondered if that said something about the priorities of humanity.

He and his team had radios but weren't using them, to avoid making any noise. Instead, they were communicating the way most humans did these days, via texts on their cell phones.

From this, Semel knew his people were in position. He had given them orders to stand down. No one was to make a move until he said so.

None of his team questioned this. Semel was the leader. But he knew they must be wondering if he was making the right call. After all, they had the CIA outnumbered. Even though Dante Garcia and Milana Moon were top agents, they were distracted. It would be easy enough to ambush them and grab the girl. Then, it would only be a matter of time before she coughed up Pandora.

But Semel was determined to find out what Charlie was looking for now, to learn what the source of Cleopatra's power was. And then perhaps he could deliver *that* to Israel too.

To that end, he had brought night-vision goggles and a highly sensitive directional microphone, which he was using to watch the CIA and eavesdrop on their conversation. He was a bit too far away for the goggles to be effective: Charlie, Dante, and Milana were only greenish blobs. But the microphone was working well. Depending on which way his targets were facing, he could hear a decent amount of their conversation.

So he knew that they had just found another clue and that they were excited about it. Semel stayed as still as he could, watching and listening.

And waiting for the right moment to ambush.

THIRTY-ONE

Dante and Milana gathered around Charlie as she shone her flashlight on the underside of the marble disc, revealing the Latin words etched there.

Ubi unum invenis, ibi totum reperies.

"Where you find one, you will find all," Charlie translated.

The others looked to her. "That's it?" Dante asked, sounding annoyed. "What does that even mean?"

"I don't know," Charlie admitted. The thrill of finding the next clue had already faded, replaced by disappointment. She had hoped for something less cryptic, or possibly even blatantly obvious: a map, or a distinct set of directions. But now she had yet another riddle to solve.

She looked around the ruins, trying to deduce what Cleopatra meant. Unfortunately, except for the section of floor she stood on, nothing else of the temple remained. The landscape around her had been repeatedly looted, razed, and built upon again over the past two thousand years. It was a stroke of luck that Cleopatra's clue had remained hidden here all this time. But everything else was long gone.

Which meant that if Cleopatra's clue was pointing to something that had been in the temple, then Charlie had come to a dead end.

But what if the clue pointed to something that *wasn't* in the temple? Charlie tried to imagine what that could be. What would Cleopatra have referred to simply as "one"?

Off in the darkness, a feral cat hissed angrily.

By Charlie's side, Dante tensed. He cased the ruins around them carefully.

Milana suggested, "Maybe we should go someplace else to figure this out. Seeing as we're breaking the law by being here. We've found all that we came for, right?" She looked to Charlie for confirmation.

Charlie sighed in frustration. She felt as though she was missing something. Something that should have been obvious. And yet every moment she and the CIA stayed there was a risk. If they got arrested for trespassing— especially with an ancient artifact in their hands—it might turn into an international incident. They had narrowly avoided this at the Parthenon, and she didn't want to press their luck. "Sure," she agreed. "Let's go."

Charlie started back the way they had come, but Dante suddenly blocked her path with his arm, keeping her there.

In the distance, the feral cat hissed again.

Dante couldn't be sure that it was the same cat that had hissed at him earlier, but it sounded similar. The cat had only made that noise when he had come too close to it.

Which meant that someone else was there with them.

"Get down!" Dante ordered. Then he pulled Charlie to the ground, ducking behind an ancient marble wall. Milana dropped right beside them.

A second later, someone started shooting.

THIRTY-TWO

The bullets came from all around. Which meant there was more than one shooter, and they had the CIA surrounded. They were using silencers, but Charlie could still hear the bullets as they ricocheted off the ancient relics, showering her with splinters of marble.

Charlie realized that if it wasn't for Dante's quick actions, she might have been hit. The medieval wall they were crouched behind was shielding them from the gunfire—but it wouldn't protect them for long. If the enemy circled to another position, the three of them would be exposed.

"Who's shooting at us this time?" Charlie asked, failing to keep the panic from her voice.

"I don't know," Dante replied. "You've got more enemies than anyone I've ever met."

He had his gun drawn, but there was no way he could risk even taking a shot. To do so would leave him open to enemy fire.

He locked eyes with Milana. They had worked together long enough to be able to form a plan without speaking. Both knew what they had to do.

Milana gripped Charlie's arm tightly. "When I move, *you* move, all right?"

"Wait," Charlie said, worried. "Are we leaving Dante behind?"

The shooting stopped as suddenly as it had begun. In the ensuing silence, Charlie heard distant voices and footsteps, moving quickly through the ruins.

Milana snapped to her feet, dragging Charlie behind her, and ran.

Charlie followed the orders she had been given; she knew better than to question Milana and Dante in a situation like this. She sprinted as fast as she could, staying by Milana's side. Although as she did, she yelled back to Dante. "Track me!"

Before Dante could ask what she meant, the gunfire began again. The enemy was shooting at Milana and Charlie now, either targeting them specifically or unaware that Dante hadn't moved as well. Bullets pocked the ground around them.

Dante sprang from where he'd been crouched and

fired back, aiming at where the shots were coming from. There was a cry of pain in the darkness, and then at least one of the shooters stopped.

Milana and Charlie made it to the shelter of a colonnade of brick arches, remnants of a building that was a thousand years younger than the Temple of Venus. They raced through it, the gunfire echoing hollowly behind them. The colonnade only extended a hundred yards, after which the building had crumbled, so beyond that, they would be exposed again.

Charlie nearly stopped, fearing leaving the protection of cover, but Milana pulled her onward. "If we stay put, we're trapped," she said urgently.

So Charlie kept on running. They emerged into the open and dashed through the ruins. For a few moments, they appeared to have slipped past their attackers, but then there was a cry of surprise from somewhere close by. Charlie heard footsteps coming after them.

"Keep going," Milana ordered, then took cover in the shadows, preparing to confront the enemy.

As scared as Charlie was, she continued on alone, aware Milana was far more prepared for this situation than she was. Milana had been trained to fight, whereas Charlie had not; if she stayed behind and tried to help, she would only get in the way.

In the darkness, Charlie had to focus on what was

in front of her, not what was behind her. The ground in the Forum was uneven, full of ancient debris and poorly marked excavation pits. Charlie worked her way through it, desperately trying to come up with a plan.

If she escaped—and Dante and Milana did too—then they had chosen a location to meet up again: a hotel near the Spanish Steps. But that arrangement meant nothing if Charlie didn't get away, and right now the chances of that seemed slim. She had no idea how many of the enemy were around her—or who they were. Was it the Mukhabarat? The Mossad? The Shah family again? Or someone else entirely?

For the moment, no one was chasing Charlie or shooting at her, but that could change quickly. And to make matters worse, she was now in a section of the Forum with no easy way out. Like many European cities, Rome was built upon layers of ruins. Charlie was fifteen feet below street level, surrounded by brick walls with railings at the top. Jumping down into the Forum had been simple; climbing back out again would not. Charlie could only discern one place where she might be able to escape, a series of tiered ruins that led back up to the street.

There was a howl of pain from the darkness behind her, followed by the muffled sounds of a scuffle. Charlie *hoped* this was Milana getting the jump on whoever was pursuing them, but she had no way of knowing that for sure. Charlie glanced behind her—a dumb reflex, she knew, but she couldn't help it—and stopped watching where she was going.

So of course, she immediately stumbled over something. She didn't even see what it was. She *felt* it, though. A shock of pain went through her right foot as she bashed her toes, and the next thing she knew, she was sprawled on the ground. She scraped her arms and legs on rocks, and whacked her shoulder on something hard as well. Worst of all, she cried out as she fell, which surely alerted the enemy to her presence.

Charlie quickly got back to her feet, cursing her stupidity, then ran onward. Her foot was hurting badly, making her limp, but she tried to fight through the pain. She reached the tiered ruins and scrambled up them.

Her foot hurt even worse as she did this. Pain radiated up her leg. She finally arrived at the top of the ruins and found herself facing another five feet of brick wall to get back to the street. Normally, this wouldn't have been much of an obstacle, given her rock-climbing skills, but now she struggled with it, taking longer than she could afford. By the time she clambered back over the railing to the modern-day street level, she was in agony.

She couldn't keep running, not with her foot like this.

In the distance, down the sidewalk, two of the enemy were racing toward her, silhouetted against the streetlights.

Charlie looked toward the Via dei Fori Imperiali. At the moment, it was devoid of cars . . .

But there was someone on it. The man dressed as a gladiator who she had seen earlier, back in the city, was riding his homemade chariot down the street, perhaps heading home after a night's work, or maybe heading to the Colosseum at the far end of the road, hoping to find more tourists there. The horse was plodding along slowly, in no great hurry. It didn't appear to be a particularly young horse, but at the moment, Charlie figured it could still go faster than she could.

She ran toward the gladiator, yelling for help in Italian. The man looked at her, surprised, as she emerged into the glow of the streetlights—although Charlie wasn't sure if his surprise was due to her age, how banged up she was, or perhaps just general shock that anyone was along this stretch of road at all.

The gladiator didn't stop his horse, not that he was moving very quickly anyhow. He just stared at Charlie as she ran toward him.

Behind her, the enemy was coming fast.

Charlie leapt into the chariot, told the gladiator that she was sorry—and then shoved him into the street. The man was big and would only weigh her down. His homemade armor clattered on the asphalt and he shouted after her angrily, but she ignored him and snapped the reins.

The horse responded by breaking into a gallop. Burdened by the chariot, it didn't move extremely fast, but for the moment, it was fast enough, whisking Charlie down the Via dei Fori Imperiali. The two people chasing her quickly fell behind.

Charlie didn't get a good look at them in the darkness, but she could tell from their silhouettes that they were men—and well-built, athletic men at that. As they faded into the distance, one took out a phone and made a call, although Charlie couldn't hear him over the clatter of the horse's hooves on the street and the creaking of the chariot's wheels.

The chariot was built more for show than speed. Now that Charlie was riding it, she discovered that much of the body was only spray-painted Styrofoam. It was really just a crude construction of scrap wood and didn't look like it would hold together much longer.

But for the moment, Charlie was actually fleeing along the Roman Forum in a chariot, which probably hadn't been done in at least 1,500 years.

Ahead of her, at the far end of the Forum, the road curved around the Colosseum. Given the building's popularity during the daytime, it was surprisingly dark at night. But Charlie figured there might be a few tourists there, or maybe even a police officer, which would make it far safer there than where she was now. There was also a subway entrance close to it, which could be another means of escape.

Charlie now had the freedom to glance back the way she had come.

The two men who had been chasing her had stopped. Their silhouettes grew fainter and fainter as Charlie raced away from them.

She did not see anyone else, which made her worry. Where were Dante and Milana? Were they all right? Or had they been overwhelmed? If something had happened to them, what was Charlie supposed to do then?

Behind her, a car swerved onto the Via dei Fori Imperiali, then braked by the two enemy men. The men leapt inside it, and then the vehicle sped toward Charlie.

After which, another car turned onto the road and dropped in behind them.

Charlie urgently snapped the reins. Her horse picked up its pace a bit but not enough to outrun two cars. The chariot's wheels wobbled dangerously, while its spindly wooden framework creaked and split.

Charlie sprang from it onto the horse. A second later, the left wheel broke loose and the rest of the chariot dropped, sparking on the asphalt. This and Charlie's sudden weight on its back spooked the horse, which now ran in earnest, although it was hampered by the remains of the chariot dragging behind it.

The two cars were hurtling down the road toward her.

Charlie found the cheaply made belt that attached the chariot to the horse and undid the buckle. The chariot came free and collapsed in the street behind her.

Freed from it, the horse gained speed, but it was still an old horse without much stamina. It was already breathing heavily and breaking into a sweat. Plus, Charlie hadn't ridden many horses in her life, and never one without a saddle. She had no idea what to do except cling to its mane and fight to stay atop it, which was no easy task. She was being jostled roughly, aggravating her wounded leg.

The Colosseum was getting closer.

The cars were bearing down.

And her horse was wearing out. It stumbled in a pot-hole and nearly fell. Then, obviously hurt, it stopped running altogether.

Still, it had gotten Charlie far enough away. She leapt off the horse, grimacing at the jolt of pain as her sore leg hit the pavement, and then ran again.

A pedestrian-only plaza stretched between the Colosseum and the southern end of the Forum. To Charlie's dismay, this area was also closed to visitors at night; it was devoid of tourists, police, or anyone else who could help her. The Colosseum was locked off with metal gates, and the closest subway station was too far away from her to reach for safety. She was out in the open with no place to hide, not a good position at all.

The first car veered off the Via dei Fori Imperiali and onto the plaza, barely missing the horse. Then it bore down on Charlie, as if the driver intended to run her over.

At which point the second car slammed into it. It caught the first car by the rear right tire, sending it skidding out of control.

Until that moment, Charlie had thought both cars were pursuing her, bearing members of the same enemy team, but now it appeared that the drivers were working against each other. The second car struck the first again, sending it into a low embankment, where it flipped and landed upside down.

The second car was badly damaged as well. Its front axle snapped and it ground to a halt in the plaza in front of Charlie, blocking her escape.

Isaac Semel and another three Mossad agents climbed out.

The agents immediately aimed their guns at Charlie. "Don't try anything stupid," Semel told her.

"I never do." Charlie reluctantly raised her hands in surrender, allowing one of the Mossad agents to grab her from behind.

Charlie looked to the first car, lying upside down in the plaza nearby. The two passengers had been knocked unconscious in the wreck, while the driver was trying to escape through a shattered window. He was only halfway out when Semel clubbed him on the back of the head with the butt of his gun, knocking him cold as well.

Sirens wailed in the night, indicating the police were on their way. Charlie figured the man whose chariot she had stolen had called them. Or maybe someone had witnessed the gunfight at the Forum.

Semel looked from one ruined car to the other, then directed his agents to head toward the Colosseum. "Take her there."

The agent holding Charlie tried to drag her away, but she held her ground. "Wait," she said, then nodded to the man Semel had just knocked out. "If he's not with you—and he's not with me—then who is he? Mukhabarat?"

"Even worse," Semel said knowingly. He reached down, fished something from the man's suit, and tossed it to Charlie.

She caught it, then gaped at it in surprise. It was a badge. A badge she had seen quite often recently.

The man was from the CIA.

THIRTY-THREE

Back at the Temple of Venus Genetrix, Dante and Milana were making the same startling discovery. They had defeated the men who had ambushed them at the ruins, although it hadn't been easy. Which made sense, now that they found the badges on them. The men had received the exact same combat training that Dante and Milana had.

Dante and Milana had just been a little bit better.

Still, they were banged up and bloodied from the fight. Dante had a split lip, a wrenched arm, and a burn across one bicep where a bullet had nicked him. Milana had a gash from a knife in her left arm and an ache in her ribs where she had been sucker punched. She had wrapped a torn piece of cloth around her arm to stanch the flow of blood. She probably needed a few stitches, but at the moment, there were other concerns.

Their own agency had ambushed them.

They could hear the Italian police on their way.

And Charlie was gone.

Dante and Milana left the CIA agents where they had knocked them out, although they took their IDs and badges. When the police found them, it would take the agents longer to prove they were CIA without identification, which would stall them for a while.

Then Dante and Milana fled into the Forum.

They stayed clear of the Via dei Fori Imperiali. As it was the main road, the police would gather there in force. Sure enough, as Dante and Milana slunk off into the ruins, a half dozen cars flashing bubble lights and emblazoned with the word "Carabinieri"—Police—skidded to a stop on the side of the road closest to the Temple of Venus. Other police cars continued on toward the Colosseum, in the direction Charlie had gone.

Dante and Milana went that way too, skulking through the shadows. They found a staircase that took them up the Capitoline Hill, past the ancient latrine from where Isaac Semel had spied on them.

"Arthur Zell double-crossed us," Dante said, at once enraged and dismayed. "After everything we've done for the Agency . . ."

"Obviously, he doesn't trust us to deliver Charlie to him," Milana observed.

"I told him we were coming to Rome!" Dante said angrily. "Didn't that show him that we could be trusted? And he responds by trying to take us out! I'll destroy him when I get the chance!"

Milana grabbed Dante's arm, forcing him to stop and face her.

"You're getting emotional," she said.

"Darn right I am! My own agency just tried to kill me!"

"Emotions cloud judgment. We have to focus right now. We need to find Charlie."

Dante knew she was right. He tried to calm down. But he was seething.

Arthur Zell had been lying to him all along. Most likely, the director of the CIA wasn't in Rome at all. He had never been on the jet. Instead, he had merely told Dante he wanted to meet and pretended he was on his way. Then he had sent a black ops team to take them out. The CIA had probably arrived in Rome long before Zell had claimed it would. That way, the operatives could have been lying in wait when Dante, Milana, and Charlie arrived and tailed them from the airport. They had followed them to the Forum, where it was dark and quiet and easy to set up an ambush. The plan would have been to execute Dante and Milana, then spirit Charlie back to the United States and . . .

Dante shuddered, imagining what people who didn't care about Charlie might do to get her to cough up Pandora.

The thought of it incensed him. As did the idea that he'd been betrayed. Arthur Zell had cared more about Pandora than his life. Or Milana's.

Which meant that, as far as the CIA was concerned, he was no longer an agent.

He was a rogue. He had spent his entire life working for the United States, and now his country had turned on him.

It was a lot to handle.

Milana slipped her hand into Dante's and squeezed. It brought him back. He looked into her eyes. Instead of anger, he saw sadness there.

He wasn't the only one who had been betrayed. Milana had too.

She was only in this mess because of him. He had chosen her for his team. He had made her look bad when they lost Charlie and Pandora—and when he covered up what they had found in the Amazon. If it hadn't been for Dante, Milana would have been on other operations, probably scoring one success after another.

Instead, she was here in Rome, disavowed by the Agency and on the run.

"We need to find Charlie," Milana said again. "How do we do that?"

Dante focused on her and let the anger slide away. It wasn't gone, he knew. It would come back. But for the time, at least, he could keep it from clouding his judgment.

At the base of the Capitoline Hill, the Italian police were gathered at the railing along the Via dei Fori Imperiali, sweeping their flashlights across the Forum. One of them spotted the prone body of a CIA agent and called to the others, who quickly scrambled over the railing, dropped into the ruins, and went to investigate.

Dante started running again before anyone noticed them. Milana fell in beside him. Even though both were aching from their fights, they ignored the pain and moved quickly.

They headed south, toward the Colosseum. Dante had seen the CIA chasing Charlie that way. With any other kid Charlie's age, he would have expected the worst. He would assume she had been captured.

But Charlie was no ordinary kid. Maybe she had escaped.

Although, even if she had, she was still in grave danger.

Dante picked up the pace and ran as fast as he could, hoping they could find Charlie before their enemies did.

THIRTY-FOUR

Charlie took it as a bad sign that the Mossad had dragged her into the Colosseum.

The iron gates that barricaded the entrances had simple locks. A member of Semel's team had quickly picked one, and then they had all slipped inside before the police showed up.

While the Colosseum was possibly the most renowned tourist attraction in Italy, Charlie was well aware that it had been the site of a staggering amount of suffering and death. The sporting events that took place there were brutal. For its inaugural games in 80 AD, the emperor Titus had arranged for the slaughter of over six thousand animals, including hundreds of lions, leopards, elephants, giraffes, rhinos, and hippos. Ultimately, over one million animals would be killed at the Colosseum. Within a hundred years after its construction, most of the wild animals in northern Africa were extinct.

But it was the human slaughter that really bothered Charlie. At the Colosseum, prisoners had been executed in front of eager crowds, and gladiators had routinely fought to the death. Most gladiators were captured slaves, although a few actually volunteered. At the height of Rome's power, there had been four hundred gladiator arenas across the Empire, in which about eight thousand gladiators were killed per year—although the greatest venue for the battles was the Colosseum, where hundreds of men could die in a single day, solely for entertainment.

Despite Charlie's fears, she was still amazed by the construction of the building. Originally known as the Flavian Amphitheater, it was designed to hold up to eighty thousand people at once—a considerable portion of the population of the city. Like many modern-day stadiums, it was an oval of tiered seating, surrounding a central arena. When first built, it had been coated with marble and had an enormous retractable awning to protect the spectators from the sun.

In the shadows of the massive stone arches that supported the building, the Mossad quickly frisked Charlie. The three agents with Isaac Semel patted her down and rifled through her clothes. They came across the rubbing of the stone tablet, the coin that Charlie had recovered at the Parthenon, and the marble disc from the floor at the Forum, then passed them all to Semel, who pocketed them.

Charlie wasn't carrying anything else.

"She's clean," an agent announced.

Semel nodded, then led them into the center of the Colosseum, where there was less chance that they would be seen—or heard—by the police outside. In its heyday, the floor of the arena had been wood coated with sand—which was needed to soak up all the blood that was spilled there. The wood had rotted away long ago, revealing the hypogeum, a labyrinth of tunnels and rooms that had been a sort of basement for the Colosseum. It was down in the hypogeum that gladiators and wild animals had waited for their time to fight. Archaeologists had found evidence of human-powered, winch-driven elevators that would lift the combatants up through the wooden floor, allowing them to burst through the ground dramatically—as well as sluices that diverted river water through the hypogeum to clean it. On a few occasions, the Colosseum had even been flooded and mock naval battles had been staged inside.

In ancient times, the hypogeum had been a terrifying place, dimly lit by oil lamps, crowded with condemned men, scalding in the heat of the sun, reeking of wild animals and excrement and blood. The gladiators had referred to it as hell.

This was where the Mossad brought Charlie now.

The labyrinth of narrow passages was claustrophobic and confusing in the darkness; Charlie quickly became disoriented. Even if someone had known that she was in the Colosseum, it was hard to imagine they could have found her down in the hypogeum.

Eventually, Isaac Semel pointed to a small brick alcove. To Charlie, it looked as though back in Roman times, it might have been a holding pen for prisoners who were about to be thrown to the lions. The Mossad agents dragged Charlie inside and roughly seated her on the ground.

The brick walls of the room stretched two stories above them, showing a mere sliver of sky. There was only one exit, which the Mossad agents blocked.

Despite the air of menace, Isaac Semel smiled at Charlie. He knelt down, looked her in the eye, and spoke in a surprisingly friendly manner. "I know we didn't really start our relationship off on the right foot. I'm sorry about that. I'm not a bad person—and neither are any of my agents. I think you know that. I mean, we just saved you from the CIA. That was *your* agency trying to kill you out there. Not us."

"What's with the kindly old grandpa act?" Charlie asked. "You really think I'm going to fall for this?"

"This isn't an act. . . ."

"Of course it is. If you were actually nice people, you wouldn't have dragged me down into the bowels of the Colosseum to talk to me," Charlie said. "You would have taken me out for gelato."

"We brought you here to protect you," Semel said. "The game has changed. You're out of time to hunt for whatever Cleopatra left behind—if it even exists. Your own country has turned on you. Do you think those are the only agents the CIA sent to Rome? Do you believe that if the police had you instead of us, the CIA wouldn't be able to get to you? Plus, the Mukhabarat is still on your tail, and who knows how many other agencies? You're no longer safe. Except with us. We can protect you. All we ask is that you give us Pandora."

Charlie studied Semel carefully, looking into his eyes, trying to assess whether she could trust him.

The betrayal by the CIA had caught her by surprise. It wasn't so much that the Agency had turned on her— but that it had turned on Dante and Milana. Both of them had devoted their lives to the Agency, and it had repaid their loyalty by trying to execute them.

Or maybe, Charlie realized fearfully, the Agency *had* executed them. She had no idea if either Dante or Milana had survived.

And if they hadn't, then maybe she really did need someone to keep her safe.

"I know you're worried," Semel said. "You put on a good act, being tough, but you're still only a kid. I have a granddaughter your age. If she was in your position, I would hope that she could find someone to look after her, too."

"So . . . ," Charlie began cautiously. "You'll protect me . . . but only if I give you Pandora? If I don't, you'll just throw me back out there and leave me to fend for myself?"

Semel blinked, caught off guard by this response. "Charlie, we don't want to use Pandora to make weapons. We only want to keep it out of our enemies' hands. We want to keep it safe."

"It *is* safe," Charlie assured him, then tapped her skull. "Right here. If you really want to protect it, then you should just protect *me*. I'm sure you came here on your own plane, right? Get me to the airport and fly me back to Israel with you."

"And what proof do I have that you won't just run off with Pandora when we get there?" Semel asked. "Only your word."

"What proof do *I* have that you won't try to weaponize Pandora?" Charlie replied. "Only *your* word."

One of the Mossad agents, a burly, strapping man, stepped forward and spoke to Semel brusquely in Hebrew. "We've wasted enough time. I can get her to talk." In his hand, a knife blade glinted in the moonlight.

Charlie recoiled, but there was nowhere to go. Her back was to the wall.

Semel was suddenly on his feet, moving with startling speed and power for a man his age. He wheeled on the Mossad agent and unleashed a flurry of moves. The knife clattered to the ground by Charlie. And then the Mossad agent dropped as well, writhing in pain.

"I don't care how important Pandora is," Semel said angrily. "We do not hurt children."

There was a brief, soft sound, like that of a bird flying through the night. Something struck Semel in the neck.

The other Mossad agents went on the alert, but they were quickly struck as well. Then the agent on the ground was hit too.

Charlie was close enough to him to see he had been struck by a small sedation dart. She turned to Semel, who had pulled the dart from his own neck. There was resignation in his eyes—and then his eyelids drooped shut and he slid to the ground.

The other Mossad agents collapsed behind him.

Charlie looked up. High above her, balanced precariously on the walls at the top of the small chamber, were Dante and Milana.

Charlie was thrilled to see they were still alive. "What took you so long?" she asked.

"It wasn't that easy to find you in here. Even with *this*." Dante holstered his gun, then held up his phone, displaying the tracking app.

Charlie struggled to get back to her feet. Her leg still hurt, and she was shaken from the events of the night. "Do you guys know how to get out of here?"

Milana pointed to the east. "There's a set of stairs that way."

Charlie knelt by Isaac Semel and went through his pockets until she found the rubbing of the stone tablet, the round piece of marble from the Forum, and the coin from the Parthenon. She took everything back, then stepped over the fallen Mossad agents and entered the maze of passageways again.

Above her, Dante and Milana walked along the tops of the walls of the hypogeum, keeping tabs on her from above.

"Why didn't you tell us you were carrying the tracking bracelet again?" Dante asked.

"I *did*. When I told you to track me after the CIA ambushed us."

"I meant before that."

"It was only in case of emergencies."

"The Mossad didn't frisk you?" Milana asked, surprised.

"No, they did. But I hid the tracker where they wouldn't find it. I swallowed it."

High above, Dante gave a short laugh of surprise. "When?"

"On the jet tonight. I found it back in the hotel in Athens, then figured maybe I should hold on to it in case of trouble. I ate it along with my gyro. It wasn't that easy to swallow, but it went down okay with a little tzatziki sauce."

Dante suddenly felt foolish, realizing that he had completely lost track of the tracking chip. After finding it in the gutter in Athens, he had brought the clasp of the bracelet that contained it back to the hotel to show to Milana, but then hadn't seen it again. He noticed Milana looking slightly ashamed herself; obviously, she had lost track of it too. Still, there was no point in being upset about it. "Good thinking," Dante called down to Charlie. "Looks like we got here just in time to save you."

Charlie glanced back at the prone bodies of the Mossad. "Actually, if it hadn't been for the Mossad, your friends at the CIA would have captured me. What are we supposed to do about *them*?"

There was a pause before Dante answered, and when

he did, there was a weariness in his voice. "We obviously can't trust them anymore."

"Is there *anyone* we can trust?"

Dante and Milana shared a look. "Perhaps," Dante said. "I don't know for sure."

"For the time being, we're fugitives," Milana said.

"Welcome to the club," Charlie told her.

She reached a junction in the hypogeum. An archaeological dig was underway, although the work had been covered with tarps to protect it at night. Holes had been dug in the ground, with wooden beams laid over them to allow people to get across. A warning sign was taped to the wall close by: *Una persona alla volta.*

One person at a time.

Charlie found herself staring at it. In all the excitement that evening, she'd had no time to think about Cleopatra's latest clue. Now she took the piece of marble from the Forum out of her pocket and looked at the engraving on it:

Ubi unum invenis, ibi totum reperies.

Where you find one, you will find all.

Find one.

Charlie unrolled the rubbing of the stone tablet and examined it. It didn't take her long to find what she was looking for.

Suddenly she understood. She understood *everything*.

"Charlie!" Dante hissed from above. "Why aren't you moving? What's going on?"

Charlie grinned up at him, her eyes gleaming in the moonlight. "I think I know where to find the philosopher's stone."

THIRTY-FIVE

Langley, Virginia

Arthur Zell was not pleased with the news from Rome.

The choice to take out his own operatives had not been an easy one. He knew that Garcia and Moon were top agents, but he also believed they had lost sight of their objective. The United States needed to control Pandora, pure and simple. It couldn't be left in the hands of a young, impetuous girl while they traipsed all over the world looking for other ancient artifacts. Perhaps Cleopatra had truly hidden something of great power, but Zell assumed that it still couldn't be as important as Pandora.

And yet he was sure that Garcia and Moon wouldn't see things the way that he did. They were too close to Charlie Thorne. They certainly wouldn't approve of the drastic measures Zell might use to get Charlie to give up Pandora.

It was a tough call, but Zell had ultimately decided his agents were expendable.

He had set them up, telling them he would meet them in Rome but sending a black ops team to ambush them instead. It should have been a relatively easy operation.

But it had failed.

Garcia, Moon, and Thorne had escaped. Even worse, they certainly knew that the CIA had betrayed them.

Which made them an even bigger problem than before.

Thankfully, they hadn't killed any of his agents in Rome. They had only knocked them cold, showing more respect for their lives than Zell had shown them. Zell wasn't sure how Garcia and Moon had managed that, taking out six agents, although it appeared that they had help. From who, Zell didn't know yet. That was a concern in itself.

The leader of the black ops team was now on hold, on a secure line from Rome, waiting for orders after having delivered the bad news.

Zell paced his new office, trying to come up with a plan. He hadn't even had time to unpack yet. Everything he had intended to put on the shelves was still in cardboard boxes. The furniture was still what Jamilla Carter had picked out—and, given what Zell knew about bureaucracy, it would probably be another six months until he could replace it all.

He wondered if he would even last in this job that long.

He had been here just over a day, and he already had a massive failure that now needed to be covered up. Charlie Thorne had been Jamilla Carter's undoing, and if Zell wasn't careful, she would be his as well.

His plan had been to turn things around quickly, to prove that he could succeed where Carter had not. The black ops would neutralize Garcia and Moon, apprehend Charlie Thorne, and bring her back to the States, where the CIA would take whatever measures were necessary to make her cough up Pandora.

Zell considered his options.

Then he returned to the call with the leader of the black ops team.

"We'll need to paint Garcia and Moon as rogue agents," Zell said. "Notify the Roman police and Interpol. Tell them Garcia and Moon ambushed *you* in the Forum, not the other way around. And ask for their help in finding them. We need people posted at airports, train stations, car rentals . . . If there's a way out of Rome, I want it under surveillance."

"We're already working on that, sir."

"Good. And I assume you've impounded the jet they arrived on?"

"Yes sir. But, not surprisingly, we haven't seen any sign of them."

"Of course." Zell didn't expect that Garcia or Moon would return to the jet. That would be far too risky. But still, it made sense to cover all the bases.

"Sir?" the black ops leader said. "I've just received some more intel on who might have been helping Garcia and Moon. My team was able to trace the car that rammed ours by the Colosseum. It was rented by a shell company used by the Mossad."

"The Mossad?" Zell exclaimed, despite himself. "They're back in this mess again?" He sat at his desk and ran his hands through his thinning hair in exasperation. If Garcia and Moon were in league with the Mossad, then the Israelis might have Pandora already.

In theory, the US and Israel were allies, but as far as Zell was concerned, anyone who had Pandora was a threat.

The longer Charlie Thorne was out in the world with that equation, the more dangerous she became.

As much as Zell wanted Pandora, sometimes the best way to neutralize a threat was to make sure no one had it. And there was only one way he could do that for sure.

"We need to change the objective of the operation," Zell said.

"Yes sir?" the black ops leader asked. "How so?"

"The objective is no longer to bring in Charlie Thorne and recover Pandora. The objective is now to terminate her."

There was a long pause. Then the black ops leader said, "If we do that, then Pandora will be lost forever."

"I know. But the world will be safer that way. The only way to prevent anyone else from having Pandora is to kill Charlie Thorne."

THIRTY-SIX

Rome

Charlie, Dante, and Milana returned to the touristy section of Rome and found a crowded restaurant. They knew they couldn't return to their jet, because the CIA would be staking it out, and they knew they had to keep a low profile, because the Roman police and maybe even Interpol might be looking for them now. But they still needed a place to talk, and they were hungry.

Even though it was nearly eleven at night, the restaurants around the Piazza Navona were bustling. Rome was a city that stayed up late. The crowd seemed to be equal parts tourists and locals.

Most of the restaurants had tables set out on the wide sidewalks, but it made sense to eat inside, where there was less chance of being noticed by a passing police officer. They found a table in a quiet corner of an otherwise busy café, ordered some pizzas, and sat so that Dante and Milana could keep an eye on the front door. Each of them made a trip to the bathroom to wash all the dirt, grime, and dried blood off themselves. Then Charlie laid out the rubbing of the stone tablet for them all to look at. After everything the rubbing had been through, it was now crumpled, torn, and faded but, thankfully, still legible.

MEA CÆSARION CARISSIMA

PIS PHARAONIS SVNT TALIA VT VRBAE
T ECCILAM OMNEM POTESTATVM HOS
H NONNE BELLVM NOSTRARVM AN II
XVIR QVÆSITVM AD FONTEM IVVE EN
S A REGNO AMBVLABVNT ET PVNGNAB
I GISTRVM FIENT ET ORIGINEM MONSTR
ER ES ROGANT QVID INVENIAS ET ALIQ
VENE VOS QVIDEM GLORIAM LAVDVE
ET NOSCE TE IPSVM ET QVARE PARERE
RGO EX SVNT ET VNDE QVINQVAGINTA R
ORATORES ILLZA PVLCHRÆ NAVES MINAS
D DEVM FACVT MVLTA VESTI ATRÆ HABE
VS HOSTES AD FEMINÆ PROFECTÆ CONS
R HOC SERVI REGINÆ IN DOMO SVNT ETS
E T FO CONSILIO REFVGIEBANT ET CIVES
A ERB I ES MEMENTO STATVS QVO ET CLA
C A EST ET VINCIET OMNIA VNVM VERIT
MAGNÆ OBORTÆ VNDÆ VELVM PELLVN
COR ET ANIMA VIRAGINIS ATRVM SVNT
EM DIVVS MAGNVS ME REDIIT PHAR

"We're back to this again?" Dante asked.

"Yes," Charlie said. "Every time I've looked at this rubbing, I've had the sense that there's more to it than I realized, but it wasn't until we were at the Colosseum that it finally hit me what that was."

"Care to enlighten us?" Dante asked.

Their waiter set a basket of freshly baked bread on the table, along with a small bowl of olive oil and balsamic vinegar, glasses of wine for the adults, and a soda for Charlie. Charlie greedily grabbed a hunk of bread, dipped it in the oil and vinegar, and wolfed it down.

"This isn't just a tablet," she said. "It's also a map."

Dante and Milana stared at the rubbing, trying to make sense of it.

"Look at the crack," Charlie told them. "What does it remind you of?"

Understanding came to Milana first. She stared at the thin line, noting the wandering path it took through the stone, then gasped in surprise. "It's a river."

"Not just *any* river." Charlie grabbed another hunk of bread. "The Nile. The center of the Egyptians' world. The source of life and wealth and power for their entire civilization."

"Of course," Milana said. "And therefore, this entire tablet is a map of Egypt."

Dante squinted at the crack. He could see how it followed the general course of the Nile, wending from south to north through the stone. And yet . . . "That's not quite the Nile," he pointed out. "The path it's taking is slightly off."

"This map was made two thousand years ago," Charlie reminded him. "Rivers change course over time. Back in Cleopatra's day, the Nile flooded almost every year. They *needed* it to. The floods brought new nutrients and soil down from the headwaters in the rainforests of Central Africa. A bad flood year meant tough times. A good flood year meant the gods were smiling on the Egyptians. But it would also lead to the river overrunning its banks and maybe even shifting course."

Milana added, "It's also possible that whoever made this tablet didn't know the exact route of the Nile. It *was* two thousand years ago. So maybe they just gave the best representation that they could."

"All right." Dante held up his hands in mock surrender, conceding the point. "It's a map of the Nile. I don't suppose that it also shows us where the philosopher's stone is hidden?"

Charlie beamed excitedly. "It does."

Before she could say any more, Milana and Dante both stiffened, on the alert.

Charlie froze, wanting to turn around and look behind her, but knowing that would probably be a bad idea, for then she would be showing her face to whoever was there.

"Police," Milana said.

There were two of them, walking past the café. She and Dante could see them through the open doors: a man

and a woman, casing the café carefully, as though searching for someone.

Milana slipped her arm through Dante's and began
speaking Italian to him in a lively way, as though they were
a local couple out for a late dinner with their daughter. She
told a long story about the hard day she'd had at work at
the hospital, pausing now and then to take a sip of wine.

Dante didn't speak Italian, but he played along, pretending to hang on her every word.

Charlie noticed he did an extremely good job of looking at Milana like he was enamored with her.

Eventually, the police continued on without even
bothering to come inside. There were hundreds of cafés
in Rome, maybe thousands. They couldn't possibly search
them all top to bottom. There was a chance that they
weren't even looking for Dante, Milana, and Charlie at
all—but if they were, coming into the restaurant probably
seemed like a waste of time. What fugitives would stop
for dinner in a place like this?

Once the police were gone, Milana dropped the act
and asked Charlie, "Where's the stone?"

"*Ubi unum invenis, ibi totum reperies,*" Charlie said.
"Find one and you will find it all."

Dante and Milana looked back at the rubbing, letting
their eyes wander over the words that had been inscribed
into the stone.

Dante was the one who saw it first. "There!" he exclaimed, and thumped a finger down on the word "unum." "That means 'one'! That's the 'one' Cleopatra wants us to find!"

Charlie grinned. "Exactly."

"So the stone must be located somewhere in this area of the Nile," Milana deduced, inspecting the rubbing closely. "It looks like there's a mark on the western bank of the river just above the word 'unum.'"

"Yes," Charlie agreed. "At first, I thought that was just a chip in the rock, or a mistake I made when I did the rubbing, but given the clue, I think it must be the site of the philosopher's stone."

Dante pulled out his phone—it was CIA-issued, with no tracking chips, so he could use it without fear of being traced—and quickly brought up a satellite map of Egypt. Even though the Nile's course was somewhat different from what was depicted on the rubbing, Dante was still able to pinpoint the approximate location of where the mark would have been on the modern map. "Looks like the stone would be located right about here," he said, displaying his phone to the others.

The spot was quite far south in Egypt, along the banks of Lake Nasser.

Milana immediately grew concerned. "That's not good."

"Why not?" Dante asked.

"That lake didn't exist in Cleopatra's time," Milana explained. "It was only formed in the 1960s, with the construction of the Aswan Dam. Which means that anything built along the banks of the Nile there two thousand years ago will now be underwater."

"That's not insurmountable," Dante said, sounding surprisingly upbeat. "We're both certified scuba divers. The lake can't be that deep. It won't be *easy*, but we could handle an underwater salvage operation."

"I'm not so sure," Milana said dourly. "Diving into an archaeological ruin that could be a hundred feet or more below the surface is exceptionally dangerous. I don't think either of us is qualified for that. Plus, there's the question of how we could even mount such an operation, given that we're now wanted by our own agency."

"Charlie can pay for it," Dante suggested. "She's loaded."

"And there's the issue of how we would get back into Egypt in the first place," Milana reminded him. "Our passports have certainly been flagged."

"The stone isn't in Egypt," Charlie said.

The others turned to her, surprised.

"But we just figured out it's at that spot on the map . . . ," Dante began.

"That's only showing where Cleopatra left it," Charlie told him. "But if she put it where I think she did, then it isn't in Egypt anymore."

"Then where is it?" Milana asked.

"You'll never believe it," Charlie replied.

THIRTY-SEVEN

The pizza arrived just as Charlie began to explain things. Charlie eagerly grabbed a slice, then pointed to the spot they had located on the map, doing her best not to drip any grease onto the precious rubbing. "There used to be a temple dedicated to Isis here. And as we know, Cleopatra identified with Isis. In fact, lots of Egyptians thought she *was* Isis in human form. So it makes sense that if she was going to hide the philosopher's stone somewhere, she would do it in an Isis temple."

"You can't guarantee that," Dante countered.

"No," Charlie admitted, "but if you were Cleopatra, what safer place would there be? She couldn't bury the philosopher's stone, because the landscape of Egypt is constantly changing. The sand dunes in the desert move around thanks to the winds, and like I said, the Nile shifts course all the time. So if Cleopatra really wanted to protect something, she'd need to put it in a structure of some sort, and she had plenty of reason to believe that a religious building like a temple would stand the test of time. After all, the pyramids of Giza were already well over two thousand years old. Plus, Cleo hid the original stone tablet that I got this rubbing from in a different Isis temple, so she obviously felt it worked."

"Makes sense," Milana said, wolfing down her own slice of pizza.

"There was already a big Isis cult in this area," Charlie continued, pointing back to the spot on the rubbing. "The main Isis temple in all of Egypt was located relatively close by, on an island called Philae. Cleopatra—and her ancestors—made pilgrimages there every year. They had these enormous royal barges that were like floating palaces, with dozens of rooms. Some even had gymnasiums, libraries, and gardens. And that was just for the queen. When Cleopatra took Julius Caesar down the Nile, they had four hundred other boats in their procession."

Dante asked, "So if Cleopatra wanted to hide the stone, wouldn't she have hidden it in the main temple? Why hide it in this other one?"

"Well, technically, the smaller temple didn't exist the first time Cleopatra visited the area," Charlie replied. "Cleo commissioned its construction. It wasn't even finished until after she died—although she ended up dying quite a bit earlier than she planned, thanks to Octavian. So I'm thinking, maybe Cleo had this temple specially constructed for hiding the philosopher's stone. Maybe she even thought her descendants would store the stone there forever. After all, it was relatively safe: a remote location with a large group of priests keeping an eye on it. At the very least, it was a decent place to stash the stone until Caesarion showed up to claim it. I'm sure it never occurred to Cleo that, at some point twenty centuries later, men would have the power to dam the Nile and flood the whole valley."

"So what happened to the temple?" Milana asked.

Charlie dug into a second slice of pizza. "When the time came to build the Aswan Dam, the Egyptians knew they'd be flooding the whole area behind it. And they knew there were lots of important archaeological sites that would end up underwater. The United Nations started a major campaign to document the sites and protect whatever monuments they could. Over fifty countries helped out—although the United States made some of the most significant contributions. At some point, it was suggested that instead of letting the Isis temple be submerged, it could be moved somewhere else entirely. They just had to take it apart, block by block, and then put it back together again, like a set of really old Legos. They could even ship it off to another country. Which is exactly what the Egyptians did. As a thanks for all the help, they sent the Temple of Dendur to the United States."

Milana dropped her slice of pizza in surprise. "Oh my. I know where it is."

"Where?" Dante asked.

"It's in the Metropolitan Museum of Art in New York City," Milana said.

"Exactly," Charlie agreed.

Dante gaped at them in shock. "How could an entire temple be inside a museum?"

"You've never been to the Met?" Milana asked, sounding disappointed.

"No," Dante said defensively. "Art museums really aren't my thing . . ."

"It's like the most famous part of the museum," Milana told him. "They built an enormous addition just to house the temple. It has a whole wall of windows that look right out onto Central Park."

"Oh!" Dante said, recognition dawning on him. "I know the room you're talking about! They've filmed a lot of movies there."

"That's the place." Charlie polished off her second slice of pizza.

Milana looked to her. "And you think the philosopher's stone would still be inside it?"

"I've been inside that temple," Charlie said. "It's not that big. It's not like the Great Pyramid, which has a whole lot of hidden chambers deep inside it. If I was going to hide a stone there, I'd probably hide it *inside* one of the blocks that the temple was made out of. And they moved all the blocks from Egypt to New York. So it's probably still there. All we have to do is find the right block."

"All right," Milana said gamely. "I've been to the temple too. There are hieroglyphics all over it. So, in theory, there's a final message from Cleopatra explaining where the stone is hidden."

Dante made a time-out sign with his hands. "Hold on. Let's think about this. The CIA just turned on us. We are fugitives. And you want to go back to the United States— right into the heart of the biggest, most crowded, most heavily policed city in the country—and then try to steal an ancient artifact from the most popular attraction in the middle of the city's most popular museum?"

"What else are we supposed to do?" Charlie asked. "Go into hiding?"

"Yes!" Dante exclaimed, then caught himself and lowered his voice before he started making a scene. "We should be lying low."

"For the rest of our lives?" Milana asked pointedly. "That's not what I signed up for when I took this job."

"Neither did I," Dante said. "But we don't have jobs

anymore. And if we want to get them back, this isn't the way to do it . . ."

"You want to get back into the Agency?" Milana asked him, stunned.

"You *don't*?" Dante replied with equal surprise.

"The Agency just tried to *kill* us," Milana reminded him. "I know you devoted your life to it. So did I. And I'm upset to see it all come to this. But there's no way I'm ever going back. Not after what they've done. I'd never be able to trust anyone there ever again."

Dante took some time to think. Charlie watched his eyes as he realized Milana was right. It was as though something had died in him. It seemed as if, for the past few hours, he'd been clinging to a dream that he could make things right—and now he was realizing that it would never work. He would never be a CIA agent again. He finally sagged in resignation. "If that's the case, then why take chances at all? Going after this stone is insanely risky. And for what?"

"For the same reasons we went after Pandora," Charlie said firmly. "Because we need to get to it before anyone else does."

"I think it's safe," Dante said miserably. "No one has even come close to finding it for two thousand years . . ."

"But now, thanks to our actions, that's not the case anymore." Charlie took another slice of pizza. "The CIA, the Mossad, and the Mukhabarat are in this hunt. And the Shah family too."

Dante waved this off. "The Shahs are a bunch of fools . . ."

"And yet they caught us by surprise in Athens," Milana reminded him.

"What happens if they get their hands on the stone?" Charlie asked. "Fools with the power to generate as much gold as they want would be incredibly dangerous. That's what the whole story of King Midas was about."

"That's a myth," Dante said dismissively.

Charlie asked, "Do you think it's a coincidence that while everyone was trying to create a philosopher's stone, a cautionary tale was told about what would happen if someone had the power to turn everything into gold? Cleopatra was clearly very careful in how she used the stone, but other world leaders might not be. Obviously, Cleo feared that would be the case with the Romans, which is why she hid it from them. She loved Caesar and Mark Antony, but she still didn't share her secret with them. In the wrong hands, the philosopher's stone could destroy world economies or make armies unstoppable . . . or even be deadly."

Dante drained his glass of wine. "But the CIA and the Mossad and everyone else don't even know about the stone. You've got them all thinking this is about the Library of Alexandria."

"It doesn't matter what they *think* they're looking for," Charlie replied. "If they figure out the clues, they'll find the stone. And since I've done most of the work already, there isn't too much left to figure out. If we don't get the stone, someone else will. And soon." She finished the final piece of pizza and tossed the last remnant of crust onto the table.

Dante looked to Milana, trying to read her. "You agree with this?"

"Isn't this what our mission was all along?" Milana asked. "To track down all these items and keep them out of the wrong hands?"

"Well . . . yes," Dante agreed cautiously, then shifted his gaze to Charlie. "And to recover Pandora. Eventually."

Milana said, "I don't see why we should stop just because the CIA turned on us. If anything, we ought to be more dedicated to this. Because our own government has now proved that they can't be trusted with these things either."

"And we can?" Dante asked.

"Better us than someone else," Charlie replied.

Milana nodded in support.

Dante sat back in his chair, stroking his chin in thought. Finally, he said, "Not that I'm agreeing to any of this, but . . . given our newfound position as fugitives, exactly how would you plan on getting back into America?" He looked to Charlie. "Are you going to blow another million dollars on a private jet for us?"

"I don't think that'd work," Charlie said. "Since I've done that once already, the CIA would be expecting it. They've probably got tabs on every private jet in Europe by now."

"And flying commercial is out of the question," Milana added. "Seeing as we'd never get through customs. In fact, we'd probably get busted before we got near the plane."

"Then what are we supposed to do?" Dante asked testily. "Swim to America?"

"Not quite," Charlie said. "We're going to put some of your hidden talents to the test."

PART FOUR
THE TEMPLE

Cleopatra stood at one of the most dangerous
intersections in history: that of women and power.

—STACY SCHIFF,
"Rehabilitating Cleopatra"

THIRTY-EIGHT

North Cat Cay
The Bahamas
Four and a half weeks later

When Milana returned to the boat, she found Charlie preparing the barbecue for dinner.

Even though there was a cramped but decent kitchen on the boat, Charlie preferred to make dinner outside. Over the course of their voyage, Charlie had spent as much time on the deck as possible. She hadn't ever been to sea for a long period before and had discovered, a bit late, that she got slightly nauseated inside the cabin. She felt much better when she could breathe fresh air and watch the horizon. Plus, it was nicer up on deck anyhow. "If you're going to sail across the Atlantic Ocean," she'd said, "you might as well look at it."

Her favorite place was sitting on the bow with her bare feet dangling above the water, although once she had mastered steering, she also liked being at the helm. On a few nights, she had even slept out on the stern, though that had made Dante uneasy. He feared that, in the middle of the night, Charlie might tumble off the boat into the sea. His discomfort had made Charlie that much more eager to sleep outside, because she still enjoyed doing anything that got under his skin.

The sailboat was a fifty-foot Beneteau that they had bought in Naples, Italy. It was fifteen years old, but the owner had kept it in good shape. Charlie had paid the woman 175,000 euros for it, which wasn't cheap but was still far less than what hiring a private jet would have cost. The high-end Swiss bank where Charlie kept all her money had a branch in Rome; Charlie had made a significant withdrawal to cover the cost of a boat, new clothes, and six weeks' worth of supplies.

Dante was an adept sailor. He had grown up in Miami, raised by a single mother, because his father—and Charlie's—had left her while she was three months pregnant. Dante had grown up poor, but he was smart. When he was in middle school, he had found work at a local marina, and it wasn't long before many of the boat owners took a shining to him. They taught him to sail and would then pay him to take their boats over to the Bahamas, so that they could just fly in and have the boats waiting. For Dante, it was easy money; it only took about eight hours to make the crossing and he enjoyed being out on the ocean. By the time he was in high school, he was spending most of his summers in the Bahamas, crewing for rich people who didn't even know how to steer their own boats. He had learned to sail over longer and longer distances, taking boats across the Caribbean as far as the British Virgin Islands and Anguilla. And while he had never done anything quite as ambitious as sailing across the entire Atlantic, the fundamentals were the same. He knew how to do it, as long as he had a willing and able crew.

Even though their target destination was New York City, in a sailboat, they had to follow the trade routes. The winds in the Atlantic moved in a clockwise direction, so to get to the Americas, you traveled the exact same course that Columbus had. They had sailed through the Mediterranean Sea from Italy to Gibraltar, then gone south along the northwestern coast of Africa to the Cape Verde Islands, and finally crossed the ocean itself to the Caribbean. Thankfully, they were just ahead of hurricane season and had only hit one minor squall. For the most part, the weather had been clear, the ocean had been calm, and the winds had been with them.

Now they were an easy day's sail from Miami. The way Charlie had figured things, sneaking into the United States from the water was much easier than from the air. Private jets could be tracked; they had registration numbers and left heat trails—and there were a limited number of places they could land. Meanwhile, someone with a sailboat was free to travel almost anywhere; boats weren't monitored the same way that planes were. Technically, you weren't supposed to be able to simply dock wherever you wanted and walk into the United States, but it was relatively easy to do. Florida alone had thousands of marinas, and there was very little policing of the coasts. Plus, Homeland Security and the Coast Guard didn't pay much attention to private sailboats, which were too slow to smuggle contraband and too expensive to be a chosen route for illegal immigrants.

After days of hectic travel and danger, the four-and-a-half-week journey aboard the sailboat had been a welcome relief. Milana felt sorry that it was coming to an end. Although they were still trying to get to New York as fast as they could, they had been able to take a little time in the Caribbean to catch fish and get fresh provisions in small towns. The boat was now anchored along the edge of a shallow reef, miles away from anyone else.

Milana had been snorkeling along the reef, hunting for dinner. She climbed the ladder at the stern of the sailboat and triumphantly held up the large red snapper she had caught with her speargun. "Got a big one!" she announced, and then noticed there were already three other fish laid out by the grill. Charlie had even had time to fillet them all.

"Oh," Milana said, slightly disappointed. "I guess Dante beat me to it."

"He's awfully good with a speargun," Charlie said.

Milana gently removed the spear from the snapper and set the fish by Charlie. "Did he go out to get more?"

"He's just swimming for fun now." Charlie pointed to the edge of the reef, where Dante was snorkeling.

Milana smiled. "The guy's practically a fish. I had no idea he enjoyed this so much."

Charlie said, "Well, it's not like you two have had a chance to go on vacation together. Although, Rome might have been more romantic if your own agency hadn't tried to kill you there."

Milana kept staring out at the ocean, watching Dante. Even though it was getting toward sunset, it was still brutally hot and humid. Meanwhile, the water was warm and crystal clear, and the reef was healthy and populated by teeming schools of fish. Milana was tempted to dive right back in again.

Only, she wanted to talk to Charlie while Dante wasn't around.

There had been plenty of leisure time for all of them on the trip. They had spent hours playing cards and board games—which Charlie had always won—or practicing martial arts on the rocking deck—which Milana and Dante were much better at, although Charlie was learning quickly. At night, they had lain out on the bow, looking at the stars, sharing stories and getting to know each other better. Milana had come to think of Charlie more and more as a little sister. But there were still things that they hadn't discussed.

Milana took a knife and started filleting the snapper she had caught. "You never got the chance to be a kid, did you?" she asked.

Charlie looked up from tending the coals of the barbecue. She thought about denying this but then realized Milana was right. "Not really. But it's no big deal. I mean, most kids my age are still stuck in school, studying for math tests and having to write book reports."

"They also get to have friends their own age and play sports and have sleepovers. It *is* a big deal that you've missed out on that. And to be saddled with Pandora . . . It's not fair to ask that of anyone, let alone someone your age."

Charlie resumed poking at the coals. "I can handle it."

"Still, I'm sure it's not easy. I just want you to know, I'm here to help in any way that you need. And . . . I'm sorry."

"For what?"

"Back when we were at Mount Wilson a few months ago, I pulled a gun on you. I thought it was the right thing to do at the time. I thought Pandora would be better off in the CIA's hands than yours. In retrospect, that was the wrong call. So I apologize. I want you to be able to trust me."

"I do."

"Do you really? A hundred percent?"

Charlie met Milana's eyes. She realized that, up until that point, she *hadn't* trusted Milana fully. But now that had changed. "A hundred percent."

Milana smiled. "Good. Because the moment we set foot back in the United States tomorrow, things are going to get dangerous again."

"I know."

"If you want, we can still change the plan. We could just stay here on the boat, sailing around the Bahamas, off the grid, playing it safe."

"For the rest of our lives?"

"For a good long while, at least. It's not so bad out here, is it?" Milana gutted the snapper, then tossed the entrails into the water. A small dogfish shark raced over and scarfed them down.

Charlie took a few moments to think about their situation. She had enough money socked away to easily cover the cost of provisions for the rest of her life. They could keep on sailing, going anywhere they wanted around the world, and if they were careful, they could most likely keep anyone from tracking them down. Lots of people probably dreamed of having a life like that.

But it seemed wrong to Charlie. "Shortly after Dante blackmailed me into hunting for Pandora, he told me he was disappointed in me. Because I had been wasting my gifts. If we just stayed on the boat, that'd be doing the same thing."

"The situation has changed. Back then, Dante thought he could protect you. And Pandora as well."

"We need to go after the philosopher's stone. We have to get to it before anyone else does. And then, after that, we need to find the other things on Einstein's list."

"All right," Milana said supportively, although Charlie sensed a hint of disappointment in her voice.

The coals were now glowing red-hot, ready to cook dinner. Charlie spread them across the base of the barbecue, set the grill on top, and then laid out the fresh fillets of snapper. "Do *you* want to play it safe and just keep sailing?"

"No. I think you're right about our obligation. But I didn't want to force you into it. Plus, I'm getting kind of sick of fish." Milana flashed Charlie another smile, and Charlie laughed.

"Honestly, I'm dying for a hamburger," Charlie admitted.

"Me too," Milana agreed. "Now, since we're *not* going to play things safe, could I give you some advice?"

"Sure."

"I know you've spent much of your life acting older than you are. But there's nothing wrong with acting your age on occasion."

"Like what?"

"You don't have to put up a front all the time. You can let your guard down. Dress like a thirteen-year-old. Listen to popular music. Read young adult fiction. Lose a game of cards now and then."

Charlie nodded thoughtfully. "I might give that a shot. Except for the losing. That doesn't sound like fun at all."

"It builds character."

"I have plenty of character as it is."

"True." Milana squeezed a lemon over the fillets on the grill, then dusted them with salt. "Also, there may be an occasion soon when acting your age could be an advantage."

"How so?"

"Like when the time comes to locate the philosopher's stone," Milana said. And then she told Charlie about the plan she'd been hatching.

THIRTY-NINE

Tel Aviv, Israel

Isaac Semel was looking at his notes for what was possibly the thousandth time when something just clicked.

He had no idea why it had happened then rather than at any point in the weeks before. Since Rome, he had spent days on end poring over the clues Cleopatra had left behind to no avail.

He was supposed to be focusing on other things, of course. So far, his mission to recover Pandora—and whatever else Charlie Thorne was looking for—had been an abject failure. Twice, the CIA had gotten the jump on him. Twice, he had returned home empty-handed. He knew that, behind his back, the younger members of his team had been questioning his decisions. He knew there were rumors around the Mossad that he was losing his edge. And even though his superiors hadn't said so, he knew they were disappointed with how things had gone. He had been given another assignment, tracking some rebels in the West Bank, and was quite sure that someone else had been tasked with locating Charlie Thorne, although no one had said as much to him.

But he couldn't keep his mind off the operation. Thanks to Charlie, he knew the clues that Cleopatra had left behind. Now he just had to figure out what they meant.

He had photographed the rubbing of the stone tablet, and Charlie had told him what the original key to the code was. The technicians at the Mossad's photography lab had enlarged the photo and enhanced it so that he could see every grain of the stone.

He also knew what Charlie, Dante, and Milana had said in the Forum, right before their own Agency had ambushed them. Semel had recorded their conversation. The quality of the sound wasn't perfect, given that he had been quite far away at the time, but he was using the highest-quality long-distance microphone available.

First of all, they had revealed what they were actually looking for: the philosopher's stone.

Semel had been surprised to hear it then, and it still shook him every time he listened to the recording.

He had passed the news up to his superiors at the Mossad. To his disappointment, they had been dismissive, thinking there was no way that ancient people could have found what modern scientists had not. But Semel didn't agree. Like Charlie, he understood that the philosopher's stone would explain the power and influence of Cleopatra's family—and he knew it still had the potential to alter history. With unlimited wealth, Israel would no longer be dependent on the United States—or any other country. It could become a world power in its own right.

But for that to happen, he had to find the stone.

At the Forum, Charlie had translated Cleopatra's final clue: "Where you find one, you will find all."

Semel had been trying to understand that ever since. He had pondered it on his morning runs through Tel Aviv, and at nights when he was supposed to be focusing on other things. He had sat in his home study, staring at the photograph of the rubbing, desperately trying to comprehend it.

And then, suddenly, it came to him.

As was the case with many moments of inspiration, this one seemed to come out of nowhere, like a lightning bolt on a clear day. Semel had returned home from work and merely taken a cursory glance at the photograph, which had sat in the center of his desk for weeks. But this time, he understood.

His eyes fell upon the word "unum," sitting directly on the crack in the tablet. He immediately realized that might be the "one" that Cleopatra meant, grabbed a magnifying glass, and took a closer look. He found the fleck along the crack and grasped that it was a possible location for Cleopatra's treasure.

As a member of the Mossad, Semel was well versed in Egyptian history and geopolitics. He knew that the Nile had changed course over the centuries, and that the spot the fleck represented was now deep under Lake Nasser. He had spent much of the last few weeks researching Cleopatra, and so he was aware of her connection to Isis. Therefore, it didn't take much time to figure out that the location on the map corresponded with the Temple of Dendur, and then to learn where the temple had been moved.

Semel grabbed his phone, called Yitzhak Levin on a secure line, and shared the news. The head of the Mossad listened carefully, skeptical at first but gradually growing more intrigued. After Semel explained everything he had found, Levin fell silent for a while, thinking.

Finally he said, "Assemble a team and head to New York City immediately."

"Yes sir."

"However, I want to make things very clear: Your objective is not whatever you think might be hidden in this temple. Your objective is to recover Pandora."

Semel paused a moment before answering "Yes sir" once again.

"I know you don't agree with this, but I don't want any distractions. Forget about this nonsense with the philosopher's stone. As far as I'm concerned, the only value of whatever is in that temple is that Charlie Thorne wants it. If she shows up, I want you to be waiting for her. Can I count on you to carry these orders out?"

"Yes sir."

"Very good. Do whatever it takes to bring us Charlie Thorne."

FORTY

Miami, Florida

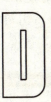ante Garcia had spent much of his teenage years sailing around Miami, and so had visited many of the marinas in the area, but the place he was heading now was new to him.

It was up the coast from the heart of the city, north of the glitzy condos and nightclubs of Miami Beach. They had furled the sails and were using the Beneteau's small motor to cruise up the Intracoastal Waterway, which separated the barrier islands from the mainland. Along the way, the large expensive waterfront estates gave way to more modest homes on smaller properties, although all of them had private docks with at least a small sailboat or fishing boat. The speed limit was only five miles an hour, to prevent wakes that would bang the boats against their docks—and to avoid harming manatees. The large, slow-moving mammals often rested by the surface in the Intracoastal, where reckless boaters might ram into them or slice their bodies with the propellers of their outboards. The last thing Dante wanted to do was attract the attention of the police, so he stayed a bit below the speed limit for the whole journey.

Charlie was at her favorite place, at the bow with her feet dangling, for the entire trip up the Intracoastal. After so many days at sea, so far from land, it was overwhelming to see how much civilization there was along the southern coast of Florida. Only two weeks before, out in the middle of the Atlantic Ocean, Charlie figured they had been hundreds of miles from any other humans. Now they were surrounded by millions.

At the wheel, Dante looked like a different man from the one he had been back in Italy. His skin was much darker than usual and he had grown a thick beard during the journey. Charlie and Milana couldn't change their looks quite as dramatically, but in the hot summer sun, it made sense to have broad-brimmed hats and sunglasses, so their faces were well concealed—not that anyone would have been looking for them here anyhow.

After a few miles, Dante turned into a branch of the Intracoastal that cut west, away from the ocean. The homes got smaller and the boats older and more weatherbeaten. Finally, they arrived at an old pier with a few small, two-person sailboats docked at it. The building behind it was colorfully—although somewhat amateurishly—painted, and a homemade sign announced BOYS AND GIRLS SAILING CLUB OF NORTH MIAMI.

A middle-aged woman was waiting on the dock, also in a broad-brimmed hat and sunglasses, as well as a tan sundress and sandals. She regarded them sternly as they approached, although Charlie thought the woman might be trying her best not to smile.

Dante expertly brought the sailboat in alongside the pier. The woman made no attempt to help them tie it up; she seemed to be out of her element around boats. So Charlie leapt ashore with the bowline and cinched it around a cleat on the pier, while Milana did the same at the stern.

Dante cut the motor. Now that they were far inland from the ocean, there was no breeze, so it was hot and humid. The sounds of the city were all around them: the roar of cars, the blare of music, and the chatter of humans. It was more noise than Charlie had heard in weeks. She had forgotten how loud civilization was. Or maybe she had never noticed.

She finished tying up the boat, then turned to the woman on the pier and said, "Nice to meet you, Director Carter. I'm Charlie Thorne."

Jamilla Carter tilted her nose down so that she could look at Charlie over the tops of her sunglasses. "I'm not the director anymore, thanks to you."

Charlie shrugged. "You never tried to kill my brother and Milana. So I like you better than the other guy."

You wouldn't say that if you knew what I'd planned to do with you, Jamilla thought. And then it occurred to her that Charlie probably *did* know. "It's nice to finally meet the young woman who caused me so much trouble," she said, then checked out Dante's new look as he climbed off the boat. "No one's going to mistake *you* for an agent. That's for sure."

"You've changed yourself, ma'am," Dante replied. "Retirement agrees with you."

"Liar," Carter said, then sighed. "I'm so sorry. I never imagined Zell would do something like this. The fool . . ."

"No need to apologize," Dante said. "*He* did it. Not you."

"Even so, I should have considered the possibility. I could have protected you . . ."

"You're doing more than enough right now."

Back in Italy, Dante had returned to his old-school methods of contacting Jamilla Carter. He was sure that the CIA had her phones tapped, her email scanned, and her home under surveillance. So he'd sent a delivery of flowers to her house with a card that offered congratulations on her retirement from her friends at Denise's Hair Salon. Denise's was a fictitious business, a code that Dante and Jamilla had arranged, and the phone number

Dante had put on the card went to a burner phone he'd bought in Rome. Jamilla had called that line from her own burner phone.

By that time, Dante was already at sea, and his stops on land were rare, but on those occasions, he and Jamilla had been able to hatch a plan.

Jamilla was breaking several laws by helping him now, but she had always liked Dante and Milana and she hated what Arthur Zell had done to them. Plus, retirement was boring. She needed some excitement.

So she had flown down to Miami, which was about the least suspicious thing a retired person in the United States could do. She had rented a nice room at a beach-front hotel and spent most of her time lounging by the pool, reading crime fiction, although every once in a while, when she was sure no one from the CIA was tailing her, she'd done a little work for Dante.

Now she tossed him a manila envelope. He opened it to find reservations at a motel in North Carolina for that night, fake driver's licenses for him and Milana, keys to a rental car, three radio earpieces, and five hundred dollars in cash.

"The car's parked in front," Jamilla explained. "It's in my name, so you'd better not do anything dumb and get yourself pulled over."

"Of course not," Dante replied.

"Sorry I couldn't manage more cash. I was only a government employee. I'm not as loaded as she is." Jamilla nodded toward Charlie. "I assume she can get you more as you go."

"I'll pay you back," Charlie said.

Jamilla waved this off, like it was ridiculous. "I'll tell you what you *can* do for me, though. Let me know what it is that Cleopatra has you chasing all over the globe."

Charlie looked to Dante.

"You can trust her," Dante said.

Charlie looked back to Jamilla. "The philosopher's stone."

Jamilla's eyes went wide in surprise but only for a second. Then she chuckled softly. "Well, we certainly can't have *that* falling into the wrong hands. If it really exists." She returned her attention to Dante. "What's your exit strategy?"

"It's probably best for all of us if you don't know."

Jamilla thought about that, then nodded. "I suppose that makes sense."

After tying up the boat, Milana had been inside the cabin, gathering their bags, which they had already packed. Now she emerged with them and stepped onto the pier. The bags were all quite small, as they didn't have many clothes. "We're good to go," she said.

Jamilla told them, "The Boys and Girls Sailing Club

is very appreciative of your donation. As you can see, the boats they have are very small and barely seaworthy. It will be quite a treat for them to learn to sail something like this. And maybe someday, one of those kids will be able to parlay those skills into a career the way you did, Dante."

"I hope things work out better for that kid than they did for me." Dante couldn't keep the bitterness out of his voice as he said this.

"So do I," Jamilla agreed. "I put some snacks and drinks for you in the car. And a few books." She looked to Charlie. "To keep you occupied. It's a long drive."

"Thanks," Charlie said. "For everything."

"Godspeed," Jamilla Carter told them. "Now get a move on."

FORTY-ONE

Dubai, United Arab Emirates

Ramses Shah was halfway down the ski run when he got the phone call.

Ramses was well aware of how bizarre it was to have a ski slope in Dubai, one of the hottest cities on the planet. But Dubai was flush with cash and a tourist haven for the extremely wealthy from all over the world. So its mall had an indoor ski slope and penguin exhibit, there were man-made islands in the shape of palm trees in the bay, and the world's tallest building, the Burj Khalifa, dominated the skyline.

Ramses had been in a conference room at the Burj all day, having meetings. Everyone else had gone to dinner, but he wanted to get a few runs in.

Skiing was one of Ramses's favorite hobbies. Every winter, he spent one week in the Alps, another in the Rockies, and yet another in Canada. But now, in summer, the only place to ski was Chile, and he didn't have the time to schlep all the way down there. As long as he was in Dubai, he figured he'd grab some time on the slopes. It wasn't nearly as good as a *real* mountain. The run was short and crowded with tourists, most of whom had never been on skis before. But still, it was something.

As Ramses was slaloming through his fifth run, his phone rang. Caller ID said it was Zara Gamal, his contact at the Mukhabarat.

Even though it was 118 degrees in Dubai, the ski slope was so heavily air-conditioned, it hurt to take your gloves off. Normally, Ramses wouldn't have answered a call until he was somewhere warmer. But he quickly removed his gloves and answered this one. "What do you have for me?"

"The Mossad thinks the objective is in the Temple of Dendur."

"The Temple of Dendur?" Ramses repeated, thinking he hadn't heard it right. "The one in New York? At the Metropolitan Museum of Art?"

"That's the one. Some Mossad agent worked it out, and a mole there tipped off the Mukhabarat."

Now that Ramses thought about it, Dendur made sense. An Isis temple in a remote area of Egypt would have been an excellent place to hide something. He said, "So the Mossad and the Mukhabarat are both going after the scrolls from the library?"

"Turns out, the treasure isn't the Library of Alexandria after all. It's the philosopher's stone."

Ramses almost dropped his phone in surprise. His hands were so cold, he was already having trouble holding it. But he no longer cared. He was too busy imagining what it would be like to have an unlimited amount of gold.

He looked around him, at the people skiing in the middle of a desert. Dubai was filled with rich and powerful people from all over the world. People with so much money, they had no idea what to do with it all.

And with the stone, Ramses would be richer than all of them put together.

He could buy the Burj Khalifa. Heck, he could buy Dubai. He would have power and influence like no one else in history. . . .

Well, no one since Cleopatra.

The Shah family could become the new royal family of Egypt, immune to politics, able to do anything they wanted.

He asked, "When is the Mukhabarat heading to New York?"

"Immediately."

"Thank you. I won't forget this."

"You'd better not. If you really find the stone, you owe me a palace."

Ramses hung up. And then, even though his hands were freezing and the snow machines were blowing ice crystals all over him, he stayed right where he was and made another call.

"How's Dubai?" Ahmet asked.

"I'm leaving right away. Something more important has come up. Pack a bag and meet me at the private terminal at the airport."

"Why? What's going on?"

"I'll explain when I see you." Ramses already had Omar, Baako, and Lembris with him in Dubai. They'd fly the private jet to Cairo, then to New York. Although the stop in Cairo really wasn't about Ahmet, who was useless. "And I need you to do one more thing."

"What's that?"

"Stop at my house on the way to the airport. And go to the room with my snakes . . ."

FORTY-TWO

The Metropolitan Museum of Art
Central Park
New York City

The Metropolitan was one of the largest art museums in the world. It had over two million separate works in its collection, and the main building, which was the size of four city blocks, had over six hundred thousand square feet of display space. More than six and a half million people visited it every year, easily making it the most popular art museum in the United States.

It sat on Fifth Avenue, on the eastern edge of Central Park, at a point that was almost the dead center of Manhattan. It was bounded on the north, west, and south by the park itself, which was lush and green in the middle of summer, and bounded on the east by some of the most expensive real estate on earth.

The front entrance of the museum was monumental and imposing, a great stone staircase flanked by fountains.

Slightly over twenty-four hours after arriving in Miami, Charlie, Dante, and Milana headed up the steps, into the grand entry foyer, and approached a ticket booth.

The salesperson pointed out that it was late in the day and asked if they really wanted to buy tickets then, as the museum would only be open for another hour. Maybe they would prefer to come back the next morning instead?

"I wish we could," Dante said with fake regret. "But we're leaving tomorrow. This is our only chance to see the museum at all."

"Then I hope you get to see as much as possible." The salesperson took their cash and slipped them three tickets. "Be sure to visit the Temple of Dendur. Kids love that."

"Thanks for the tip," Dante said.

They had woken up in North Carolina before sunrise and been on the road ever since, racing through Raleigh, Washington, DC, Baltimore, and Philadelphia to get to New York City as fast as possible. They had only stopped for fast food, bathroom breaks—and one quick trip to a mall in New Jersey, where Milana had purchased the outfit Charlie was now wearing.

Entering the museum, Charlie looked extremely different than she had when sneaking into Ahmet Shah's apartment weeks earlier. The idea wasn't merely to disguise herself, so that her enemies wouldn't recognize her. It was to make her look significantly younger.

In the past, Charlie had often sought to present herself as much older than she truly was, which allowed her to access events—like Ahmet Shah's party—where she normally wouldn't be allowed. Now Milana wanted to produce the opposite effect. Charlie had balked upon seeing the clothes at first, but she knew Milana's plan made sense, so she allowed herself to be made over.

Charlie was wearing a rainbow skirt and a T-shirt with a sparkly unicorn logo. Her hair was pulled back in a ponytail and cinched with a baby blue scrunchie. She slouched to make herself look shorter and carried a small pink backpack. Normally, visitors to the museum were supposed to check bags, but Charlie looked so young and innocent, no one stopped her. She slipped into her role with skill, enthusing about the things she wanted to see and acting morose around the things she didn't. Milana wondered how much of it was true acting ability, and how much was Charlie reveling in the chance to actually be a kid for once.

They made a beeline through the Egyptian galleries, passing sarcophagi, large granite sphinxes, and glass cases full of papyrus scrolls, until they came to the enormous room that held the Temple of Dendur. The room and the temple were both impressive pieces of architecture, built two thousand years apart, one designed specifically to showcase the other.

The room was vast and spacious, with a soaring ceiling and a slanted wall of glass to the north, facing the summer greenery of Central Park. The temple sat atop a large raised platform, bordered at one end by a shallow reflecting pool, which was supposed to represent the Nile. In the enormous room, the temple itself was surprisingly small, taking up less space than the average coffee shop. It was a squat block of beige limestone, although back in Cleopatra's time it had probably been festively painted, like most temples.

The exterior walls were covered with engravings depicting Egyptian gods and goddesses, like Isis, Osiris, Horus, Thoth, and Sekhmet—although there were also depictions of real people, such as Pedesi and Pihor, the sons of a local Nubian chieftain—and Cleopatra's rival Octavian, who had coopted the construction of the temple after Cleopatra's death and wanted himself depicted as a pharaoh.

"It's ironic," Charlie observed, looking at the engraving. "Octavian had himself sculpted on this temple but never realized that the thing he wanted most on earth was hidden inside it."

"We *think*," Dante reminded her. "We still don't know for sure yet."

"Oh, it's here," Charlie told him. She couldn't say why she knew, but she had an overwhelming sense that she was right. The temple seemed like the perfect place for Cleopatra to hide the philosopher's stone. Charlie could imagine the queen of Egypt on one of her many trips down the Nile, selecting the site and approving the design of the temple—if not designing it herself. Although Cleopatra would certainly have been stunned to learn that the temple would one day be moved halfway around the world.

Unfortunately, there was no way to examine the temple closely—yet. As the ticket seller had indicated, it was one of the most popular exhibits at the museum, and so there was a good-size crowd around it. Its interior was even worse; the single room was so narrow that only five or six people could fit inside at a time, and there was always a line waiting to get in. But then, the plan had never been for the three of them to inspect the temple during normal museum hours.

After surveilling the room that held the temple, Charlie, Dante, and Milana wandered through the nearby galleries. Although the art was incredible, they were far more focused on the layout of the museum. They noted emergency exits and escape routes, hoping they wouldn't need them but still planning for worst-case scenarios. While other families discussed artists and cultures, the three of them discussed self-defense techniques and backup meeting places.

Fifteen minutes before the museum was due to close,

a message was played throughout the galleries, a woman with a pleasant voice letting everyone know they should start toward the exit.

Charlie, Dante, and Milana headed back to the Temple of Dendur instead.

There was another message at ten minutes to closing, and another at five. By this point, Charlie, Dante, and Milana had returned to the gallery with the temple. The room was mostly empty, although there were still a few other guests. A museum guard was calmly ushering everyone out.

As they headed for the door, Milana came to his side, pretending to be a befuddled foreign tourist. She unfolded a museum map in front of him and pleaded, "I'm sorry. This museum is so big. We've been trying to find our way out for fifteen minutes. Can you please show us the way? We are here, right?" She pointed to a spot on the map that was entirely wrong.

"No, you've got yourself all turned around," the museum guard replied good-naturedly. "Let me show you how to go."

While Milana fumbled with the map in front of him, providing a distraction, Charlie dropped behind the exiting guests and slipped back into the temple. By the time the guard had set Milana straight, Charlie had disappeared from view.

"Thank you so much," Milana said, then looked around, concerned, like a mother who had lost track of her daughter. "Where's Imogen?"

"She ran ahead," Dante informed her. "She wanted to use the bathroom before they closed the museum."

Milana feigned a look of relief, thanked the guard again for his help, and then hurried with Dante in the direction of the exit.

Charlie was now safely inside the temple. The museum had many security cameras around the exterior of the temple, but none inside it. Now that Charlie had the small room to herself, she had plenty of time to examine the hieroglyphics.

The ancient walls had taken a beating over the centuries. Visitors had been carving their names into the stone for almost as long as the temple had existed; the first instance dated to only five years after its completion. Now the interior walls were protected by clear plexiglass shields, which allowed tourists to see the art but not touch it.

It didn't take Charlie long to find what she was looking for.

One of the stone panels depicted Isis, recognizable with her sun-disc headdress and royal staff—although the goddess also had Cleopatra's thin nose and protruding chin. By her feet, a meter above the floor, there was a small engraving of an Ouroboros.

Charlie knew what to do—although she had to bide her time first.

Fifteen minutes after the museum had closed, she heard the first set of footsteps approaching the temple. It wasn't hard to detect them, as they echoed loudly throughout the cavernous room.

Just inside the entrance to the temple, Charlie pressed her hands against the plexiglass panel along one wall of the narrow room, braced her feet against the other, then walked herself up eight feet to the ceiling. It was a relatively easy rock-climbing move, especially with flat walls. Then, with her back against the ceiling, looking down at the floor, she waited.

Thirty seconds later, the guard stepped into the room below her, gave it a cursory glance, and ducked back out again.

He hadn't even bothered to look up. He had probably cased the small room hundreds of times before, if not thousands, and it was routine. He obviously had no concern that someone might be up at the ceiling, over his head.

Charlie stayed where she was, listening to his footsteps fade away, then lowered herself back down to the floor again.

In her pocket, Charlie had one of the three radio earpieces Jamilla Carter had given them. She placed it in her ear and said, "The guard just came through on rounds. I'm safe."

"We saw," Dante replied. He and Milana were now sitting on a park bench on the north side of the museum, keeping an eye on the temple through the great glass wall of the exhibition gallery. The plan was for them to stay there all night. "Go to radio silence. No talking unless it's an emergency."

"Okay," Charlie said. Then she went back to waiting.

A half hour later, there were more footsteps. Once again, Charlie climbed up the walls of the narrow room in the temple to the ceiling.

This time the guard didn't even bother looking inside the temple. After all, he had already checked it once. He merely wandered through the gallery.

Inside Charlie's backpack were a sandwich, a cookie, a bag of chips, two glass bottles of water, and a book. Since there was no way out of the museum that wouldn't set off any alarms, the plan was for Charlie to stay in the temple until the first visitors arrived in the morning, then file out with them. Charlie ate her dinner, although she only drank one of the bottles of water, because if she had to pee, it would make for a very long night.

Then she read her book for an hour, waiting to see if the guards made any more passes through the gallery.

They didn't, which was what Charlie had expected.

She couldn't guarantee a guard wouldn't return to the temple later in the night, but now that security had confirmed there was no one inside it, they would probably stop checking. After all, the museum was locked and full of security cameras. No one could get to the Temple of Dendur without being seen.

Now Charlie went to work.

In addition to her dinner, she had also brought along a few tools, a flashlight, a small piece of lead, and Cleopatra's coin from the Acropolis.

With the tools, Charlie removed the plexiglass panel over the Ouroboros. Although Dante had taught her how to dismantle an alarm system, there was none. She set the panel down gently on the floor, then held the coin up against the engraving.

It was the exact same size, although the Ouroboros on the temple wall was a tiny bas-relief rather than an etching. It was almost as though the coin had been cast from the very stone Charlie was looking at.

It was a good thing she had gone through all the trouble to get the coin back from Ahmet Shah.

Charlie pressed the coin against the Ouroboros.

There was a click as they fit together perfectly.

A secret panel, so flawlessly crafted that it had been invisible, popped open in the stone, releasing a gust of two-thousand-year-old air.

Charlie felt a rush of emotions: relief that she had decoded Cleopatra's clues correctly, the thrill of discovery, and a surge of excitement.

The secret panel was a foot across and four inches tall. Upon closer inspection, it was the front of a stone drawer. Pressing the coin into the proper spot had triggered the release of a latch. Charlie grasped the edges of the panel and slowly pulled out the drawer, which groaned as it scraped along the ancient stone.

The drawer was only a few inches deep. Inside was a papyrus scroll.

The stone drawer had been expertly designed by Cleopatra's masons. It had formed a perfect seal against the elements, so the papyrus looked brand-new, even though it was more than two thousand years old.

Charlie carefully lifted it out of the drawer, realizing that she was the first person to touch it in generations.

The scroll was heavier than she expected. Something was hidden inside its rolls.

Charlie cupped her hand around one end and tilted the scroll.

A small glass vial slid into her palm. The stopper at the top had been sealed to it with red wax.

Charlie could feel liquid sloshing in the vial.

As she had told Dante and Milana, back on the plane from Athens to Rome, there was a good chance that the philosopher's stone was not a stone at all, but a chemical compound. Charlie wasn't surprised to find it was a liquid—although she had to test it first to make sure.

She set the scroll aside, placed the piece of lead she had brought on the floor, then cracked the wax seal on the vial.

Fumes wafted out. It was a smell that Charlie had never encountered before, at once sweet and metallic.

Charlie carefully dripped a tiny bit of the liquid from the vial onto the piece of lead.

The liquid was almost as clear as water, but it moved more sluggishly, like mercury.

When the drop hit the lead, it immediately began sizzling. A small, dark cloud enveloped the metal, shielding it from Charlie's eyes for a few seconds, and then it quickly dissipated.

Where the lead had been, something gleamed on the floor.

It was smaller than the lead had been, and the sheen of it was unmistakable.

Gold.

"Whoa," Charlie said. "Guys, I found the philosopher's stone. And it works!"

She knew Dante would be annoyed at her for using the radio when it wasn't an emergency, but she was too excited to keep the good news to herself.

There was no response.

In fact, now that Charlie thought about it, there seemed to be something wrong with the radio. She had been too distracted before to notice, but there was a faint crackle of static, as though the transmission had been cut off.

"Hello?" she asked. "Dante? Come in, Dante."

She only got static in return.

Charlie's excitement quickly turned to fear.

Something had gone wrong.

FORTY-THREE

Isaac Semel had spotted Charlie, Dante, and Milana in the gallery that housed the Temple of Dendur right before closing time.

The Mossad team was outside, in Central Park, watching through the great glass windows.

They had arrived too late to enter the museum, just after ticket sales had ended for the day, but there was still plenty of daylight left to case the museum from the outside. It was particularly easy to monitor the gallery with the temple because of the windows. In addition, the summer foliage in Central Park offered ample cover. And since the park was popular with bird-watchers, Isaac Semel didn't even look out of place with a pair of binoculars. In fact, he saw two other regular people carrying them.

He didn't even recognize Charlie Thorne at first.

The girl was so smart and competent, he sometimes forgot she was only thirteen. In her unicorn T-shirt and ponytail, she looked even younger. Dante and Milana appeared somewhat different as well—Dante now had a full beard, and both were dressed down in tourist clothes—but Semel had done plenty of stakeouts over the years and was able to identify them quickly.

He watched Milana distract the guard with her map, then saw Charlie duck into the temple.

Semel guessed what their plan was. His team had their own radios, so he called them and had all four quickly assemble with him on Fifth Avenue, across the street from the grand entrance of the museum. There, they blended in with a large crowd of tourists who had just left the building.

It wasn't long before Dante and Milana emerged from the Met. As Semel expected, they immediately turned north on Fifth Avenue and headed to the section of the park where he had just been. Then they sat on a park bench facing the gallery with the temple, where they could keep an eye on Charlie through the windows.

The two of them didn't look like CIA operatives. They looked like a young couple on a date.

Although Dante and Milana were wanted as rogue agents, they were paying far more attention to the museum than their surroundings. Either they didn't expect anyone to be looking for them in Manhattan, or they were so concerned for Charlie's safety, they weren't thinking about their own.

Semel had a camera with a telephoto lens—which also wasn't uncommon in Central Park. Plenty of tourists and bird-watchers carried them. Semel was easily able to take a few photos of Dante and Milana without them noticing.

"Let's take them out," one of the Mossad agents said, fingering the weapon she had hidden beneath her jacket. "Once it gets dark, we can dump their bodies in the park. The girl will be helpless without them."

"There's no need for us to get our hands dirty," Semel told her. "I have a better idea."

And then he called a contact at the CIA.

Outside of Washington, DC, the largest CIA office in the United States was in New York City. Even though the CIA was tasked with investigations outside the United States, New York was a center of international commerce and diplomacy, as well as home to the United Nations. Semel had made many connections at the Agency over the years, one of whom was high up in the Manhattan field office.

He didn't waste time on pleasantries. He simply said, "I thought you'd like to know that rogue agents Dante Garcia and Milana Moon are currently in Central Park, less than a mile from your office." Then he texted the photos of them on the park bench, along with their exact location.

The CIA operative had plenty of questions, like how it was that Semel knew about Garcia and Moon's location, and why he was in New York City, but for the moment, the priority was the rogue agents. He notified Washington and within five minutes, he had a response directly from the office of Arthur Zell himself: Apprehend Garcia and Moon immediately.

A team of eight operatives was promptly dispatched to Central Park.

When the CIA arrived, it was dusk. The park was shifting from the bright greens of day to the shadows of night.

Dante and Milana had changed their method of surveillance. Dante was now alone on the park bench, keeping an eye on the gallery with the temple, while Milana was on the move, taking a lap around the museum. As far as the CIA was concerned, having them split up was a better scenario. It was easier to capture them on their own than as a team. The mission leader decided to hit them when they were farthest apart, while Milana was on the south side of the museum and Dante was on the north. Four ops would go after each one of them.

Dante and Milana were still using radios, though. The CIA could see that. Therefore, the CIA decided to cut their communication so that one couldn't tip off the other. They used a transponder that blocked the transmission frequency.

Less-seasoned agents might not have noticed anything, but Dante and Milana both recognized the static hiss on their radios and realized something was wrong.

Milana was already on edge, as she had noticed some men exhibiting strange behavior on the south side of the museum. They were watching the employee entrance closely, which was an odd thing for anyone to do. There were still plenty of tourists around, but they were mostly gathered at the main entrance of the museum, sitting on the steps or taking pictures of the fountains. To Milana, these men looked like they were trying to figure out a way into the Met.

She couldn't get too close to them without attracting attention, but she thought she heard them speaking in Egyptian Arabic.

Mukhabarat, she thought.

And then her radio went dead.

She instantly took evasive action, bolting into the park, thinking that the Mukhabarat had set her up, using one team as decoys to distract her attention while the other ambushed her.

But the people who came after her were CIA.

She could tell by the way they attacked. They already had her surrounded, one on each side of her, the way that recruits were taught at the Agency. While three of them gave chase, one stepped from the trees into her path, aiming a gun with a silencer at her. "Agent Moon, stand down!" the woman shouted.

Milana didn't stop. Instead, she dropped and rolled. The other agent didn't shoot; she wasn't part of a kill squad, like the one Arthur Zell had sent to Rome. She was a field operative trying to arrest a rogue agent, and she was in the middle of Manhattan, so she wasn't going to gun Milana down in cold blood. Although the agent did try to incapacitate her. She fired at where Milana's thigh would have been, if Milana hadn't dropped. As it was, the bullet sailed over Milana, who then came up out of her roll on the attack.

In a flurry of movements, she disarmed the stunned CIA operative and threw her to the ground. There was no time to knock her out. Milana raced onward into the park. The downed agent quickly got back to her feet, then produced a second gun from her ankle holster and joined the other three agents in pursuit.

• • •

Dante ran in the other direction, away from the park, having bolted from his position outside the museum the moment the radio went dead. The four CIA agents tasked with apprehending him took up the chase.

Not far from where Dante had been sitting, 84th Street cut through Central Park. It was currently jammed with cars, mostly taxicabs, waiting at the traffic light at Fifth Avenue, although the light had just turned green. Dante dodged through the stalled cars, sliding across the hood of one, and reached the other side of 84th as the traffic began to surge forward. The pursuing agents were caught in the middle of it. Car horns blared. Tires screeched. One agent was clipped by a cab and knocked to the ground.

Dante made it to Fifth Avenue, where traffic was now stopped at the same light, and cut across it, the three remaining agents still on his tail.

He couldn't take down three agents at once. He had to keep running. But each step took him farther away from Charlie.

The kid was on her own.

Inside the Temple of Dendur, Charlie was concerned, but Dante and Milana had discussed this scenario with her. If she wasn't directly threatened, she was to stay put inside the temple. There were alarms and security cameras everywhere in the museum. Any attempt to leave would trigger them and bring security running, probably even the police as well.

Charlie had ideas about how to evade security and get out of the museum, but if Dante and Milana were compromised, she'd be running toward trouble rather than away from it. The temple might have truly been the safest place for her to be.

She was still anxious, though. She hated not knowing what was going on. She hated the idea that Dante and Milana might be in danger, and that her orders were to just sit and wait until morning. But there was nothing she could do about it.

Besides, there were still things she needed to take care of.

First, she had to hide the fact that any theft had taken place. She slid the ancient stone drawer shut again, then bolted the plexiglass panel back in place over it. With a rag, she wiped her fingerprints off the plexiglass as best as she could.

She tucked the brand-new piece of gold into her pocket, then set about placing the philosopher's stone in her backpack, taking precautions to make sure that the precious elixir was kept safe. She was toying with the idea of wrapping the glass vial back in the papyrus scroll when she realized that, in all her excitement, she hadn't taken the time to read what was written on the ancient paper.

There turned out to be two pieces of papyrus, one rolled inside the other. Both had writing on them in Latin, Greek, and Egyptian hieroglyphics. Charlie could only read the Latin, but she assumed it was the same message, written three times over, so that it could be read by almost anyone.

The first scroll had the recipe for making the philosopher's stone.

Charlie was astonished.

Although she was even more amazed to see what was written on the second scroll.

"Whoa," she gasped. "That's a surprise."

"What is?" asked a voice behind her.

Charlie wheeled around to find a man blocking the exit of the temple and trapping her inside the narrow room.

Ahmet Shah.

FORTY-FOUR

Ramses Shah hadn't expected Ahmet to try to take measures into his own hands. In fact, he hadn't even realized what his son was doing until it was too late.

They had visited the museum that day, hoping to figure out how to get inside the Temple of Dendur. To their surprise, they had spotted Charlie Thorne, Dante, and Milana there as well. At first, Ramses had been concerned, fearing that others would get to the philosopher's stone ahead of them, but then he realized that wouldn't be so bad after all. Just like at the Parthenon, he could let them take the risks, then swoop in to seize the treasure afterward.

He told his men to clear out before they were spotted, but as they were leaving the museum, Ahmet had said he needed to use the bathroom and would meet them outside. Only, Ahmet never came out. Instead, he sent Ramses a text saying, Don't worry. I've got this under control.

Livid, Ramses texted back, What are you doing?

Ahmet replied, Making you proud. And then went silent.

There was no way to go back into the museum without making a scene. The last of the visitors had been ushered out, and the doors were now locked. Ramses could only bide his time and hope his son wouldn't screw anything up.

It occurred to Ramses that every time Charlie Thorne's name had been mentioned lately, Ahmet had reacted strangely. A darkness had come over him. At those times, Ramses had thought it was anger, but now that he really thought about it, he realized there was something more to it.

Ramses wasn't merely angry at Charlie Thorne. He loathed the girl. Which made sense. The girl had bested him twice and proved him to be a fool. Ahmet's pride had been wounded—and now, Ramses feared, he wasn't merely after the philosopher's stone.

He wanted revenge.

Charlie was seeing this for herself. The hatred in Ahmet's eyes was clear—although he was actually smiling as he came toward her. It was a cold, cruel smile, as he knew she had no escape.

Ahmet had jimmied the lock on a storage closet in the

nearest men's room, then hidden inside. The closet was for the janitorial staff, holding mops, buckets, cleaners, and extra toilet paper. It was a tight space and it smelled awful, but the guards didn't bother checking it when they searched the bathrooms at the end of the day. Ahmet had waited in there for two hours, figuring that after a while, the guards would stop making sweeps of the museum. Sure enough, the guards had come into the bathroom twice more—although once, it was for the guard to actually *use* the bathroom. After that, Ahmet presumed it was safe to return to the temple.

He had removed his shoes so as to not make any noise and moved as quickly as possible. He knew there were security cameras in the galleries but hoped that maybe the guards weren't monitoring them constantly. And if there were guards on patrol, then there couldn't be motion sensors, because the guards would trigger them. So Ahmet hadn't encountered any trouble getting to the Temple of Dendur.

He hadn't really worked out what he was going to do *after* confronting Charlie. He had given no thought at all to how he would get back out of the museum again. His mind had been entirely consumed with seeking revenge.

"Hello, Charlie," he said. He spoke quietly, but his voice echoed ominously in the small chamber of the temple. "I brought something for you."

He held up a syringe. He would have preferred a knife or a gun, but he couldn't have brought those through museum security, whereas the syringe was too small to be noticed. And what was in the syringe would work just as well as a bullet.

"What is that?" Charlie asked, unable to hide the fear in her voice.

"Cobra venom," Ahmet replied proudly. "The same thing Cleopatra used to kill herself. It's funny when you think about it. Here you are, in her temple, and you're going to die the same way she did."

"Cleopatra didn't kill herself with cobra venom," Charlie told him. "That's a myth. And also, I'm not going to die today."

She still had the glass vial in her hand. There hadn't been time to place it in her backpack yet. Now she flicked the stopper out with her thumb and whipped the vial toward Ahmet, like a young wizard with a wand.

Charlie hated to use the elixir to defend herself, but she had no other choice. The remaining drops of liquid flew through the air, caught Ahmet in the face, and instantly began to react. His flesh smoked and sizzled.

Ahmet screamed in pain, dropping the syringe and desperately trying to wipe the elixir off his face. This only resulted in him getting it on his hands, which began to burn as well.

Charlie grabbed her backpack and stomped on the syringe, shattering it and releasing the venom. Then she barreled past Ahmet, knocking him aside, and fled into the museum.

For Ahmet, the pain the elixir caused was excruciating, so bad that he wanted to curl up in a ball and cry. He had no idea what Charlie had done to him, but he had the horrifying feeling that she had just disfigured him for life. And yet he realized his suffering would all be for naught if he let her get away.

So he spun around and went after her.

As he did, he stepped on the jagged glass of the syringe with his bare foot. It cut into his flesh, and he suddenly realized that, in addition to everything else, the very cobra venom he had brought with him to kill Charlie Thorne was now in his system as well.

He desperately needed to go to the hospital.

But he was even more desperate to catch Charlie Thorne first.

So he plucked the piece of glass out of his heel and ran after her.

Adrenaline was now surging through his body, fueled by pain and rage. He charged after Charlie as she fled from the Temple of Dendur. She had gotten a good lead on him when she had caught him by surprise, but he was bigger and faster and gained on her as she ran through the next few rooms. Ahmet dashed past numerous works of art, focused only on Charlie, then rounded a corner into a new gallery . . .

Only to have something smash him in the face with startling force.

It was heavy and made of metal. Ahmet felt like he'd been hit with a wrecking ball. He staggered sideways and slammed into a medieval knight.

Between the wounds he had already suffered and the blow to his head, Ahmet wasn't quite sure if he was seeing things or not. Ahead of him, in the center of the gallery, were four other knights astride horses, all in shining armor, carrying wooden lances, looking as though they were on their way to battle.

Ahmet had not taken the time to explore the museum the way that Charlie had, so he hadn't come upon the Arms and Armor Galleries. To him, it made no sense that any of this would be in an art museum at all.

In fact, the Metropolitan Museum had one of the most extensive collections of such objects in the world. Throughout human history, metalworkers had crafted incredibly beautiful weapons for wealthy patrons. Several rooms surrounded the central gallery, their walls lined with swords, scabbards, halberds, and lances, while glass cases contained knives, daggers, rifles, and other weapons. Mannequins stood silently throughout, wearing elaborate armor from Europe, China, and Japan.

Ahmet had stumbled into one of the mannequins, and he now noticed it was missing its helmet.

The helmet was in the hands of Charlie Thorne. That was what she had clubbed him with.

The cobra venom in Ahmet's foot was now just as painful as the burning in his face. He felt as though the flesh in both places was being eaten away. His leg could no longer support his weight, and he sagged to the floor.

Charlie approached him warily, ready to hit him again if she had to. "You really need a doctor," she said, sounding legitimately concerned. "Sorry. I was only acting in self-defense." Then she ducked away into the shadows.

A few seconds later, Ahmet heard one of the glass display cases shatter. Then alarms started ringing.

The case must have been wired, Ahmet realized. And now the museum's security system had been triggered. A steel door began to drop at the entrance to the gallery, sealing it off to lock the thieves inside.

Ahmet's vision was blurring, though whether that was due to the elixir or the venom, he didn't know. He thought he saw Charlie race through the shadows, still clutching the helmet—and maybe something else as well—and then slide under the steel door just before it thudded to the floor.

He was now trapped in the museum. His body hurt everywhere. And Charlie Thorne had gotten away.

The girl had bested him again.

Ahmet had failed once more.

Now he could only hope that the guards would find him in time to get him medical attention.

His whole body was throbbing. The pain from his foot was racing through his leg. He hurt so badly, he thought he might throw up.

It took every ounce of strength he had to call his father.

"Where are you?" Ramses demanded angrily.

Ahmet didn't bother to answer, knowing it would only disappoint his father. Instead, he said, "Charlie's on her way out of the museum. Be ready to grab her."

And then he passed out from the pain.

While casing the museum earlier in the day, Charlie had spotted several doors for the employee area. She went through the closest one to the Arms and Armor Galleries. This led to a staircase, which she followed down one floor. The employee area turned out to be expansive, taking up almost the entire ground level of the enormous museum.

There were offices for curators and staff, laboratories, framing workshops, and storage areas. A significant amount of the museum's collection wasn't on display but instead locked up in temperature-controlled rooms. As opposed to the visitors' galleries, which were spacious and airy, the employee area was cramped and confusing. Charlie found herself in a seemingly endless warren of hallways.

The alarms were still ringing down there. Charlie suspected that the security staff would be much more focused on the upstairs, where she had broken the glass on the display case, but she still worried about running into anyone. After all, she was carrying objects she had taken from the museum—like the glass vial and the helmet. She hadn't wanted to drop the helmet, as her fingerprints were on it, and it made for a handy weapon as well. But it was very obviously stolen, and she couldn't exactly hide it in her backpack.

So she raced through the halls as fast as she could, figuring that sooner or later, she would find an exit.

Eventually, she came to a fire door. It was alarmed, but that hardly mattered now. Charlie burst through it and found herself at the rear of the museum, in Central Park. While Fifth Avenue was still bustling on the other side of the building, this side was dark and empty.

There was only one person there: Lembris, the biggest of Ramses Shah's thugs. Charlie recognized him from the Parthenon; he was the one who had grabbed Eva. He came around the corner, on the lookout for her, just after she emerged through the door.

Before Lembris could react, Charlie launched herself at him. Her weeks of training on the sailboat had taught her the best places to strike in a fight. First, she smashed the helmet into his gun. The weapon flew from his grasp and disappeared into some bushes. Then, Charlie brought the helmet down onto Lembris's head, dropping him to his knees.

She didn't have the time—or the power—to knock him out for good. But while he was down for the count, she raced onward.

Lembris yelled out at the top of his lungs in Arabic. "Mr. Shah! She's getting away!"

Ramses Shah was close by. He saw Charlie fleeing into the park and went after her, determined to get the philosopher's stone at any cost—and avenge his son while he was at it.

FORTY-FIVE

Since she was outnumbered, Milana Moon headed for terrain she could use to her advantage.

The Ramble was known as the wildest section of Central Park, nearly forty acres of winding trails, thick woods, and rocky outcrops, set on the northern edge of a small lake. Of course, it wasn't true wilderness at all; in fact, it had only been sculpted to look like wilderness by the park's designer, Frederick Law Olmsted, but it was close enough. Milana felt much more at home in the jumble of hackberries and locust trees than she did in the streets.

The Ramble wasn't far from the art museum. Running flat out, Milana arrived there in just over a minute, with the CIA agents close behind. The moment Milana reached the trees, she stopped fleeing and changed her tactics, melting into the shadows.

The first three agents ran right by her, passing within only a few feet. The last, bringing up the rear, wasn't quite so lucky. He was out of shape for an agent, already wheezing from exertion, and Milana easily got the jump on him.

By now, the other three had realized their mistake and doubled back. One caught a glimpse of Milana knocking out the trailing agent, pulled her gun, and yelled at Milana to freeze.

Milana didn't. Instead, she darted into the trees.

The second agent came after her, but she was used to the city, not the woods, and quickly found herself out of her element. She heard a rustle in the leaves and spun toward it; by the time she realized it was only a squirrel, it was too late. Milana slammed into her from behind, whacked her on the back of the neck, and left her slumped in the bushes.

The remaining two agents were harder to deal with. They were more cautious and seasoned. Milana lay in wait for another few minutes, hiding in the trees, knowing they were out there somewhere. She wanted to get back to Charlie but feared that, if she ran, she would leave herself open to an attack.

Finally, the third agent came along, creeping stealthily down one of the Ramble paths. Milana ambushed her and took her down.

"Put your hands up, Agent Moon," a voice behind her said.

Milana had no choice but to comply. She turned around to find herself facing the fourth agent. He had his gun aimed directly at her.

"You're making a mistake," Milana told him. "I'm not the enemy here."

"Feel free to explain that at the office," the agent told her. "You're under arrest for treason."

Dante was less than a quarter mile away but in a place that felt like a different world. He was racing down crowded sidewalks and crossing streets filled with cars. While the Ramble was quiet, the city was a cacophony of voices, car horns, and blaring music.

The three CIA agents came after Dante, shoving their way through the crowds.

Dante arrived at Park Avenue, two blocks east of Fifth. It was the widest street in the city, because, as its name indicated, it had once had a park running through the center of it. Nowadays, to accommodate traffic, the park was mostly gone. Only a thin median strip remained, bounded on each side by three lanes of traffic.

For the moment, the light was green, and pedestrians were crossing the avenue, but Dante could see that was about to change.

He ran as fast as he could, charging into the street,

making it across three lanes of traffic and the median before the light changed.

Dante ran on anyhow, dashing in front of the last three cars just as they began to move. The drivers stomped on their brakes, pounded their horns, and screamed at him. And then, once Dante was past, they hit the gas and roared down Park Avenue, livid at having been held up for an extra second. The flow of cars blocked the road in both directions.

The CIA agents could only watch helplessly from the other side.

Dante flagged a cab, leapt inside, and said, "Drive."

The driver pulled away from the curb and started the meter. "Where to?" he asked.

"The Metropolitan," Dante said, having no idea that Charlie wasn't even there anymore.

Charlie was at a castle.

Belvedere Castle was one of the most beautiful attractions in Central Park. Built in the 1860s, it was designed in gothic style and perched atop a dark stone cliff, overlooking a large pond. The castle was relatively small, only two rooms, one on top of the other, with a narrow staircase that spiraled through a thin turret. It was like a tiny piece of medieval Europe in the midst of New York City.

Ramses Shah cornered Charlie at the base of the castle. For an older man, he was in much better shape than Charlie had expected, and she was tiring after all her exertion.

There was a large viewing balcony beside the castle, at the top of the cliff, ringed by a low stone wall. Charlie considered leaping into the pond, but in the darkness she couldn't tell how deep the water was. If she landed on rocks, she'd break her legs or snap her neck and kill herself. It was too big a risk. So she turned to face Ramses instead.

Knowing he had her trapped, Ramses approached her cautiously. He clutched a second syringe.

"Do you know what this is?" he asked menacingly.

"Yes," Charlie replied. "It's cobra venom. Your son already tried to kill me with some of it. It didn't work out so well for him."

"That's a lie," Ramses said.

"No it's not. Ahmet is in really bad shape right now. The venom is attacking his nervous system and shutting down his organs. Soon, he's going to have trouble breathing, and then his heart will stop. If you really care about him, you ought to forget about me and take him to a doctor."

To her surprise, Ramses didn't seem the slightest bit concerned. Instead, he almost seemed pleased. "Yes, this venom is extremely fatal. Just a tiny bit will cause an agonizing death. Cleopatra might not have died from it herself, but she tested the venom on many of her enemies. Now, if you don't hand over the philosopher's stone, you too will die from the curse of Cleopatra."

Charlie sighed, annoyed, and shook her head. "That's not what the curse of Cleopatra is."

Ramses faltered, surprised by her comment. And her attitude. He had expected her to be frightened. But instead, she seemed disdainful of him, as though he was a fool. "What?"

"The curse of Cleopatra wasn't some mystical hex she put on the philosopher's stone to prevent people from finding it. There's no such thing as magic. Instead, the curse was on Cleopatra herself. She was cursed by being a woman. History treated her terribly for it."

"How so?" Ramses continued coming toward her, his thumb poised on the plunger of the syringe.

Charlie was backed up against the stone wall with no place to go. "Think about Julius Caesar. He was a brute who killed thousands of people without mercy. A significant portion of Europe died at his command. He did away with democracy in Rome and installed himself as emperor, which led to a succession of insane rulers. Because of his power grab, his own friends turned on him and assassinated him. And he had dozens of affairs, with men and women alike. But most people still think of him as a great leader. Meanwhile, Cleopatra actually *was* a great leader. She ruled Egypt wisely, she kept the peace for decades, and she was brilliant. She only had two relationships, both of which lasted for many years and really might have been loving. And yet she is remembered by history as a scheming seductress. It's not fair."

"Life isn't fair," Ramses said. He was almost upon Charlie now. "Give me the stone."

Charlie shrugged off her backpack and reached into it. "However, there *is* one advantage to being a woman."

"What's that?" Ramses asked almost tauntingly.

"Men are always underestimating you." Instead of removing the philosopher's stone from her backpack, Charlie removed the other item she had stolen from the Arms and Armor Galleries, the object she'd had to break the glass display case to get.

It was a mace. A medieval weapon that consisted of an iron ball on a foot-long chain attached to a wooden handle. This particular one was exquisitely crafted, with a sheath of silver around the handle, and even after a few centuries, it was still in perfect working condition.

Ramses Shah was now within easy striking distance. Although Charlie didn't attack yet. Instead, she held the mace at the ready, as a warning.

"I really don't like hurting people," she said. "So why don't you just back off and leave me alone?"

Ramses considered her for a moment, daunted by the mace. But then, his greed overwhelmed him. Even though he already had plenty of money, he wanted more. He wanted the wealth of Cleopatra herself. And so, rather than backing down, he lunged at Charlie, trying to stab her with the syringe, thinking that he could easily overpower her.

He was wrong.

Charlie hit him with the mace. She didn't smash him in the head, as that would have crushed his skull and killed him. Instead, she aimed for his wrist, hoping to disarm him. The heavy iron ball struck his forearm, snapping both bones. Ramses howled in pain, although he somehow managed to keep a grip on the syringe. He shifted it to his other hand, glaring at Charlie with loathing.

Charlie readied the mace again. "Now, be sensible," she said.

Only, Ramses wasn't. He wasn't about to let himself be defeated by a girl. He cursed at Charlie and charged toward her, leaving her no choice but to defend herself.

She leapt aside and swung the mace at him once more. She was only trying to hit his other arm, but he shifted his attack at the last second, going for her throat.

The iron ball glanced off his head, sending him reeling.

Ramses slammed into the stone wall and, carried by his own momentum, pitched over it and tumbled down onto the rocks below.

Charlie dropped the mace, shocked and saddened by how everything had played out.

"Freeze!" a voice yelled from the darkness.

Isaac Semel and the Mossad had arrived. And so had Anwar Zafadi and the Mukhabarat.

They had come from different directions and caught up to her at the same time. Everyone had guns, and they were all pointed at Charlie.

She raised her hands over her head and said, "What took you guys so long?"

FORTY-SIX

The CIA agent who had captured Milana Moon marched her through the Ramble at gunpoint. He had cuffed her hands behind her, but he still stayed a few feet back, so that she couldn't get the jump on him. He had read Moon's file and seen what she had done to the other agents. He wasn't going to give her a chance to attack.

Both of them kept silent as they walked. The CIA agent didn't want to drop his guard, engaging in conversation. And he was sure that anything Milana told him now would be a lie anyhow.

They were nearing the edge of the Ramble, close enough to see the lights of Fifth Avenue in the distance, when someone suddenly lunged out of the trees, catching the agent by surprise.

Dante Garcia hit him like a truck, slamming him to

the ground, then wrenched his gun away and turned it on him. "I'm really sorry about this," he said. "But I can't let you arrest my girlfriend." He took the keys to the handcuffs and, holding the agent at gunpoint, freed Milana, who promptly used the cuffs on the agent himself.

They left him sitting with his back to a tree, his arms locked behind him on the other side of the trunk, with one of his own socks stuffed in his mouth to keep him quiet.

Milana gave Dante a quick kiss on the cheek as they ran off. "My hero," she said teasingly.

Dante pointed to the tracking bracelet on Milana's wrist. "Good thing you were wearing that. Or I never would have found you."

"We should probably check on Charlie," Milana told him.

"I'm sure she's fine," Dante said. "She's much safer in the museum than we are out here." But he checked the tracking app anyhow, just to make sure.

That afternoon, before entering the museum, he had asked Charlie to put on a new tracking bracelet. This time, she hadn't made a fuss.

Charlie's location came up on Dante's phone.

"Oh no," he said. And then he started running for Belvedere Castle.

• • •

"I assume you found the philosopher's stone?" Isaac Semel asked.

Charlie was still backed against the wall at the edge of the viewing balcony. The Mossad and the Mukhabarat were slowly closing in on her, guns raised. The Mukhabarat had sent two agents down to the bottom of the cliff to check on Ramses Shah, but everyone else was surrounding Charlie, eight men in all.

"No," Charlie replied. "The stone doesn't exist. But I found something better."

Semel gave her a skeptical look. "And what might that be?"

"I'll tell all of you, but you have to share." Charlie started to reach into her backpack.

"Put that down!" Anwar Zafadi yelled. "And step away from it!"

Charlie followed his orders. "I'm not trying to pull anything here. Feel free to look for yourself."

Zafadi kicked the mace away from Charlie, so that she couldn't use it, then knelt and dug through her backpack. The first items he came across were the two glass water bottles, one still capped while the other was almost empty, with only a tiny bit of fluid at the bottom.

"That's only water, obviously," Charlie said. "From my dinner."

Zafadi set the bottles aside. It never occurred to him

that the tiny bit of fluid in the second bottle might not actually be water. After all, it *looked* like water. Although it was, in fact, the remaining bit of elixir. Back in the Temple of Dendur, Charlie had split up what she had left, leaving some in the original vial, then pouring the rest into the empty water bottle, just in case things went wrong. That had turned out to be a good call, as she'd been forced to use all the elixir from the vial on Ahmet Shah.

Zafadi then found the papyrus scroll. Although he didn't find *all* of it. While fleeing to Belvedere Castle, Charlie had tossed the piece with the instructions for making the philosopher's stone into some bushes beside the pond. She figured it would merely look like a scrap of garbage rather than one of the most important discoveries of human history, and that she could come back and retrieve it later. She had done her best to memorize it when she first saw it, but it always made sense to have the original copy.

The piece of the scroll that Zafadi now held was the piece that Charlie had wanted him and the Mossad to find.

"That's it," Charlie said encouragingly.

Zafadi used the flashlight from his phone to illuminate the text. He had only read a few words before he gasped in surprise. Then he looked to Charlie, unable to conceal his shock. "Is this for real?"

"I think so," Charlie said. "That's what all of Cleopatra's clues were leading to."

"Where did you find it?"

"Hidden in a stone block inside the Temple of Dendur."

Isaac Semel could no longer control his curiosity. He lowered his gun and moved to Zafadi's side to look at the piece of papyrus. "What is it?"

"The location of the scrolls of the Library of Alexandria," Zafadi said breathlessly. "According to this, Cleopatra hid them before the library was burned."

Now it was Semel's turn to be amazed. "Where are they?"

"In the Sinai Desert," Charlie replied. "I'm not sure how accurate her references to the landmarks are, because things might have changed over the past two thousand years. But I'll bet if you put your best people on it, you can work it out."

Semel and Zafadi exchanged a glance. They were still wary of each other, having been adversaries for their entire careers, but now the thrill of discovery appeared to be stronger than their suspicion.

Semel looked back to Charlie. "But at the Forum in Rome, you distinctly said you were looking for the philosopher's stone."

"All I knew was that I was looking for a great treasure

of Cleopatra's. I *thought* it was the philosopher's stone. It turned out to be the library instead."

Zafadi asked, "And after all the time you spent looking for it, you're just giving it to us?"

"The library doesn't belong to me," Charlie replied. "It belongs to the world. I assume you'll make sure that happens."

"Of course," Semel said.

"Great!" Charlie exclaimed. "Well, I'm glad that's settled. If you don't mind, I really need to get going." She grabbed her backpack and the glass bottles. "I'll recycle these on my way out of the park. Do you guys mind returning that mace to the museum? It's pretty expensive . . ."

She tried to slip past Semel, but he grabbed her arm. "Not so fast, Charlie. There's still one more thing you have that I need."

"Pandora?" Charlie asked, surprisingly pleasant about it. "I'd love to help you, but that got destroyed in the fire at Mount Wilson."

"But you memorized it first," Semel asserted.

"No I didn't."

"I don't believe you."

"Well, it's the truth," Charlie said. "You can torture me all you want, and I won't be able to tell you a thing. Not that you'd do that, of course, because you're a Mossad agent illegally running a mission on American soil, which is a violation of international law. If you so much as *threatened* me, Dante and Milana would have no choice but to shoot you." She yelled out, "Isn't that right, guys?"

"Sure is!" Dante called back from the darkness, catching the Mossad and the Mukhabarat by surprise.

"Sorry, Isaac!" Milana shouted from a slightly different location.

They had come upon the scene while the Mossad and the Mukhabarat had been distracted, learning about the library. Charlie had seen them, but no one else had. Dante and Milana had then slipped into the forest around Belvedere Castle, where they remained hidden.

The members of the Mossad and the Mukhabarat all turned their guns toward the trees, ready for battle.

"Stand down!" Zafadi ordered sharply. "We're not starting a firefight in the middle of New York City! We're not even supposed to be operating here."

His men reluctantly lowered their guns. Although the Mossad kept theirs raised and looked to Isaac Semel.

"Zafadi's right," he said. "Stand down."

His men lowered their guns as well.

"Good call," Charlie said.

Semel turned back to her. "You really never memorized the equation?"

"I never even had a chance to see it," Charlie replied,

sounding honest even though it was a lie. "I realize every-one at the Mossad is expecting you to return with it, but maybe the Library of Alexandria is a decent condolence prize?"

"I suppose it is," Semel agreed, then released Charlie's arm and waved her through the crowd. "Go in peace, Charlie Thorne."

"Thanks," Charlie said, and then before Semel could change his mind, she raced off into the night, taking the philosopher's stone with her.

FORTY-SEVEN

Washington, DC
Four weeks later

Arthur Zell was in his home office, reading about the discovery of the Library of Alexandria, when the email arrived.

It was five thirty in the morning. As CIA director, he always had to wake early to get his security briefings. He was reading the news while eating his breakfast.

The library was the biggest story of the week, heralded around the world as one of the most significant archaeological finds of all time—as well as a landmark display of international cooperation. The leaders of Egypt and Israel had appeared at a press conference together to announce the news, along with noted scholars from both countries.

Zell had to admit, the results were exciting and astounding. Nearly three thousand papyrus scrolls had been recovered from a previously unknown archaeological site in the Sinai Desert, where the combination of dry weather and a cleverly designed storage area had preserved them perfectly. There had not been time for the scholars to closely examine all the scrolls yet, but a cursory inspection had indicated they would be a treasure trove of information about life in ancient times.

However, Zell was also bothered by the news. It seemed like too big a coincidence that the discovery had been made so shortly after Dante Garcia and Milana Moon had gone to Egypt, looking for Charlie Thorne and something that Cleopatra had hidden.

There were still many loose ends with that operation. After the debacle in Rome, Garcia and Moon had shown up in Manhattan—which the Agency had only learned of thanks to a tip from the Mossad. On the same night, Charlie Thorne had broken into the Metropolitan Museum of Art—Zell had seen the security footage as proof—and two Egyptian billionaires had ended up in critical condition. Ramses Shah was still in a coma at Mount Sinai Hospital in Manhattan, having been badly wounded in a fall off a cliff in Central Park, while his son, Ahmet, had nearly died after somehow being poisoned by cobra venom. Zell had attempted to question Ahmet, but a team of high-priced attorneys was stonewalling the investigation.

Meanwhile, Charlie Thorne, Dante Garcia, and

Milana Moon had all disappeared after that night and had not been heard from again.

Until the email showed up.

It arrived in Zell's secure inbox, the one that only other CIA agents should have been able to access.

```
Hi Arthur!
    I assume you've seen the news about the
Library of Alexandria. The USA would have
been part of that discovery if you hadn't
been such a jerk and tried to kill your own
agents.
                              Sincerely,
                          Your nemesis
P.S. Jamilla Carter was a much better CIA
director than you. I have proof.
```

Attached to the message were classified internal memos from Zell, authorizing the termination of agents Garcia and Moon.

To Zell's horror, he now realized that the email had been sent to other people besides him. Charlie Thorne didn't only have access to his secure account; she also had access to the accounts of the Director of National Intelligence, the chairman of the Senate Select Committee on Intelligence, the director of the Smithsonian

Institution—and the president of the United States.

Zell was so stunned, he didn't know what to be most concerned about first. He had no idea how Charlie Thorne had breached the system, or how she had obtained the classified memos, or how she had engineered things with the Israelis and the Egyptians.

In the midst of all those worries, another one struck Arthur Zell. He quickly accessed his secure files, which were triple-encrypted.

The files from Project Prometheus were gone. All the notes that Albert Einstein had collected about the discoveries of other great thinkers from history had been erased.

The original copies that Jamilla Carter had given him were still locked away safely in a vault at CIA headquarters, but Zell was shaken to see that Charlie Thorne had such access to his files. The girl was far more troublesome than he had imagined. And now he had made an enemy of her.

His phone rang. He checked the caller ID.

It was the White House.

Arthur Zell sighed heavily, realizing he was in for a long day of defending his actions, then reluctantly answered the phone.

EPILOGUE

Madalena
Ilha de Pico
The Azores

"Did you have anything to do with this?" Dante asked.

He was reading the *New York Times* website at one of the only two internet cafés in Madalena. Charlie had just entered with Milana, their arms full of groceries.

"The discovery of the Library of Alexandria?" Charlie asked. "You know I did."

"I'm not talking about that," Dante said, then pointed to a different article. This one stated that the newspaper had obtained classified documents, which indicated CIA Director Arthur Zell had ordered the execution of two of his own agents.

"Hey!" Charlie exclaimed, faking innocence. "That's about you!"

Neither Dante nor Milana was mentioned by name in the story, but it was incriminating enough.

"How'd you get the files?" Dante asked.

"I don't know what you're talking about," Charlie lied. "Someone else must have done this."

In truth, Jamilla Carter had helped her. Charlie had called her from a pay phone in Maine, a few days after she had fled New York City, while Dante and Milana were shopping for a new sailboat.

The former director hadn't given Charlie the documents, but she had steered her in the right direction to find them.

Early that morning, while Dante and Milana had slept in, Charlie had come to this very same internet café to send the email to Arthur Zell and the other government higher-ups. She had also emailed the documents to the *New York Times*. And then she had sent a bouquet of flowers to Jamilla Carter's house.

Madalena was the first place she had been able to get decent Wi-Fi in weeks. The new boat was even nicer than the one they had sailed west across the Atlantic on, but they had chosen not to spring for a satellite Wi-Fi system—or even a portable computer. They had been off the grid for the entire journey.

Still, Charlie had been in no rush to send the email.

This was actually the second time they had been to Madalena. They had spent the last week enjoying themselves on Ilha de Pico, which was a gorgeous volcanic island warmed by the Gulf Stream, with crystal-clear lagoons and beautiful reefs.

The Azores were a remote Portuguese island chain, about four-fifths of the way across the North Atlantic to Europe. Madalena was the biggest town on Ilha de Pico, and it still only had just over six thousand residents. The small marina was filled with the sailboats of other people making the Atlantic crossing.

Dante's time ran out and his Wi-Fi connection shut down. He took a bag of groceries from Milana and they left the internet café, heading back to the boat.

Dante seemed annoyed, although Charlie had the sense that he was secretly pleased but trying not to reveal it. "I appreciate what you're trying to do," he said. "But it's not going to change anything. They'll never reinstate Milana and me. Zell's going to spin all sorts of lies to protect himself. He'll say we were double agents working for the Russians, or something along those lines. We'll have to keep lying low for a long time to come."

"Zell might go down in flames, though," Milana said. "Which is a nice touch." She snuck a smile to Charlie behind Dante's back.

"It was also risky," Dante warned. "I know you're good at covering your tracks, Charlie, but the CIA has an entire building full of computer specialists who Zell will now put to work on that email. It won't take them long to trace it to here."

"It'll probably take at least a day," Charlie said. "Assuming I *had* done this, of course. And by the time the CIA could even get anyone here to find us, we'll be long gone."

"We will?" Dante asked, surprised.

"Yeah," Charlie said. "None of us are really the sort of people who want to spend the rest of our lives hanging out on tropical islands. I mean, it's nice here and all, but we still have work to do. There's a lot more discoveries on Einstein's list. We have to find them before anyone else does. We need to keep them safe."

As it was, the remainder of the philosopher's stone and the ancient scroll with the recipe for it were tucked away in a cabinet on the sailboat. Charlie had insisted they be cautious with the elixir, although back in the United States, she had used a tiny bit on another piece of lead to demonstrate to Dante and Milana that it really worked.

They had used the gold that it created to buy the sailboat.

Dante and Milana shared a look. They had been enjoying their time in the Azores—and yet Charlie was right.

Both of them had joined the CIA because they believed in doing the right thing. The fact that they weren't agents anymore didn't change that about them.

"Charlie has a good point," Milana told Dante. "Even though she memorized all of Einstein's notes, the CIA still has the originals. And they've proven they can't be trusted."

Dante sighed, then looked to Charlie. "So where are we going?"

"England," Charlie said with a grin. "I think it's time we tracked down what Isaac Newton found."

ACKNOWLEDGMENTS

I will admit, when I first made a list of the most brilliant people from history, whose discoveries Charlie Thorne could track down, Cleopatra was not on it. I was guilty of accepting the common wisdom about Cleo myself: All I really knew about her was her love life.

Then I read *Cleopatra: A Life*, by Stacy Schiff, which is certainly one of the best biographies ever written. Schiff fully admits that, for a famous historical figure, there's a lot we don't know about Cleopatra, but she did an amazing job filling in the gaps. I now know that Cleopatra was smarter, more innovative, and a much better leader than history usually gives her credit for. Plus, her life took place at the intersection of the Greek, Egyptian, and Roman Empires, which made her the perfect historical figure to write about. That meant I had to do a lot of research for this book. So, I am indebted to Caroline Harris for getting the ball rolling on this project, Caroline Curran for doing an astonishing amount of research—and helping me develop the clues Cleopatra used—and to Catherine de Luna for helping me with the Latin translations. And thanks, as usual, to Mingo Reynolds, RJ Bernocco, and everyone at the Kelly Writers House at the University of Pennsylvania for finding me such great interns every year.

Then there's my incredible team at Simon & Schuster: Krista Vitola, Justin Chanda, Lucy Cummins, Erin Toller, Beth Parker, Roberta Stout, Kendra Levin, Catherine Laudone, Anne Zafian, Lisa Moraleda, Jenica Nasworthy, Chava Wolin, Chrissy Noh, Anna Jarzab, Brian Murray, Devin MacDonald, Christina Pecorale, Victor Iannone, Emily Hutton, Emily Ritter, and Theresa Pang.

And massive thanks to my incredible agent, Jennifer Joel, for making all this possible.

Thanks to my amazing fellow writers (and support group) James Ponti, Sarah Mlynowski, Julie Buxbaum, Christina Soontornvat, Karina Yan Glaser, Max Brallier, Gordon Korman, Julia Devillers, Leslie Margolis, and Rose Brock.

Thanks to all the school librarians and parent associations who have arranged for me to visit, all the bookstore owners and employees who have shilled my books, and all the amazingly tireless festival organizers and volunteers who have invited me to participate.

Thanks to the home team: Ronald and Jane Gibbs; Suz, Darragh, and Ciara Howard; Barry and Carole Patmore; Megan Vicente; and Andrea Lee Gomez.

And, of course, thanks to my children, Dashiell and

Violet, who helped me explore Rome, Athens, and the site of the actual resting place of Cleopatra's treasure. (I'm not saying where it is in case you have decided to read the acknowledgments before the rest of the book.) D. and V., you are excellent explorers, sounding boards, and junior editors. I love you both more than words can say.